"I DO
SEE Y

"I'm fed up with you
best for me. I'm sick of your bullying and your
and totally insensitive—advice. You know why I don't believe that anything awful is going to happen to you? Because you have no *clue* what awful is. You think awful is when your fingernail breaks!"

Caroline stood. "I'm sorry I bothered you, Liz," she said in a small, quiet voice. Then she walked out, letting in a draft of cold air and the gray promise of imminent rain.

I didn't think about Caroline again until Sunday evening, when Max phoned.

"The reason I'm calling is that I thought you'd want to know Caroline Marshall is dead."

"Dead?" I repeated, sure I'd misunderstood him. My stomach lurched. My head felt light, and the room tipped for a moment. "What happened?"

"She shot herself."

"Oh, God," I moaned, remembering those darting violet eyes. "Oh, God."

Caroline had come to me for help, and I'd sneered at her . . .

CRY FOR HELP

"A nicely executed plot . . . a very enjoyable read."
—*Dean James, manager of Murder by the Book bookstore and coauthor of* By a Woman's Hand

Don't miss this exciting debut mystery from
Karen Hanson Stuyck!

CRY FOR HELP

Karen Hanson Stuyck

BERKLEY PRIME CRIME, NEW YORK

CRY FOR HELP

A Berkley Prime Crime Book / published by arrangement with the author

PRINTING HISTORY
Berkley Prime Crime edition / December 1995

For information address: The Berkley Publishing Group, 200 Madison Avenue, New York, NY 10016.

ISBN: 0-425-15103-4

Berkley Prime Crime Books are published by The Berkley Publishing Group, 200 Madison Avenue, New York, NY 10016.

PRINTED IN THE UNITED STATES OF AMERICA

10 9 8 7 6 5 4 3 2 1

For Steve and Danny,
with thanks for their continuing love and support

CRY FOR HELP

ONE

When I saw Caroline Marshall's face through the peephole that Saturday afternoon in November my first instinct was to pretend I wasn't home. But Caroline, a crackerjack investigative reporter if no longer a stellar friend, had undoubtedly already spotted my car in the parking lot. I opened the door of my apartment.

"I need to talk to you, Liz," she said, just as if nothing had ever happened between us.

I sighed, letting the rain-filled norther nip at my bare feet. November in Houston was always unpredictable; four days ago it had been 85 degrees. I thought wistfully of the steaming bathwater just waiting for my frosty toes, the P. D. James novel calling my name from the edge of the tub. "Come on in."

Caroline marched inside, looking thin and elegant in a gray cashmere sweater and tailored black wool slacks. I watched her take in the contents of my underfurnished living room: two upholstered tub chairs, wheat colored, that I'd taken from my former apartment, along with a brass floor lamp for reading. The adjacent dining room held a small butcher-block table and two oak chairs. Otherwise the apartment had flat brown industrial carpet and bare white walls, which added to the look of vast open space. There were a coffee mug and a pile of paperbacks next to the chair closest to the lamp. They made the place look lived in, I thought.

Caroline apparently didn't think so. The expression on her

face—disapproving but trying to hide it—reminded me of the first time I met her. I'd walked into my freshman dorm room at UT. A pretty blond girl sat on the bed next to the window. "Hi, I'm Caroline Rogers, your roommate," she'd said. "Let me help you carry in those clothes."

Together we had hung my home-sewn dresses and discount store separates in the closet. When we were done, Caroline stood silently, studying my assembled wardrobe. Finally she turned to me. "We'll need to work on this," she said.

Now, fourteen years later, Caroline managed to keep her assessment to herself. She perched on the edge of one of the chairs. "Were you getting ready to go somewhere?" she asked, nodding at my faded velour robe.

"No, I was just going to take a bath." And wallow in the luxury of an undisturbed hour with Commander Adam Dalgliesh.

"I'm sorry to barge in on you like this, but I had to talk to *someone*." She spoke rapidly, all the while twisting a strand of strawberry blond hair. "I've been feeling so awful lately. It's as if everything is crumbling around me." Her voice broke. She took a deep breath. "I—I don't know if I can take anymore, Liz."

I stared at her, too surprised to respond. In the ten years since we'd graduated from college I couldn't remember Caroline once acting even remotely vulnerable. Awful was not something that Caroline Marshall felt.

I waited for more details. But Caroline just sat there, avoiding eye contact. She seemed lost in her thoughts, as if she'd forgotten I was there. "Something happened to upset you?" I finally asked.

"You might say that." The bitterness in her voice was also new. Caroline was as cynical as the next journalist; as an investigative reporter she probably had more than average reason to be. But she was never bitter. It was one of the reasons I'd always secretly envied her: Caroline had never seen a need to be bitter or even deeply disappointed. Even as a teenager she'd radiated a deep-seated conviction that whatever it was she wanted, she would eventually get.

Finally she offered an explanation of sorts. "Everything upsets me these days. I feel so strange, so unlike myself."

Suddenly, inexplicably, she seemed on the verge of tears.

I reached forward and awkwardly patted her knee. I couldn't imagine what was upsetting her.

"Is everything okay with you and Paul?" The only other time I'd seen Caroline act this way was in college, when she thought Paul was about to dump her. For one entire day she lay, practically comatose, on her bed. Fortunately Paul called the next day, and Caroline rejoined the land of the living. They were married seven months later, at the end of Caroline's junior year.

Caroline sat up straighter and dried her eyes with a tissue. She glared at me. "You'd be real amused, wouldn't you, if Paul and I broke up? After all the things I said about you and Max."

"No," I lied, trying hard to convince myself that I was above such pettiness. "Are you and Paul breaking up?"

"No, we are not," she snapped.

I tried again. "Something happen at your job?" In her work Caroline had to deal with a lot of angry people, the downside of uncovering crime, corruption—or sometimes just highly embarrassing information.

She shook her head. "I'm having trouble on a story, but nothing I can't handle. It's not that."

So what *was* it? "Damn it, Caroline, will you just tell me what's wrong?" Why did she always have to be so difficult?

She pushed a strand of hair away from her face and favored me with an unconvincing smile. "Listen, this is probably just my midlife crisis. You know, when you start questioning everything you've done for the last thirty years? You're convinced that something awful is going to happen, and there's nothing you can do to stop it."

Caroline was practically the last person I'd expect to have a midlife crisis. She'd always been too cantankerous for self doubts. But then I never would have thought of myself as a divorcée either. "What awful thing do you expect to happen?" I asked.

Her violet eyes darted around my apartment. "I—I don't know."

"Have you talked to Paul about this?" I asked. "Maybe he'd have more insight than I would." Or a clue as to what you're talking about.

Caroline bit her lower lip. "Paul's in Austin. He took Jonathan to visit his parents."

"How about Dr. Houssman? He always told me I should feel free to call him at any time. Even if you haven't seen him for a while, I'm sure he'd be happy to talk to you." Dr. Ted Houssman was the psychiatrist Caroline had recommended to me when Max and I were having problems. She'd been in therapy with him and said he'd helped her a lot.

I wasn't prepared for her reaction to what I considered a fairly orthodox suggestion. Caroline's already pale face turned a shade paler. Her lower lip started to tremble. "I can't tell him about this! I just wouldn't feel comfortable. It—it sounds too crazy."

"Listen, I've discussed more than my share of crazy feelings with Dr. Houssman," I said. "He was always reassuring. I can't imagine anything you could come up with that would shock him."

"You don't understand, Liz."

She was right. I didn't.

Caroline produced another anemic smile. "I guess this is something I just need to work out for myself."

Too bad she hadn't realized that half an hour ago. I struggled with a tangle of emotions: concern for Caroline (Was something really wrong?) mixed with intense curiosity (What *was* wrong?) and annoyance (So what the hell was she doing here if she didn't want to confide in me?).

I watched as Caroline leaned back into the Haitian cotton upholstery. She crossed her legs, exposing expensive-looking black leather boots. "So how are *you* doing?" Sounding like her old self again, wanting to know everything that was going on.

"Okay. Too busy at work, as usual. Trying to make arrangements for a family therapy conference next week that should have been made months ago." How in the world had we ended up discussing my work week?

"Don't you ever want to get back into real journalism?"

I shook my head, trying—unsuccessfully—to ignore the stab of resentment at her assumption that my public relations job at the mental health center wasn't "real journalism." "No, I like the variety of what I do: one day interviewing patients for a feature story, the next day giving tours or helping arrange a conference. And I've been at the center so long, it feels like a second family."

She shrugged. "You always had a higher opinion of families than I did. One family is more than enough for me."

At first I'd assumed that Caroline was just steering the conversation to safer topics—topics where she was in control, she asked the questions. She'd gotten cold feet about confiding in me and wanted a few minutes of face-saving small talk before she left. But now I wasn't so sure. She seemed to have recovered from her emotional outburst with amazing speed. If she was really feeling so awful, would she be sitting here now, acting for all the world as if nothing unusual had happened?

When I didn't say anything, Caroline added, "It's been a long time since I've seen you, Liz." To her credit, she didn't make it sound like an accusation.

"Yes." Seven months to be exact. The last time I'd gone to lunch with Caroline she had told me at length what an imbecile I'd been to leave Max, and suggested—no, ordered—that I go crawling back to him. I decided then that I'd had it with our volatile friendship. I was too tired and too depressed to deal with Caroline's demands and her compulsive string-pulling any longer.

I studied the poised, affable person in front of me. Just one long-time friend stopping in to catch up with her old college roommate. Could the my-world-is-crumbling speech have been just an act, a ruse to get in the door and catch my attention? Could this be Caroline's roundabout way of apologizing for her meddling and inexcusable rudeness? Caroline never, ever apologized for her actions. Perhaps this was her way of trying to say, "Forgive me, Liz. Let's be friends again."

"Jonathan asks about you," she said.

"Tell him Hi. We need to get together." My only regret about how things stood with Caroline was missing my visits with Jonathan. During a smoother phase of our friendship, she had asked me to be her son's godmother. I took this as an obligation to produce Christmas presents, birthday gifts, Valentine's cards, and regular outings to Baskin-Robbins.

"I know he'd like that. He misses you."

"I miss him too." Jonathan was a likable eight-year-old, triply blessed, with his mother's looks, brains, and a personality totally unlike hers. "How's he doing?"

Caroline's large violet eyes finally showed some animation. "He's great. He's into video games now, his new all-consuming passion."

"What? What happened to the dinosaurs?" Had the child already tossed out the plastic stegosaurus I'd spent an entire lunch hour tracking down?

"Extinct." She smiled. "Jonathan packed them all away in his closet four months ago."

She seemed to have forgotten all about her big crisis, whatever it was. Caroline leaned toward me. "So what about men? Are you dating anyone?"

"Not really. Nothing serious, in any case."

"I don't think Max is dating either. At least he came to the Stantons' Halloween party by himself."

"How fascinating." You'd think she'd learn, wouldn't you? A bright woman, astute enough when she wanted to be, someone who'd known me since I was eighteen.

But no, Caroline had introduced Max and me, Caroline had hosted our wedding, and Caroline wanted us back together. The hell with what Max and I wanted.

"You ever think about trying to get back together with

him?'' she asked on cue. ''Maybe now that you're not so depressed.''

''No!'' I could feel my cheeks burning. ''Being alone by myself is infinitely preferable to being alone and living with Max.''

Caroline considered that for a moment. ''That's an interesting concept. I wish I could feel that way. Are you sure that's how you feel?''

I stood up. When I managed to speak, my voice was shaking. ''Caroline, I don't want to see you anymore. I'm fed up with you always thinking you know what's best for me. I'm sick of your bullying and your unending—and totally insensitive advice. You know why I don't believe that anything awful is going to happen to you? Because you have no *clue* what awful is. You think awful is when your fingernail breaks!''

Caroline stood, too. ''You really believe that, don't you?'' she said quietly.

I watched her manicured hands pull on her leather gloves. She stopped at the doorway of my apartment, turned back to face me. ''I'm sorry I bothered you, Liz,'' she said in a small, quiet voice. Then she walked out, letting in a draft of cold air and the gray promise of imminent rain.

I retreated to my bath water, which by now was stone-cold with floating pools of bath oil. I added enough hot water to boil a lobster. I attempted to commune with Commander Dalgliesh. But I felt edgy and too distracted to get into the book. Confrontation was Caroline's style, not mine. I was an avoider, not a fighter. I was always too afraid of hurting anyone's feelings.

After my unsettling afternoon, the prospect of an evening with my sister Margaret, her husband, Raoul, and their three rambunctious preschoolers seemed a pleasant diversion. I arrived early, intending to tell Margaret about Caroline's strange visit. But five minutes after I walked in the door, two-year-old Maria stumbled and gashed her head on the coffee table. I ended up babysitting the four-year-old twins while their parents took Maria to the emergency room. By the time they got back, three hours later, the only thing any of us wanted was to go to bed.

I didn't think about Caroline again until Sunday evening, when Max phoned.

''The reason I'm calling,'' he explained in his careful, lawyerly way, ''is that I thought you'd want to know Caroline Marshall is dead.''

''Dead?'' I repeated, sure I'd misunderstood him.

''Paul found her body this morning. He and Jonathan had been out of town for the weekend.''

My stomach lurched. My head felt light, and the room tipped for a moment. ''What happened?''

''She shot herself.''

''Oh, God,'' I moaned, remembering those darting violet eyes. ''Oh, God.''

He told me the time and place of the funeral. I was barely listening.

It's as if everything is crumbling around me. I don't know if I can take anymore, Liz. Caroline had come to me for help, and I'd sneered at her.

TWO

Caroline Rogers Marshall was not present at her funeral. I wished, as I listened to the earnest, baby-faced Methodist minister drone on about a woman he obviously had not known, I could have said the same for myself.

". . . the tragic death of this promising young woman." I caught the end of the sentence, delivered in the minister's nasal voice.

Promising? Yes, Caroline had been promising. But it seemed a generic comment. I bet this guy thought *everyone* under the age of thirty-five was promising. The person the clergyman described was just a statistic: a thirty-two-year-old woman/wife/mother who killed herself. His eulogy transmitted no sense of the charming, cranky, brilliant, combative, funny, ambitious, crusading person Caroline had been, and that made me angry. Caroline deserved better.

I glanced around the huge, crowded church, trying to gauge reactions. In the pew on my left a tall man with a lined, angular face and longish light brown hair stared back at me: Nick Finley, a reporter who Caroline often teamed up with in investigative stories. "An aging SDSer turned muckraker," she'd called him when she introduced us at one of her Christmas parties. I'd thought the description apt. For all his wit and quirky charm, Nick seemed an angry man. I'd liked him and sensed that he liked me, but I was glad I didn't have to work with him.

Nick caught me looking and rolled his eyes at me. Apparently he shared my opinion of the eulogy.

From what I could see, we were the only ones of the assembled mourners with any visible reaction to the minister's words. I recognized several people from Paul's law firm, a couple of associates I'd met once or twice, and, across the aisle from me, Paul's secretary, Mary Louise Smythe, looking solemn in a plain navy suit. A few rows ahead of her Max sat with another attorney. Although I could see only the back of his head, I could picture the expression on Max's face: blank, appropriate. At this precise moment he was probably mentally composing his condolence note to the family.

"Yet we cannot allow ourselves to give in to despair," the minister was saying. I tuned him out. I substituted my own images: Caroline getting up at 4 a.m. the day of my wedding so she could tie hundreds of fresh roses along the staircase I would walk down. "I wanted everything to be perfect for your big day," she'd explained when I arrived at her house for the ceremony and asked why her hands were bandaged. Caroline snarling at a sidewalk heckler during a college protest march: "I may be a bitch, but at least I'm a bitch with a social conscience." Caroline in a hospital bed, holding up her newborn baby, asking softly, "Don't you think he's the most beautiful thing you've ever seen, Liz?"

The minister was now talking about what a loss Caroline's death was to her husband, her young son, her friends and colleagues. I heard sobs from the front of the church, the murmur of whispered voices. Caroline's Aunt Gertrude, a plump, white-haired woman Caroline adored, stood up. She draped her arm around Jonathan's heaving, blue-blazered shoulder, then hurried the little boy out a side entrance of the sanctuary.

Until then I'd managed to maintain my composure. But the sight of Jonathan made me lose it. Tears welled in my eyes, then spilled down my cheeks. The sobbing child made real what all of the minister's words failed to convey: a living, breathing woman, connected to so many of us, was dead. And we, the survivors, had to deal with that the best we could.

Finally the service was over. I swiped at my face with a soggy tissue, undoubtedly removing the last trace of my carefully applied makeup. I took deep breaths, trying to collect myself.

The pallbearers carried Caroline's casket out of the church. A movement to my left made me turn in time to see Nick Finley push past the couple who sat next to him. I caught a glimpse of his face—stony, pale, fighting emotion—as he strode up the aisle and out the door.

In contrast the new widower, Paul Marshall, looked somber but, as always, under tight control. He was tan, blond, and athletic-looking, with a social glibness I'd always found irritating. He was the kind of man to whom everything seemed to come too easily—an assessment that today made me feel guilty. He was talking to an elegant looking older woman in an expensive black silk suit and large pearl earrings. I'd met her only once: Celia, Caroline's stepmother. "The Shopaholic," Caroline had disdainfully called her.

I exchanged greetings with Mary Louise and lingered in my pew, waiting for Max to work his way back to me. We had ended our marriage with chilly civility, but the way I felt today, even a few minutes of polite small talk would be welcome.

I studied my ex-husband as he moved down the aisle. A new suit, almost-black navy sharkskin, identical to one he'd owned several years ago, did a good job of hiding the weight he'd gained—ten pounds maybe. The extra weight made his face look jowly, his eyes appear even smaller behind his horn-rimmed glasses. He held his body stiffly—still the brainy, unathletic kid who wished reading were a team sport—as he talked nonstop to the intense-looking young man with him.

Undoubtedly the guy with Max was a new associate at the law firm. Max only got that animated when he was discussing The Law. The two of them were almost at my pew now.

Perhaps it was naive of me to expect comfort from my ex-husband, a temporary transcending of animosity because of shared tragedy. Dealing with any of my emotions had never been his strong suit.

"Hello, Max," I said.

With obvious reluctance, he wrenched himself from his conversation long enough to glance at me. He nodded and kept walking.

I told myself I wouldn't have been so upset on another day. Seven years with the man, and he didn't even want to acknowledge my presence! I felt slapped in the face. And then I thought, Maybe that's the way Caroline felt when she walked out of my apartment that last time. The thought made my stomach lurch.

I took two deep breaths and started toward the exit. Someone behind me grabbed my shoulder. "Liz James!" The voice was instantly recognizable. I turned to face the oversized body and beaming face of Ted Houssman, my former therapist. He, at least, looked happy to see me.

"How have you been?" he asked, leaning down and peering into my face. He raised his eyebrows, an expectant expression on his face. His waiting-for-information look that I remembered well from our therapy sessions.

"I've been fine," I said. "Until Caroline died. That really shook me."

He nodded. "It upset me too. She was such a vibrant woman, so full of life. It's hard to accept that someone like Caroline would kill herself."

From the corner of my eye I could see Max in the church vestibule, watching us. He'd had one session with Dr. Houssman a few months before we decided to divorce. When Dr. H. suggested he try being more supportive of me, Max found a legion of excuses why he couldn't go back for further visits. Max also had a paranoid conviction that the only thing I ever did in therapy was complain about him behind his back, which was only partially true.

"Caroline came to see me the Saturday she died," I said. "She told me that something was terribly wrong, but she wouldn't say what. We ended up in an argument, with me telling her nothing terrible ever happened to her." I swallowed. "What if I'd been more persistent, or asked the right questions, or showed more concern? Maybe"—my voice broke—"she'd be alive today."

Dr. Houssman draped one giant arm around me and

squeezed my shoulder. "Everybody thinks that with a suicide. Always! I could have been the one who saved her, they say, if only I'd been more sensitive, if only I'd seen the signs. *I* think that. She was my patient, after all."

"But that was years ago."

He shook his head. "She came back."

Why hadn't Caroline told me that when I suggested she go see Dr. Houssman? Why had she been so vehement about not talking to him?

At the same moment, Dr. H. and I both noticed the church was almost empty. A long line of cars was heading north to the cemetery.

The doctor glanced at his watch. "I need to get back to the office. I've got a client coming at eleven-thirty." His warm brown eyes studied my face. "If you decide you'd like to talk some more about this, call me." He pressed my hand. "It's great to see you."

"I'm glad I saw you, too." I stood on the church steps for a minute, watching him hurry to the parking lot across the street.

I tried not to think about how much I'd missed his weekly dose of warm understanding in the four months since I terminated my therapy. Together Dr. H. and I had survived the roller coaster emotions of my separation and the wrenching realization that my marriage could not be resuscitated and I needed to start building a new life without Max. But finally, about three months after my divorce was final, Dr. Houssman gently suggested that I was strong enough to go off on my own. Our therapeutic goals had been met, he said. I agreed, but I still missed him.

Resolutely I turned in the opposite direction and headed for my car. I wasn't up to the cemetery, and I needed to get back to work.

I spent the rest of the day finishing the last stories for the mental health center's bimonthly newsletter, fighting a constant urge to cry.

THREE

Dr. Houssman had been listening to me for a good half hour, nodding, occasionally interjecting a question, giving me his undivided attention while I obsessed. What I did in therapy was talk a problem into the ground. By the time I was through discussing all the ramifications of the situation—listed all the "but on the other hands," worked through every "yes, but"—I was sick to death of the whole thing, and ready, usually, to move on. But not this time.

"I understand how you feel," Dr. Houssman said. He crossed his leg, resting the side of a well-polished loafer on his knee. He sighed. "Like I said, I feel guilty about Caroline, too. I tell myself, 'Come on, Ted, you're trained to recognize the signs. Why didn't you anticipate this and intervene?' "

"But what could you have done?" I asked.

The psychiatrist ran two thick hands through his tangle of curly black hair. "I could have had her committed, for one thing. She would have had round-the-clock supervision, and I'd have had the time to make sure she was on the right medication."

He leaned forward, his empathetic brown eyes peering into mine. "I guess what I'm trying to say is that despite all her charm and accomplishments, Caroline Marshall was a very disturbed young woman."

"Caroline?" I repeated. I was still trying to envision Caroline in a mental hospital. God knows I'd seen more than my share of disturbed patients in the halls of the mental health center. But somehow Caroline seemed different. Not a picture of mental health, perhaps—but then who was? "She seemed so"—I searched for the right shrink word—"reality-based."

He shook his head, sighing. "Caroline functioned well, and she did a good job of keeping her symptoms hidden. She had me fooled for a long time—too long, unfortunately, to give her the help she needed."

For a moment the pain in those soft brown eyes was so intense that I wanted to get up and give him a hug. But before I could say anything, he blinked. Instantly his face was transformed into a blank therapeutic mask.

"I keep telling myself I should have done something to help her," I said. "I wake up in the middle of the night thinking that. But that Saturday when Caroline came to my place, all I wanted was for her to leave so I could get on with my plans. I told myself I felt indifferent because I was fed up with her being so bossy and pig-headed. It was okay to cut her out of my life because I was pissed that she kept pushing me to go back to Max."

I took a deep breath. "But now I realize there was more to it than that. I was so envious of Caroline's life that I just dismissed her and all her concerns. I told her any problems she had would have to be inconsequential."

Dr. Houssman nodded. "Can you tell me more about your envy of Caroline?"

I tried to put my feelings into words. "I guess it's just that everything seemed so easy for Caroline, and so difficult for me. In college she had lots of dates; I didn't. She always had money, expensive clothes, and I worked a couple of part-time jobs and struggled to get by on my scholarship money. Then, when she married Paul, she had a baby right away, a healthy, beautiful baby. And as we know"—my voice broke as I remembered each miscarriage—"that's a touchy topic for me."

He let me cry, without comment, finally leaning toward the oak coffee table between us to pull a tissue from a box.

"That's all?" he asked, handing me the tissue.

"That's not enough?" I tried to smile as I wiped my eyes.

"Of course there were other, more recent things. I got divorced, but she was still married, living in a beautiful house. Her career seemed much more exciting than mine, real Woodward and Bernstein stuff. She even seemed to be a good mother, something I never would have expected from her."

Dr. H. raised an eyebrow. "What kind of mother did you expect her to be?"

I thought about it. "Moody, bossy, controlling—the way she was with me and everyone else. But she wasn't like that with Jonathan. With him she was affectionate, kidding him a lot, really tuned in to him."

I saw Dr. Houssman glance at the round crystal clock that faced him on the coffee table. He'd joked once that he needed to find a two-faced clock so his patients wouldn't look so disbelieving when he told them their time was up.

"I'm sorry we don't have more time left," he said. "But in answer to your earlier question, there is probably nothing you could have done that would have saved Caroline. Given Caroline's defenses, I can't see her allowing you to help her. That was her tragedy: she couldn't allow anyone to get that close. Keeping up her perfect image was more important to her than dealing with her problems."

"What problems?" I asked. I still wasn't sure what Caroline's problems were.

He shook his head. "I've already told you more than I should have."

"That's it? Go out and henceforth be guilt-free?"

He smiled. "Do whatever you need to do to feel better." His look told me we'd covered this already. For eleven months, in fact. "Why don't you work on it for a while, and come back and tell me about it—say in three weeks?"

I left his office feeling as if I were leaving a safe haven. By the time I got back to my own office, I'd resolved to phone Paul Marshall that evening to see what I could do to help. Perhaps it was the classic example of too little, too late, but at least, I figured, there was a chance that in the process of assisting Caroline's family, I might manage to help myself too.

It sounded like something one of the therapists at the mental health center would tell me in an interview for our newsletter. I just hoped it was true.

As I drove to the Marshall house I told myself that my dislike of the area had more to do with me than with any deficiencies in West University Place. West U was a tiny enclave, a nice, safe village, surrounded by teeming, heterogeneous Houston. The area had great trees, lovely old homes, and a glut of huge, new quarter-million-dollar brick boxes on $200,000 lots. There was a fifties' feel to West U. All the upper-middle-class white kids could walk to the community building that was right next door to the library and across the street from the field where a series of champion Little League teams practiced. My ex-husband, Max, would have killed to have enough money to live there.

Paul was not home when I arrived, but he had told the new housekeeper, a stooped, elderly woman named Mrs. Gates, that I was coming. She stepped aside to let me into the marble-floored entryway.

The house looked the way I remembered it: huge, with cathedral ceilings making it look even larger, and dozens of plants clustered around the row of long French windows in the living room. Everything was still spotless, of course; every pillow on the two facing white couches plumped, every frame on the bright abstract paintings dusted. It was the kind of house that always looked ready for *Architectural Digest* photographers.

"Mr. Marshall told me to tell you her clothes are all still in her bedroom, the first room on the right." Mrs. Gates pointed a wrinkled finger up the winding staircase. "He told me to get some cardboard boxes for you."

She made it sound as if she wouldn't have let me have the boxes without Mr. Marshall's permission, and both of us—Paul and I—were making unreasonable demands on her. I wondered how long Mrs. Gates had been with the family. She seemed too old and too sour-tempered to be in charge of an eight-year-old boy. I much preferred Juanita, a sunny, nineteen-year-old from El Paso, who'd been here a year ago.

Maybe, though, I was jumping to conclusions, I thought as I trudged up the stairs, carrying an armload of boxes. Perhaps Mrs. Gates was hiding a warm grandmotherly nature under that suspicious glare.

The first door on the right wasn't the bedroom that Caroline had called "the master bedroom suite" when she'd taken me on a house tour shortly after they moved in three years ago. That room was down the hall, a much larger bedroom, with its own bathroom, his-and-her dressing areas, and gigantic walk-in closets—everything necessary for the perfect yuppie couple.

This room, by comparison, was quite small, with beige walls and only a queen-sized bed, simple teak nightstand, and chest of drawers as furniture. I wondered, as I opened the closet, if Paul had moved Caroline's clothes into a guest room. Perhaps he found it too upsetting to face these reminders of his wife every morning when he got dressed. But had he removed her things immediately after she died? It was only a little over a week since Caroline showed up at my apartment—and then drove back to this house and shot herself.

I tried hard to focus on something else. Anything else. I needed to finish this job and get out of here.

Caroline's wardrobe was as elaborate as I remembered. There were several rows of clothes, all neatly arranged in categories: tailored suits with appropriate blouses, everyday dresses, casual clothes (including three pair of designer jeans), dressy daytime and cocktail dresses, and a dazzling selection of slinky beaded, sequined, and cut-down-to-here evening gowns.

I sighed. When I'd phoned Paul with my offer of help, I hadn't expected to be assigned to the clothing brigade. I'd never been very interested in clothes. Originally I had no money to buy them, and then, more recently when I had the money, I'd gained so much weight that trying on new outfits was an acutely unpleasant experience. In the past year and a half I'd gained twenty pounds—and I hadn't been skinny to begin with.

I pulled each garment from its plastic bag, folded it, and laid it in the top cardboard box. Some bargain hunter at the Salvation Army Thrift Shop was going to be one happy shopper.

By the time I'd filled two boxes, making only a small dent in the crammed closet, my back was aching and I needed to take a break. I glanced at the pile of clothes I'd laid on the bed to fold. Aside from being an enviable size six (no fat and skinny wardrobes for our Caroline), the garments didn't resemble each other in any way. Frilly, flowered dresses vied with plain, mannish suits; a denim jumpsuit lay next to a long pink chiffon evening dress. No one could play guess-the-personality-of-the-owner with Caroline's eclectic wardrobe.

I walked around the bedroom, stretching. When I came to another door at the back of the room, I opened it, hoping I hadn't found another eight feet of clothes. I hadn't.

The room had probably once been a large, walk-in closet, but Caroline had converted it into a small office. Her word processor and printer sat on a rosewood desk, along with a neat stack of papers, a mug filled with pens and pencils, and a little crystal clock. An electric typewriter rested on the desk's typing arm. Caroline also had managed to squeeze in two filing cabinets, a typing chair, and a narrow rosewood bookcase.

If the stark little bedroom gave no sense of its owner's personality, this room exuded Caroline. I walked inside to look more closely at the wall of pictures and framed certificates behind the desk. She had apparently arranged the photos chronologically: Caroline, a gorgeous bride in a lacy white gown, laughing as she fed wedding cake to her handsome blond bridegroom; Caroline and I proudly holding our new college diplomas; Caroline beaming at the new baby she held in her arms; Jonathan as a toddler, grinning gummily at the camera; Caroline, soft-eyed, watching as Jonathan blew out the five candles on his birthday cake.

I went back to study the picture of Caroline and me. The

two girl graduates, dressed in our white commencement gowns, our arms draped around each other's waists. Looking so achingly young and hopeful, our whole lives stretched out before us.

I turned away, forcing myself to read a framed newspaper story with Caroline's byline. It was the first in a series she had done exposing a bogus charity whose founders pocketed the donations they collected. It was a terrific story, well-documented and dramatic. Caroline had won an award from the state press club for the series. That certificate, also framed, hung next to the story.

A noise from the bedroom made my head jerk up. "Liz?" The voice was Paul's.

"In here, Paul." Why did I feel as if I'd been caught red-handed, the party guest snooping in his host's medicine cabinet? "I was just taking a break. I was afraid this door was to another closet full of clothes."

Paul had the look of someone who was annoyed but trying hard to hide it. Up close I could see how he'd aged since that wedding picture. His hairline had receded a couple of inches, his face was puffy and tired. His body, though, still looked like an athlete's. I remember Caroline once telling me Paul had considered becoming a professional baseball player but decided the law held a greater likelihood of big bucks over more years.

"I appreciate your coming to pack up this stuff," Paul said. "Sorry I couldn't be here when you arrived, but you know how things are at the firm. I never seem to be able to get out of there before eight-thirty or nine."

"I remember," I said, feeling irrationally grateful that he had decided to opt for civility. There was something about tall, muscular men like Paul that always made me feel uneasy. "The last year we were together the only time Max wasn't working was Sunday evenings." That was also the year, Max's seventh at the firm, when he decided his normal sixty-five-hour work week wasn't producing enough billable hours for him to make partner, so he gave up his one free day,

Sunday, in his quest for the Holy Grail.

"Well, he made partner last summer. But I guess you know that."

"Yeah, I heard." Caroline had mentioned it to me during our turbulent last lunch. "Look, now that Max has made partner, he'll have more time for you," she'd said. "He won't have to be at the office so much. And think of all that extra money . . ."

I hesitated for a moment, feeling unsure of myself. "Listen, Paul, I meant to tell you this at the funeral. I am so sorry about Caroline."

"Thanks, I appreciate that." His pale blue eyes glanced over my shoulder.

"I saw her that last Saturday. She just showed up at my apartment in the afternoon. She seemed very troubled about something, but she wouldn't say what it was."

Paul shook his head. "Toward the end she wasn't very rational. I don't think Caroline even knew what was wrong. She sure as hell never told me." Suddenly he looked exhausted. "Well, I guess I'll just leave you up here to finish your packing. . . ."

"How's Jonathan holding up?" I asked, ignoring the not-so-subtle exit line.

"About as well as you'd expect an eight-year-old to do when his mother kills herself." Frowning, he turned toward the door.

I hated myself for needing to know, but asked anyway. "She—she left a note?"

"Yeah, a typed one. 'Please forgive me.' Short and to the point." This time Paul got out the door before I could ask any more questions.

I finished the job in another hour, folding the clothes quickly, pretending I didn't know the woman who'd worn them. By the time I came downstairs, carrying the boxes to my car, Paul was nowhere in sight.

I was making my last trip to the car when I heard music from the back of the house. The family room, Caroline called the sunny, plant-filled room. About a year ago she and I had visited there, talking and sipping iced tea while Jonathan built elaborate Lego buildings on the floor.

I set my box on the bottom step and walked to the family room. The least I could do was tell Paul I was leaving.

The only person in the room, though, was Jonathan, sitting cross-legged on the floor in front of the large TV screen. He was engrossed in playing some kind of video game. On the screen a man was swinging his sword at a sniper in camouflage gear.

"Jonathan, hi!"

The boy glanced up at me. "Hi." He turned back to the TV screen.

I stooped down, noticing how pale his face looked. "Your mom told me that you'd really gotten into video games the last couple of months."

Jonathan didn't answer. Instead he stared, unblinking, at the TV screen while he pushed buttons on a control panel in his lap.

I tried again. "I've really missed seeing you," I said, patting his blue-jean-covered knee. He didn't say anything, but at least he didn't pull away. "Do you think we could go out together the way we used to? Maybe to the zoo or for ice cream. Or any other place you want to go."

At first I thought he wasn't going to respond. "Okay," he finally said, still watching the little figures jump around on the TV.

"Great. How 'bout this weekend?"

Jonathan shrugged. "If it's okay with Mrs. Gates."

"I'll ask her." I noticed the brown crescents under the boy's eyes. Probably he wasn't sleeping well.

On impulse I reached over and laid my hand on the blond hair that was the exact shade of Caroline's. "I wanted to tell you, Jonathan, how very, very sorry I am about your mother's death. The last time I saw her she was telling me all about you. She was so proud of you, and she loved you very much. I know she'd want you to remember that."

Jonathan finally looked at me. "My mom didn't kill herself," he said in a flat voice.

I didn't know what to say. How could any eight-year-old accept the fact his mother had willingly—intentionally—abandoned him? Not to mention a child who, for all intents and purposes, had had only one functioning, attentive parent—and now had none.

When I didn't respond, just looked at him, fighting back my tears, Jonathan added, "My grandmother, Mom's mom, killed herself because she was sick. But my mother wasn't sick."

Confused, I asked, "How was your grandmother sick?"

He pointed a finger at his tousled blond hair. "Sick in the head. She had schizophrenia." He pronounced the word carefully, enunciating each syllable.

"Schizophrenia? You're sure?" I knew that Caroline's mother had died when Caroline was a child, but she'd never explained how. Only once, our freshman year in college, I think, had Caroline even mentioned her mother, one time when she was angry with Celia. Celia, Caroline said, was not her real mother; her real mother had died years ago. The implication was that her real mother would have been a definite improvement. But I guess I'd always assumed Caroline had been too young to know her mother well, too young to be very affected by her death. Caroline's attitude didn't encourage questions, and I had long ago forgotten my early curiosity.

Jonathan nodded. "My mom told me. She said that her mom didn't know what she was doing when she killed herself." He stopped, looking on the verge of tears himself. "But *my* mother wasn't crazy."

I reached out for him, pulling the stiff, skinny little body to me. "No," I said softly, "your mom wasn't crazy. But maybe she was really hurting inside, and we didn't know about it."

Maybe some of us just didn't want to know.

FOUR

"Liz?" The voice on the phone was male, a pleasant baritone, vaguely familiar. "This is Nick Finley, from the *Chronicle.*"

"Hi, Nick. How you doing?" I made doodles of intersecting triangles in the margin of my notes from an art therapy interview, wondering what he wanted.

"Well enough, I guess. I'm calling to see if you know any mental health type over there who feels strongly about the ethical responsibilities of therapists."

Every therapist at the center would be happy to be quoted as saying ethical standards were important in therapy—and mothers were important to children, and flags a significant symbol of the Fourth of July. But this guy was an investigative reporter, someone more given to hatchet jobs than cozy platitudes. Someone I didn't want interviewing my coworkers. "What kind of ethical responsibilities are you talking about?" I asked, buying time until I figured out how to get rid of him.

"Oh, the responsibilities of the therapist to his patient," he said smoothly. "I'm interested in what the therapeutic community as a whole deems inappropriate. So if you could give me the name of someone who's on a national professional committee or someone who's very prominent . . ."

"I'm not going to give you the name of anyone unless you tell me what you're writing about," I said just as smoothly (I hoped). "What inappropriate behavior are you talking about: charging too much, yawning while a patient sobs her heart out, suggesting sex with the therapist as the most effective form of therapy?''

''Yeah, I'm interested in the sex angle.''

Aren't we all? ''Gee, I don't know anyone here who's qualified to comment on that.'' I was remembering one extremely sleazy story Caroline and Nick had once done about mismanagement and political infighting at a local medical school. In discussing one faculty feud they'd mentioned parenthetically which embattled department head was sleeping with which other married faculty member. I (and everyone else) had read every word of the story, all the while giving little prayers of thanks that the story had not mentioned *our* institution.

''Come on, Liz. I just need a few quotes from someone above reproach whose brain I can pick. Don't get paranoid on me now.''

''Well . . .'' I thought about my friend Amanda O'Neil, a squeaky clean child psychologist. There were no skeletons in Amanda's closet. Furthermore, Amanda enjoyed talking to the press and was very good at it.

I ended up giving him Amanda's name and office number. ''Who are you writing about?'' After all my years at the center, I knew a lot of the local therapists at least by name.

''At this point it's kind of an overview,'' he said. ''I'm trying to show how prevalent the behavior is, that kind of thing.''

''And you call *me* paranoid? What do you think I'm going to do—call up the guy and tell him you're after him?'' A terrible thought struck me. ''Tell me this at least: he doesn't work at the center, does he?''

A pause. ''You have someone specific in mind?''

''Damn it, Finley, don't you give me that shit! No, I don't know of anyone who sleeps with his patients. I think it's a dishonorable and emotionally harmful act on the part of the therapist, one that usually ends up hurting someone who's already vulnerable. Most clients are not my idea of rational, consenting adults. But that's not the point.''

''What *is* your point, Liz?''

I thought—briefly—about my ironclad rule of always being calm, pleasant, and helpful to the media. "My point is that you have the reputation of being a barracuda, and I don't know if it's wise to let you in my fish tank with the little goldfish."

He laughed. "I promise you, I never go after little goldfish, only other predators."

Why was it that I didn't feel relieved?

He paused again. "Have dinner with me some night, and I'll tell you more about the story."

"You want to pick my brain too?" I was finding it hard to remember why I'd liked Nick so much the first time I met him. Maybe the fact that he was a friend of Caroline's had unduly influenced me.

"For starters." He chuckled. "Have a good weekend."

He hung up before I could think of an appropriate reply.

Saturday morning I drove to the Marshalls' house to pick up Jonathan. I'd phoned Wednesday to clear the outing with Paul and to see if Jonathan still wanted to go out with me. The housekeeper, Mrs. Gates, took the message and called me back the next day to say Paul had given his permission and Jonathan would like to go to Pizza and More for lunch.

I was surprised when Celia, Caroline's stepmother, answered my knock. "Oh, Jonathan should be down in a minute," she said in one of those whispery Jackie Kennedy voices.

She smiled at me. "Liz, I'm Celia Rogers. I think we met years ago at Caroline's wedding."

"I remember. Nice to see you again." Standing in front of her, I felt like a "before" photo in a diet ad. Thin to the point of anorexia, Celia was wearing a black knit pants suit which revealed that she, at least, had no midriff bulges.

"I wanted to thank you for being so kind to Jonathan," she said. "I'm sure Paul would like to thank you too, but unfortunately he's not around very much." She sent me a shrewd look that said, You know how *he* is.

Despite myself, I liked the woman. I knew that Caroline

hadn't, but Caroline probably would have disliked anyone who married her dad.

"I enjoy being around Jonathan," I told her. "And it seems like a tough time for him."

"Isn't that the truth?" Celia's beautifully manicured fingers encircled my wrist with surprising strength. Her frosted blond hair bobbed as she nodded vigorous agreement. "It's a terrible tragedy for a young child to lose a parent."

"It certainly is."

"Paul wanted me to sort through Caroline's books and papers," Celia continued, "and I was wondering if there's some book you wanted to keep as a memento."

Paul certainly wasn't wasting any time in getting rid of all evidence of his wife. And of course he was much too busy and important to handle the task himself.

I refused her offer as graciously as I could, just as Jonathan walked down the stairs. He looked, I thought, almost happy to see me.

"You two have a great time," Celia called as we walked out the door. "And if you change your mind about the books, Liz, you just call me. I'm in the phone book."

"So," I said to Jonathan as we pulled out of the driveway, "are you hungry?"

He looked at me with an uncomprehending expression.

"Yeah, I guess," he said in a tone of voice appropriate to adults' absurd questions: Do you do needlepoint, Jonathan? Are you fluent in Latin?

When we reached the restaurant I understood his reaction. The minute we were inside the door he ran to a machine that produced tokens for his dollar, then headed for a video game.

" 'Double Dragon II,' " I read aloud after following him to the machine. I watched for a few minutes as Jonathan manipulated a little karate guy on the screen who was fighting off a string of thuglike opponents.

"You want me to order the pizza?" I asked, then asked again when he didn't respond.

"Okay." Jonathan did not move his eyes from the screen.

He had the look of someone in a trance, except for the fact that his fingers were rapidly punching some buttons.

"What kind?"

A look of annoyance crossed his face. "Pepperoni."

I left him to his video fix and went to place our order. I wandered around for a few minutes, watching small children jump into a pen of plastic balls and some older children bowling with small wooden balls. Near me a toddler screamed when her mother tried to pull her out of a rocket-ship ride. "The ride's over now, sweetie. Time to get out and let someone else have a turn," the woman explained in her patient-mommy voice. "See? This little boy wants to get on now."

"No! More!" The kid slapped at her mother's hands. "Nooo!"

The mother tried to pry the little girl's hands off the steering wheel, failed, and ended up yanking the child out of the rocket. So much for wholesome family fun.

I wandered over to watch Jonathan defeat evil bosses until our pizza number was announced on a loudspeaker.

"You like that game?" I asked as we started eating.

"Yeah, it's okay, but I like Terminator II better."

I waited for him to share any further thoughts about video games with me. When he didn't, I said, "I talked to your grandmother for a while. Do you see much of her?"

He shrugged. "Celia brought me a new video game today, Teenage Mutant Ninja Turtles II."

Somehow that surprised me. Celia didn't seem the doting grandmother type, but maybe that was because my grandmother had over-permed white hair and wore size 18 cotton housedresses. "That was nice of her," I said. "Did you like the game?"

His mouth full of pizza, Jonathan nodded. "Yeah, it's a lot better than Ninja Turtles. There's more stages in the new game."

Before we embarked on an incomprehensible catalogue of video games, I interjected, "I don't really know Celia, but

I've talked to your Aunt Gertrude several times. You see a lot of her too?"

"I'm going to spend the night at her house tonight."

I tried to resist the pizza's siren call—unsuccessfully. "That sounds like fun. Do you like staying at her house?"

Jonathan swallowed his Dr. Pepper. "I like Aunt Gertie a lot, but she never gives me video games." He grimaced. "Only books."

"Nobody's perfect."

"I'm going to play Super Mario Brothers now," Jonathan said, getting up.

I wished I'd thought of bringing along a book to read. I briefly considered trying out one of the games myself, but decided against it when I spotted the cluster of kids at each machine. I wasn't sure if my reluctance was due to my hatred of waiting in line or to the prospect of elementary school children snickering at my video game skills. Neither reason spoke well of me.

Twenty minutes later I managed to wrench Jonathan away from Super Mario Brothers long enough to play a game of air hockey with me. I, at least, thought it was fun. Then, since Jonathan didn't want to jump in the plastic balls or bowl, we left.

The ride back was quiet. Jonathan gave a few perfunctory answers to my inept video-game questions, then lapsed into silence.

"How are you doing?" I asked when we were a few blocks from his house. "In school and everything."

He didn't answer.

"It must be really tough for you sometimes."

Jonathan looked at me, squinting. In the sunlight the circles under his eyes resembled obscene bruises on his pale skin. He looked like a kid who had recently been very ill and still hadn't completely recovered.

I wanted to stop the car and hug him, to tell him that everything was going to be all right. An eight-year-old should be able to believe that. All eight-year-olds.

"You didn't believe me when I told you that my mother didn't kill herself," he said. "Did you?"

"How did she die, then?" I asked, keeping my eyes on the road.

"Someone killed her."

"Who?" This time I slowed down the car and looked at him.

"I don't know yet."

"Oh." My foot eased back on the accelerator.

"Somebody did kill Mom." Jonathan's voice had lost its grown-up edge; he sounded on the verge of tears. "She told me that if she ever knew she was going to die she'd tell me. Because she knew how terrible it felt when her mom didn't tell her. Mom said she'd say goodbye and make sure that I knew what to do when she was gone, and she'd see that somebody nice took care of me. And she'd tell me things I needed to know when I grew up. She *promised.*"

I turned down a side street and parked in front of the first house.

"And she never did that," Jonathan said. "She never even told me goodbye."

He started to cry, the sobs racking his small, bony body. I let him cry in my arms until he sat up and said, "I want to go home now."

I walked Jonathan to his front door, trying not to be upset at the sight of his slumped shoulders, his eyes still red from crying.

Yesterday I had interviewed an art therapist for a story in the center newsletter. She showed me a picture drawn by a child who'd been sexually abused. The girl in the picture had no head. Another abused child had drawn a family picture in which a large, smiling mother and two smiling girls were in the center of the paper, while the young artist was off by himself in the corner of the page, a tiny, unsmiling figure.

"Even though a child often can't tell me in words what's wrong, he can tell me in his picture how he feels about himself and his family and his relationship with other family members,'' the art therapist had explained. Today, watching Jonathan, I wondered how he would draw his family picture right now.

He pushed the doorbell.

''I hope you'll go out with me again real soon, Jonathan,'' I said.

He didn't answer. When Mrs. Gates opened the door he walked in without speaking to either of us.

FIVE

I don't know why I let my friend Amanda O'Neil talk me into it. I'd explained to her that I wasn't a tae-kwon-do kind of person. I had always loathed exercise classes, and the fact that someone was counting in Korean—''*hana, dul, set, net*''—while we did jumping jacks did not alter the fact.

''It's good for you,'' Amanda had replied with typical psychologist assurance. ''You'll grow to like it.''

Right. Dressed now in a shapeless white cotton uniform sashed with a yellow belt, acutely aware of the *do jang*'s prevailing odor of too many bare feet, I could think of only one thing: How much longer?

Our instructor (*sabum nim*), a muscled black belt who would have fit nicely into any Marine unit, announced we would now spar. Whoopee. Not only was I unathletic, I was also unaggressive, nonviolent. A wimp.

Avoiding my eyes, Master McCrae paired me with a gangly seven-year-old yellow belt named Seth, who glared at me from behind a mop of limp red hair. I'd always suspected the kid's parents had stuck him in here because of his bad attitude.

Amanda, I noted enviously, had a plump, frizzy-haired, motherly woman for a partner.

We began sparring. I executed a feeble side kick that swished a good five inches above the kid's shoulder. He jumped to the side and then kicked me squarely in the thigh.

I backed up, trying, unsuccessfully, to block his next kick. His foot smashed into my hip.

"Hey!" One of the *do jang*'s six dozen rules was that students were not supposed to make contact when they sparred. We were not allowed to "misuse tae-kwon-do." That was in the student oath we recited at the beginning of each class, right before we promised to be champions of freedom and justice.

"What's the problem?" Master McCrae was peering at us with disapproval.

"An accident," Seth squeaked. "I hit her by mistake." Sure he did. I allowed his explanation to pass in dignified adult silence.

"If it happens again you'll be sitting out the next class," our *sabum nim* told Seth. Then, turning to me, he added, "Put more energy into those kicks, Liz."

Seth managed to keep the rest of his kicks off of my body, but when Master McCrae yelled for everybody to get back in formation—our four perfectly straight lines—the little sweetheart left me with a middle-finger salute. So much for Courtesy, Integrity, Perseverance, Self Control, and Indomitable Spirit, the virtues, the class brochure explained, that each student gained from the course.

"I've had it with tae-kwon-do," I told Amanda in the dressing room while we changed into our street clothes. "I'll finish out the month—I already paid for it—but then I quit."

"Oh, but you've made such great progress!" Amanda, a tall, angular woman who'd once been an athletic tomboy, still said things like, "Jogging could be fun, Liz, if you only gave it a chance." I liked her anyway.

I rubbed my aching thigh, knowing there'd be a big black and blue mark there tomorrow. "Amanda, five-year-olds are making better progress than I am. Master McCrae is always on my back about trying harder. After four months of class I have reached the undeniable conclusion that I do not now nor will I ever give a flying fuck about mastering the art of tae-kwon-do."

"Okay," Amanda said. "So where do you want to go for dinner?"

We settled on a neighborhood Chinese restaurant. Last week

Amanda had picked the restaurant, a vegetarian place, and I had no intention of eating another tofu burger. Once seated in a nondescript wood booth, I ordered sweet-and-sour pork and Amanda ordered steamed vegetables.

"You talk to Max lately?" Amanda asked as soon as the waiter left.

In a weak moment I'd told her how upset I'd been about Max refusing to speak to me at Caroline's funeral. Amanda, who has long contended that my major problem in life is a lack of healthy assertiveness, suggested I phone Max to tell him how I felt.

"And what good would that do?" I'd asked. "In seven years of marriage Max never once apologized to me, so I doubt he'll start now."

"I'm not concerned about Max. I'm concerned about you," Amanda had said. "Telling him how hurt you were by his behavior will make *you* feel better, no matter what he says."

Of course I never phoned him. "Uh, no, I haven't talked to Max," I said. "Maybe I should have, but I didn't."

Amanda shrugged, letting it go. To maintain your sanity as a therapist you have to learn to be philosophical when people don't take your advice.

I sipped the tea the waiter had just brought us. "You know I never suspected that you didn't like Max." Amanda had previously mentioned that Max was obsessive-compulsive and a classic workaholic, but since virtually all the therapists I knew from the center were constantly diagnosing everyone else's character flaws, I never thought much about it. Just because Amanda said Max was obsessive-compulsive didn't mean she disliked the man.

"Max is full of shit. I never could figure out why you didn't see it." Amanda set down her little china teacup and focused her hazel eyes on my face. "Not that what I feel is especially important here. It's what *you're* feeling that's the issue."

"Oh, spare me." Sometimes after a whole day of working with psychologists, psychiatrists, and social workers, I wondered if when they got home at night they started lecturing their jumping terriers on latent hostility.

"Anything you say." Unlike me, Amanda was capable of abruptly terminating an argument, shifting gears, and moving on. "Did I tell you I saw Nick Finley this afternoon?"

"How did it go?"

"It went fine."

"He ask you a lot of questions about therapists who sleep with their patients?"

Amanda nodded. "The only stuff I could really give him was the APA's stand on the subject—they disapprove, of course. Nick seemed more interested in how prevalent such behavior was and what the therapeutic community's attitude was toward it."

"What did you say?"

"I said I thought it was more widespread than a lot of the statistics indicated and that many therapists just kind of ignore the rumors about a colleague, particularly if the guy seems competent, bright, a good networker. When I was doing my internship at the child guidance center, this very well-known psychiatrist had a woman patient press charges against him. I was shocked. This man was one of my supervisors, someone who always seemed caring and professional. He was constantly preaching about each patient's right to respect and understanding." Amanda shook her halo of graying frizzy hair. "The woman was in her twenties, suffering from chronic depression. She said Stan pressured her into having sex with him to help her deal with her sexual inhibitions. After Stan's sex therapy, she had to be hospitalized for several months with severe clinical depression."

"That's disgusting," I said.

"It is, but you never would have expected it of this guy—at least I didn't. Not until other women patients came forward claiming he'd come on to them too."

"Did Finley give you any idea who he's writing about? He has to be going after someone."

Amanda shook her head. "He didn't mention any names, and I didn't ask. He did say he might call me again. I got the idea he was still at a preliminary stage, trying to get an overview of the situation.''

I waited until the waiter set down two bowls of rice and the platters of food. ''By the way, Amanda, I wanted to get your opinion on my friend Caroline's son.'' I described our lunch together and Jonathan's comments about his mother.

Amanda put down her chopsticks, her eyes mirroring her sadness. ''Poor kid. Children go through the same stages of grief as adults do, you know. It sounds as if Jonathan is still in denial.''

She sighed. ''A parent's suicide is terribly traumatic for a child. I think it might really benefit Jonathan to see a therapist for a while. If his dad doesn't want to use me, I can recommend several others.''

''I think it would be great if Jonathan could see you,'' I said. Though sometimes abrupt with adults, Amanda was invariably warm and patient with kids. Her husband, Daniel, claimed this was because Amanda was basically an oversized kid herself, but I thought she was the quintessential mother. ''I don't know if his father will let him, though. Paul always struck me as this macho, stiff-upper-lip type.''

Amanda picked up a snow pea with her chopsticks. ''Maybe he'll surprise you, particularly if you give him the we're-only-helping-Jonathan-through-a-difficult-transition routine. You know: No one is saying that the boy is disturbed or even having problems; he's just going through a vulnerable period.''

I knew. I promised to bring the subject up the next time I saw Paul, then turned my attention to my sweet-and-sour pork. A definite improvement over last week's tofu burger.

We spent most of our dinner discussing Amanda's sons. Adam, her older boy, was in his first year of medical school. He was working hard, doing well, continuing his career as the perfect child. Sam, the younger son, was using his sophomore year of college as a personal experiment to see how little studying he could do without actually failing. ''I told him that if he flunks out this semester he'll be spending next year working at Burger King," Amanda said. She shook her head, grimacing at the snow peas. "And you know what that little shit had the nerve to tell me? 'Well, that might be a real learning experience for me, Mom.' "

I laughed. I'd always liked Sam, a funny, creative kid who loved to needle his mother. I suspected—though never in a thousand years would she admit it—that Sam was Amanda's favorite. I washed down a mouthful of sweet-and-sour pork. "So what does Daniel have to say about all this?"

"He says, 'Let the kid sow his wild oats. Eventually he'll settle down and get to work.' " Amanda rolled her eyes at me. "And I know Daniel's right. Still, when I think of all those C's on Sam's transcript, I want to wring his scrawny neck."

When the waiter arrived with our check and two cellophane-wrapped fortune cookies, I was surprised it was already after nine. I opened my fortune cookie: "You must help out in an awkward situation."

"What does yours say?" I asked Amanda.

" 'Prepare yourself for a romantic encounter.' "

I sighed. "Why am I not surprised that you picked that one instead of me?"

"Because you're an inveterate pessimist?" Amanda smiled sweetly at me.

"Listen," she said as we walked together to our cars, "I was thinking you should call up this Nick Finley and ask him out. He mentioned he wasn't married, and I thought he was a real sexy guy."

"He just *mentioned* that he wasn't married?"

"Well it was when I said, "My friend Liz James is on the lookout for an eligible man. Do you know of anyone who fits the bill?"

"Very funny."

Amanda stopped at my car. "I think he likes you."

"What gave you that idea?"

"Have you forgotten that I'm an omniscient psychotherapist?" She leaned down to give me a hug. "I enjoyed the evening, Lizzy. See you tomorrow.''

I drove home wondering if my fortune cookie was advising me to phone Paul Marshall. Any time I was around him it felt like an awkward situation. I never could understand why Caroline had married such a jerk. Granted, he was handsome in a bland sort of way and a partner in one of the city's most affluent law firms. But he was also totally devoid of humor, imagination, or social conscience—all traits that Caroline, for all her faults, had in abundance. Paul was the kind of guy who inspired all those lawyer jokes.

Gritting my teeth, I walked into my apartment and phoned him. I knew he'd be as happy to hear from me as I was to speak to him.

''Thanks for taking Jonathan out Saturday,'' Paul said after I identified myself. Then he paused, waiting for me to answer the unasked question: What is it that you want, Liz?

I told him Jonathan thought that someone had killed Caroline.

A pause. ''Who?''

''He doesn't know—someone, anyone. He just can't accept that Caroline would leave him.''

Paul sighed. ''A lot of us have trouble with that.'' The smooth voice was now palpably bitter.

I took a deep breath and made my pitch. Perhaps a few sessions with a therapist could help Jonathan with his grief. I knew a child psychologist who was great at getting kids to open up to her.

There was another pause before Paul answered. ''I don't think that will be necessary.'' He sounded like someone dismissing an especially persistent phone solicitor. ''Jonathan will be fine. It just takes some time, that's all.''

I took another deep breath. ''I know he'll be fine. But maybe you could speed up the process a bit, help Jonathan recover more quickly, if he talked to someone who specializes in this kind of thing. I'm not talking about anything long-term, you understand. Even a few sessions with a child psychologist could help him a lot.''

"I don't have a hell of a lot of faith in therapists right now," Paul said, sounding annoyed. "The one Caroline was seeing didn't do her much good, did he?"

Before I could respond, he said, "But thanks for calling." And hung up.

I stared at the receiver, wishing I could ram it down Paul Marshall's throat. After seven years of working at the mental health center I still hadn't got used to many supposedly well-educated people's ignorant attitudes about psychotherapy.

Still furious, I did what I always do when I'm angry. I marched to the freezer and pulled out an almost empty carton of Häagen-Dazs. I managed to scrape a small bowl of rum raisin ice cream from the bottom, and ate it immediately.

I was standing at the kitchen sink, licking the spoon, when the phone rang. Paul Marshall wanting to get in a few more jabs?

"Hello?"

"Liz, this is Nick Finley."

I wished I hadn't answered. "Hi, Nick."

"I wanted to thank you for suggesting Amanda for the interview. She gave me a lot of helpful background information. A nice, savvy woman—I like her."

The two of them were a regular mutual admiration society, I thought sourly. "Glad she helped," I said, wondering if it was too late to go out for more ice cream.

"How about the two of us going out for that dinner this weekend? Say, Saturday night?"

I set down the spoon. Was he asking me for a date? No, certainly not. He just wanted to pump me for insider information about the sexual habits of Houston psychotherapists. A professional dinner.

I hesitated. Mr. Finley was going to be in for a big disappointment if he thought I knew a lot of salacious gossip about the psychiatric community. Still, wasn't it in the best interests of my institution to find out what Nick knew?

"Fine," I said. "What time?"

"Great. I'll pick you up at your place at seven fifteen. What do you want to eat: Chinese, Italian, Tex-Mex?''

All of the above. ''How about Italian?''

As we said goodbye I tried to figure out what it was about Nick that Amanda thought was so sexy. Maybe it would come to me before Saturday.

SIX

For my dinner with Nick I wore a long batik print skirt, a gauzy white blouse, and low-heeled pumps: the kind of clothes you'd wear when going out to dinner with a female friend or your sister and brother-in-law. Not a "date" outfit.

Nick, however, didn't seem to notice what I was wearing. He was too busy peering over my shoulder to look at my apartment. "My place was like this a couple of years ago," he said. "The early-divorce look, I call it."

In preparation for his arrival I'd picked up the books on the floor and the pile of work papers on the butcher-block table. Unfortunately this made the place look empty rather than neat. "Oh, how long have you been divorced?" I asked.

"Three years. Enough time to buy new furniture, though I was getting to like the minimalist look."

"It reminds me of college," I said as I buttoned my coat. "You know, your first apartment where everybody pools their parents' old furniture. I keep thinking that all I need is a couple of bean-bag chairs."

We walked companionably enough to the parking lot and his several-years-old black Maxima. It was not the car I expected Nick to drive. For some reason I saw him in one of those open Jeeps—the rakish adventurer stalking his journalistic prey. Obviously I was having some stereotyping difficulties here.

I told myself I needed to set the tone for the evening, make clear my expectations. "Dr. O'Neil said she enjoyed talking to you,'' I said in my best cooperative-PR-officer tone.

''Good, 'cause I want to talk to her again. Amanda's forthright and opinionated, not your typical shrink who hides behind unintelligible jargon and all the while is mentally dumping you into some insulting diagnostic category.''

''You don't sound like a big psychology fan. Caroline always used to say that a story had to speak to her—really intrigue her—before she'd go after it.''

Nick kept his eyes on the road. ''This story *did* intrigue her. It was Caroline's story, not mine. I just felt I needed to finish it for her.''

''It was *Caroline's* story?'' Why hadn't she mentioned that to me? Certainly she was preoccupied on the day she showed up at my place, but she had always phoned me before when she had ideas for mental-health-related stories.

''And you're right,'' Nick said. ''It's not my kind of story. Caroline worked on it on her own while I was doing a story on a scam to bilk city employees out of their pension money—something more in my line.''

''I read those articles,'' I said. ''They were great—well written, well documented.'' I returned his smile. ''So now you're just taking over Caroline's story from her notes? How far had she gotten?''

Nick sighed. ''Only Caroline could answer that. She certainly wasn't anywhere near being finished. I'm having a hard time making sense of her shorthand.''

I'd seen Caroline's shorthand. For anyone other than Caroline, deciphering it was next to impossible—precisely what she'd intended. ''So are you going to have to reinterview everyone?'' I asked, feeling unexpected sympathy for him.

''Unfortunately, yes. Of course by the time I get to them they'll have had time to wonder if they really want to stick their necks out or, in the case of the shrink, figure a way to weasel out of Caroline's allegations. At this point, though, I'm just trying to gather enough background information so I don't look like a fool when I ask my questions.''

I thought, but did not say, So why not drop the story? It

was what I would have done if I was basically uninterested in the topic and couldn't read my predecessor's notes. The story wasn't the Watergate scandal, after all. Nick had mentioned allegations against only one therapist.

He pulled the car into the parking lot of a white frame house that had been converted into an Italian restaurant. Diners were seated at small round tables with glass-enclosed candles, and the place had the garlicky smell I've always liked.

We'd ordered and made substantial progress on our bottle of Chianti when I mentioned Caroline's last visit to my apartment. I wasn't sure why I wanted to tell Nick about it. Maybe just because he was the only other person I knew who understood how much Caroline would have hated that funeral.

Nick was a good listener, nodding, maintaining eye contact, interjecting occasional questions to clarify my story. "I couldn't believe that Caroline would kill herself either," he said when I was done. "Not intentionally anyway."

"You think she could have shot herself accidentally?" I asked, incredulous.

"You don't usually type an apology before an accidental death." Nick considered a bread stick, then snapped it in half without eating it. "I just meant that Caroline had this sort of kinky need to flirt with danger, to take big risks. You know if someone said Caroline was playing Russian roulette and shot herself—that wouldn't surprise me."

He waited until the waiter set down our food: chicken Parmesan with fettucini Alfredo for me, and veal Marsala for Nick. "You know Caroline called me too that Saturday. I was out of town and didn't get the message until Sunday. She wanted to have brunch with me Sunday morning."

"Do you know what time she phoned?"

"Early in the evening, I think. She made some crack about me being out on a date. She didn't sound upset, but it was a fairly short message."

"Funny to commit suicide after you've just made plans for the next day," I commented. Unless, of course, you decided in the interim that you couldn't bear the pain any longer.

Didn't a lot of suicides make last desperate phone calls, a final plea for help?

"That's what I thought," Nick said. "Of course I also told myself that if I'd been there and had a chance to talk to her, she wouldn't have killed herself."

"Oh, God, not you too." My hand hovered over his arm, but I decided I didn't really want to pat it and instead picked up a bread stick. "If it makes you feel any better, a psychiatrist told me that everyone who knows a person who commits suicide feels they should have done more. He said he felt guilty about Caroline too."

A funny look crossed Nick's face. "You talking about that Houssman guy, Caroline's therapist?" When I nodded, he asked, "How do you know him?"

"He used to be my therapist too." Past tense because I viewed my recent session as a follow-up visit, not the start of anything new.

"What's he like?"

"Warm, understanding, funny. A big guy, late forties or early fifties, with lots of curly black hair." A sudden thought made me return my forkful of fettucini to my plate. "Why do you want to know?"

"Oh, I'm always looking for shrinks to interview. I told you I need to gather background information."

You'd think investigative reporters would be more adept at lying. Nick was doing everything except stand on his head to avoid meeting my eyes. "Nick, you've got to tell me this. Was Caroline writing about Dr. Houssman?" It might explain her strange reaction when I suggested that she phone him.

Nick looked genuinely startled. "No, not in the notes I have. Why? Has this Houssman come on to you?"

"No! He wouldn't do anything that sleazy."

"You said he was warm."

"Not that warm." Then, getting defensive, I added, "Dr. Houssman is *very* professional."

Nick looked amused. "I'm glad to hear it."

It seemed time to change the subject. "I really like this

place. My food is great. How's yours?'' Not exactly your inspired dinner conversation, but gee, guys, I hadn't been out much lately.

Nick studied me with intensely blue eyes. ''Glad you like it. I come here a lot.''

By himself? With newspaper friends? Or a special girlfriend who happened to be visiting her sister in San Antonio this weekend? I was surprised that I wanted to know, then embarrassed by my curiosity. Wasn't I here only because of my interest in Nick's story?

Over cappuccino Nick told me his ex-wife was a surgery resident this year. They'd divorced during her third year of medical school ''when I realized I saw more of my landlady than I did of Melissa. Melissa was a nice woman—funny, smart, concerned, just the kind of person you'd want to take care of you if you were sick. But when you weren't sick, it was kind of hard to catch her attention.''

He looked at me, checking my reaction. ''Now you're going to tell me I'm a disgusting, sexist pig who doesn't want my woman to realize her full potentional, right?''

''No.'' I sighed. ''I was always pissed off at my husband for never being around, for caring more about his work than he ever cared about our marriage. So I can hardly say it's unreasonable when you feel the same way.''

''Your ex an M.D. too?''

I shook my head. ''Lawyer.''

''Maybe the two of them should get together. They could have Christmas and Thanksgiving together—that is, if Melissa's not on call.''

''And in his free time Max could handle Melissa's malpractice cases,'' I said, getting into the spirit of the thing. ''The two of them could forge a real working partnership.''

''I hope Max isn't interested in having kids, though. That's one of Melissa's requirements of a man. Prospective surgeons don't have time to become mommies.''

Instantly I was less amused. ''I don't think kids are a high priority for Max; he can take them or leave them. I wanted very much to have children, and he was willing to go along with me on that. Not enthusiastic, but willing."

Nick looked puzzled. "I didn't realize you had kids."

"I don't. We tried, but I kept miscarrying." Four times, to be exact. Once at four weeks, twice at eight weeks, once—the last time—at fifteen weeks. The last time I'd even started wearing maternity clothes.

"You didn't consider adoption?" That was one thing about reporters, they never knew when to stop asking questions.

"I did. Max didn't. He was afraid we'd get a baby from a tainted gene pool. An inferior product."

"Sounds like a great guy." Nick, mercifully, let it go at that. He didn't seem to notice—or, at least, pretended not to—how my hands were shaking when I picked up my cappuccino.

I could feel one of my bleak moods coming on, a description that would have caused Dr. Houssman to start yelling at me. He maintained—over and over again—that I was not a passive victim of this black cloud of depression, that I could control my moods, control my thoughts. In short, fight back.

Except sometimes fighting back didn't work. Like tonight, for instance. I could take note of what I was thinking, recognize the depressive conclusions I was leaping to, and try to replace them with "realistically optimistic alternatives" (Dr. Houssman's phrase—I found those three words in combination a contradiction in terms). And I could still feel like hell. Suddenly all I wanted to do was go home and go to sleep, preferably as soon as possible.

"You okay?" Nick asked, looking concerned. I wondered if I'd missed something he said.

"Sure," I lied. "Just tired. I guess I need to get home."

He didn't imply, as Max would have, that I was ruining his evening with one of my ridiculous moods. Nick didn't make me feel that any normal, *reasonable* woman would try to hide her unhappiness from her companion and at least, damn it, *try* to act perky. Of course he might very well have been thinking exactly that, but he had the decency not to show it. In many ways Nick was not the man I expected him to be. He was nicer, more sensitive, and—yes, Amanda, I could see it now—sexier than I'd anticipated.

On the drive home Nick seemed to sense my need not to talk. He turned on the car radio to a classical station. Occasionally he interjected a comment, and I managed a monosyllabic response.

When he pulled into my apartment complex's parking lot, Nick turned to me. "I suppose I should tell you: Dr. Tom Fowler. He's the shrink in Caroline's notes."

It took me a minute. "Fowler?" The name sounded vaguely familiar. Fortunately the guy wasn't connected with the place where I worked. Under other circumstances I would have been enormously relieved.

"You know him or anything about him?" Nick asked.

I shook my head. "Not really. I think he's some big shot in the medical society, maybe a past president. I think that's why I recognize his name. If you want me to ask around, though . . ."

"Maybe later."

"Sure, it's your story." I was surprised Nick had even told me Fowler's name. I wondered why he had.

He walked me to my apartment, but declined my halfhearted offer of coffee or a drink. Standing in my white-walled, brown-carpeted living room, he said, "You look like you could use some sleep."

Before I could reply, he leaned down and kissed me lightly on the lips. "Take care, Liz," he said as he walked out the door.

SEVEN

My sister woke me Sunday morning with her phone call. "How come you're not awake yet?" she asked suspiciously. "It's ten fifteen. I've been up for over three hours."

"Don't blame me," I muttered. "I would have let you sleep." I rolled over to check my digital clock to see if she was telling me the truth. A lifetime of sisterly proximity will do that to you, particularly when Margaret, with her inborn feistiness, had, almost from birth, usurped the bullying, bossy, surrogate-mother role traditionally reserved for the older sister.

"So why are you sleeping so late?" Margaret, true to character, inquired. "Were you out late with that reporter?"

"Not really. I went to bed early, Mom. I'm just tired, that's all."

"Oh." Margaret sounded disappointed. "Did you have a good time?"

Did I? I wasn't entirely sure. "Yes, it was a pleasant meal. And"—before she had a chance to ask—"Nick Finley is a nice guy and a good reporter. Our business together is finished, and I doubt that I will see him again for a long time."

I swung my legs out of bed. "I can't talk anymore. I need coffee."

"Now if you'd gotten one of those timers I was telling you about, it would automatically turn on your coffee maker and . . ."

I hung up. My sister waited long enough for me to turn on

the burner under my teakettle and spoon instant coffee into a mug before she phoned again.

"I just wanted to tell you," she said, "you're invited for dinner tonight. I'm having ham and scalloped potatoes like Mom used to make."

Except Mom would have burned the potatoes into little black crescents or served them hard and raw and cold. Margaret, at least, could cook. "What time?" I asked, wondering if I really wanted to do this.

"Six," Margaret said. "The kids start to whine for dinner around four thirty. I can hold them off till six if I give them apple slices and Cheerios."

"Okay, I'll be there," I said as my kettle began to shriek.

"Come a little early so you can tell me all about this Nick," Margaret said. This time she was the one who hung up first.

I sighed, then drank my coffee while reading the Sunday newspaper I'd retrieved from my doorstep. I toasted a bagel, covered it with cream cheese, and ate it while I read the paper. I wished I had the medical society's pictorial roster at home so I could look up Dr. Tom Fowler, but my only copy was at the office. I finished the newspaper, showered, and strongly considered going back to bed.

Usually I felt okay in the mornings. My depression tended to start in late afternoon, getting worse as the evening progressed. Dr. Houssman had assured me that I was not clinically depressed, just suffering from your garden-variety post-divorce blues. Feeling shitty, helpless, and sapped of energy were standard symptoms. I'm sure he meant that to be comforting, but it's rather like telling someone who's throwing up every twenty minutes that her stomach virus isn't terminal.

I decided it was probably best to try to ignore that bone-tired feeling I knew had nothing to do with lack of sleep. Instead I did my laundry, went grocery shopping, and chatted with Amanda on the phone about a news release I'd promised to write to publicize her professional organization's latest workshop. I felt like everything required too much energy, and

I didn't want to do any of it, but I tried.

Dinner at Margaret's was an ordeal. The ham and scalloped potatoes were good (I was not one of those depressives who lost her appetite), but Margaret was testy because I was "holding out on her" (her words) about Nick. Afterward I played Chutes 'N Ladders with the twins until I thought my eyes would cross. I came home headachy and ready for bed. Tomorrow I could see Dr. Houssman. The thought of that session was the light at the end of a long, dark tunnel.

At 9:59 Monday morning Dr. Houssman ushered me into his office. He hung my damp raincoat over his desk chair, then waited until I took my familiar seat on the tweed couch before sitting across from me in his black leather chair. "So how have you been doing the last three weeks?" he asked.

I looked at those sympathetic brown eyes, wondering why it was that therapists all had such great voices—soothing, mellifluous. Did they give voice lessons in therapy school?

"Not great," I admitted. I told him how Nick's innocent question—Did I have children?—had pushed me into a downward spiral. "I started thinking about my last miscarriage, and afterward lying in the hospital room staring at the ceiling while Max made small talk." I blinked away tears, remembering that day.

"What are you thinking right now?" Dr. H. asked in a gentle voice.

"That I'll never have children. That I should have insisted that Max and I adopt a baby. If I'd been really vehement he probably would have given in. But no, as always, I did what Max wanted. So here I am: thirty-two years old, divorced, and probably not making enough money to convince any adoption agency that I can support a child." In short, my chances of ever raising a baby were now almost nil.

Dr. Houssman leaned forward in his chair. "Now, wait a minute. A lot of single women these days adopt children. Do you think they're all independently wealthy?" When I just shrugged, he added, "And who knows, you might remarry in a year or two."

Right. And I might win the grand prize in the Texas state lottery. "Another thing that set me off," I continued, not in the mood to think positively about the future, "was that last week Margaret and Raoul ran into Max at a fancy French restaurant. He introduced his date to them: Lisa Somebody-Or-Other, an associate from the law firm. I met her once. Twenty-seven, Harvard Law Review, tall, thin, and sexy with long auburn hair."

Dr. Houssman waited for more. "So how do you feel about that?"

"Oh, I'm totally indifferent. Not even mildly interested, which, of course, is why I'm telling you about it in such excruciating detail." How did he *think* I felt about it?

He raised his eyebrows. I raised mine back at him.

"Think about this," he said. "What are you telling yourself about this encounter? What's your message to yourself?"

"I'm saying, Look, he's dating, and you're not."

He nodded. "Okay, what else?"

"I'm saying, They're probably getting serious. Next they'll be getting married. She's pretty impressive—this brainy, successful, *thin* woman. She can probably even have kids. Brainy, cute, successful kids. I bet Max is ecstatic."

"Which makes you feel—?"

"Like shit." I thought about this for a minute. Was what we were talking about here simple, garden-variety envy: Why should Max be happy when I'm not? Or was there an element of jealousy too: That's my man—back off? And if smart, sexy Lisa found Max attractive, maybe he wasn't such a toad after all.

"Look." Dr. Houssman was leaning forward again. "At this point I usually say, Now what are the other things you could be telling yourself? But the fact is that it hurts the first time you hear that your ex is with another woman." The brown eyes offered me warmth, empathy, understanding. "It's tough."

I could feel the tears well in my eyes. Margaret had been so wrapped up in her sisterly indignation—"That jerk, bringing this anorexic child over to meet us"—that my feelings about the encounter had been lost along the way. Here, though, was someone who understood what I felt, who accepted me the way I was, and who didn't (unlike my sister) use the experience to prod me into Getting Out There, Start Dating—If Max Can Do It, So Can You.

I used the opportunity to obsess for another fifteen minutes about Max. One minute I wanted to plant a stake through his heart. The next moment (most frequently at three in the morning, one of the few times Max was sure to be home) I wanted nothing more than to snuggle up to him in bed and listen to him snore. "A lot of the time, during the day at least, I'm glad we're divorced. I'm not so agitated, so angry, the way I was when we were married. But then at night when I can't sleep, I remember all the good times and all our plans for the marriage."

Dr. Houssman nodded.

"I guess that's it," I said after a longish moment of silence. "I have nothing more to say on this subject—at least for the moment."

"How's everything else going?" Dr. H. asked, looking as if he couldn't wait to hear my answer.

I always thought it a remarkable achievement that he managed not to look bored. The people who said they'd love to be a fly on a psychiatrist's wall clearly did not have any of my sessions in mind.

I told him about packing up Caroline's old clothes and my outing with Jonathan. Since then I'd talked to the boy a couple of times on the phone. "Every time I talk to Jonathan I see how terrible it was for him to lose his mother. I feel furious with Caroline for doing that to him."

"People who commit suicide usually aren't thinking clearly right before they kill themselves. They aren't capable of evaluating the consequences to those they're leaving behind. But you're right, a parent's suicide is devastating to a young child. How is Jonathan holding up?''

''It's hard to tell.'' I described the boy's video game fixation. ''And he's convinced that Caroline didn't kill herself, that someone else killed her.''

Dr. H. sighed. ''I guess that's not so unreasonable. Just a child's form of denial. Does Jonathan have a candidate for his mother's murderer?''

''He says he doesn't know yet. He just knows that his mother promised him that if she were dying, she'd tell him goodbye.''

Dr. Houssman raised his eyebrows. ''That sounds like Caroline,'' he said after a minute. ''Her own mother's death was terribly traumatic for her. That was one of the big issues we were working on in her therapy.''

So how come she didn't say goodbye to her kid? I knew Dr. H. couldn't answer that one—probably Caroline herself couldn't.

''Caroline was the same age as her mother when she died,'' he continued. ''They both shot themselves.'' He sighed again, gazing over my shoulder at the rain-streaked window. ''History repeating itself.''

Without his usual expression of intense concentration, his face suddenly looked tired, older. I wondered how old he actually was. I'd always assumed that he was in his late forties, but today, looking sad and defeated, he could easily be well into his fifties.

We sat there silently, both of us wrapped in our thoughts of Caroline. Finally, though, Dr. Houssman roused himself.

''I'm afraid our time is almost up. Want to come back next week to see if we can tie up the loose ends?''

I realized that I wanted to, very much. I missed the comfort of our sessions together, the assurance that someone would listen endlessly to my obsessing, my self-pity, my fears for the future. When I was seeing Dr. Houssman I wasn't scared by my bleak moods. I knew that, if necessary, he could rescue me.

"See you next week," I said before I walked out of this safe haven into the dark, rainy day.

The phone was ringing as I unlocked my office door, and I ran to grab it.

"It sure takes you long enough to answer your phone," said a deep male voice I immediately associated with the lanky frame, probing blue eyes, and sardonic full lips of Nicholas Finley.

"I did it on purpose just to annoy you."

"That's what I figured." He waited a beat. "Want to go to lunch with me? I'd like to run a few ideas by you about the therapist story."

I hesitated. I'd intended to eat my lunch—one of the tasty vending machine pimento sandwiches and a nutritious bag of Fritos—at my desk.

"Come on, Liz, this is a media relations opportunity," Nick teased. "Isn't that part of your job description?"

That and about five dozen other tasks that didn't strictly fit into the job descriptions of therapist, administrator, or clerk—the numerous, well-defined center jobs. "Okay, you convinced me."

An hour later I was walking into the crowded waiting area of my favorite Tex-Mex restaurant. When he spotted me, Nick's angular, rather sad-looking face lit up with a grin. Probably the man was hungry.

"I just finished interviewing the woman who claims Fowler coerced her into having sex with him," Nick said when we got to our table.

"What's she like?"

"Twenty-three, very shy, a little country girl who seems overwhelmed by the big city. Her roommate heard Fowler give some talk about anxiety, and she suggested that Mary Jo consult him about her anxiety attacks."

"That seems to be Fowler's specialty—anxiety." That morning I'd checked out the pictorial roster and back issues of the medical society's newsletter. Sure enough, Fowler had been president last year. "He seems to do a lot of clinical research too, testing new drugs to treat anxiety."

"Mary Jo said he gave her drugs, but only after he'd been sleeping with her for a while. In her first sessions they just talked and he taught her relaxation techniques. Later he told her that sleeping with him would help her loosen up and overcome her fear of men."

I groaned, recalling the picture I'd just seen of Fowler: graying fifties crew cut, lantern jaw, oversized teeth, and a little bow tie. Not the man *I'd* choose to help me overcome my sexual inhibitions. One of the newsletters had run a photo of Fowler standing with his wife, a gray-haired, very proper-looking pediatrician. I wondered if she knew about her husband's therapy techniques. "And Mary Jo bought it—the Fowler relaxation method?"

Nick shook his head, looking disgusted. "I asked her if she didn't realize this old guy was just coming on to her. She said she did question it at first, but Fowler gave her magazine articles about Masters and Johnson and their sexual surrogates. He convinced her that what he was doing was legitimate—look at all the diplomas on his walls. The woman *is* awfully naive, and she went into it knowing zip about psychotherapy."

I winced. "You know I can see somebody like Fowler telling a patient he'd fallen in love with her and he wanted to have an affair. But trying to convince her that screwing him was the treatment? I mean this guy has a lot to lose, and it seems like he's just setting himself up for some multimillion-dollar malpractice suit." I paused. "Is she suing him?"

"She said she's talking to a lawyer now. Apparently Caroline was so outraged when she heard Fowler billed Mary Jo for their bedroom sessions that she convinced Mary Jo to sue, even gave her the name of an attorney."

"He *charged* her?" Could any supposedly intelligent man be so arrogant, so narcissistic, that he thought he could get away with such behavior? Maybe—I hadn't spent years sharing a lunch room with dozens of talkative therapists for nothing—Fowler wanted to get caught.

"Yeah, when Mary Jo quit therapy—she still had the anxiety attacks and now she felt exploited to boot—Fowler sent her a bill for four weeks of visits at a hundred bucks a pop. When she told him she wouldn't pay, he threatened to turn her account over to a bill collector. That's when Mary Jo called Caroline. She said she read Caroline's story about the hospital board of directors who used the money reserved for indigent patients to party hearty in Acapulco. Said she wanted someone like Caroline on her side."

Caroline Marshall, White Knight. It was a role I knew she'd enjoyed, one that she'd been very good at. I watched the waiter set down my plate of tacos al carbon with refried beans and fried rice. "Sounds like an interesting story." Tapping into people's hatred of rich doctors who were only looking to screw us working folks out of our hard-earned money. Mix well with a deep-seated suspicion of those quack headshrinkers—all of them crazy as loons themselves—and you've got a winner.

"It could be a whole hell of a lot more interesting if I could find that damned journal Caroline was telling me about." Nick scowled at his chicken enchiladas.

"What journal?"

Nick chewed a bit, then swallowed. "She said she had some woman's journal that described an affair with her psychiatrist. Caroline said it was great stuff—well-written, articulate—something, incidentally, that Mary Jo is not."

"But you can't find it?"

He shook his head. "I've searched every inch of her desk, read all her files. Nothing."

I was washing down my taco with a swig of iced tea when I remembered Caroline's little closet-sized office at home. "Maybe it's at Caroline's house. Why don't you ask Paul to look for the journal?"

A funny expression, almost pained, crossed Nick's face. "Somehow I don't see Paul doing that for me. I'm not exactly his favorite person."

No, Paul's favorite person had to have money, clout, or the

inclination to do him a big favor. Still, I wondered why Nick would hesitate to ask Paul for some papers he was probably going to throw out anyway.

"Do you want *me* to ask Paul about the journal?" I intended to see Jonathan soon, and I could ask Paul then.

"Sure, if you don't mind."

"I don't mind." I finished up my refried beans and tried not to think about the meal's calorie count.

The waiter, a grinning man with a mustache, appeared to ask if either of us would like dessert. I would, but ordered coffee instead. Some modicum of restraint seemed in order.

Nick waited until the waiter cleared our table. "There's something else I've been meaning to ask you, Liz. Remember when you told me that you'd been in therapy recently?"

Quite recently. I nodded.

"You know I've been thinking a lot about the therapist-patient relationship. I've even skimmed some professional books that Amanda recommended about the therapeutic relationship. And it struck me that psychotherapy, with all these confidences and secrets, not to mention all this transference bullshit, is an atmosphere ripe for sexual exploitation."

I shrugged. "You can say the same thing about any doctor-patient relationship. Or any intimate sessions with a clergyman or even a divorce lawyer. Hell, even a college professor who gets real involved with his students. They all hear confidences, they all have some kind of authority—all powerful, helping men." I looked at him. "You are talking about men, right? Or do you have cases of women therapists hitting on their patients too?"

"Only men so far." Nick scowled at me. "I don't buy your argument about therapists being just like other helping professionals. Even if you do tell your lawyer that your ex beat you every Friday and screwed cheerleaders every Saturday night, you're not likely to have an ongoing relationship with your attorney or have much emotional dependency on him. Which you *do* have with a therapist."

"The only problem with your theory is that for the vast

majority of male therapists, the most intimate thing they ever do with their female patients is hand them a box of Kleenex. And with the popularity of short-term therapy, a lot of therapists see their patients for only a few sessions, not long enough for a big dependency thing to develop.''

Nick looked annoyed. ''Is that the most intimate thing *you* ever did with Houssman—accept a Kleenex?''

''I *told* you there is nothing even vaguely sexual in my relationship with Dr. Houssman.'' Realizing that my voice was rising, I made a conscious effort to lower it. ''He has been empathetic, supportive, exasperated, amused, and occasionally confrontational with me, but never once has he been lustful.''

''Maybe he's hiding it—ever think of that? Week after week, hearing confidences from an attractive woman like you . . .''

I was so taken aback that I barely managed to defend Dr. Houssman's professional ethics.

It was only when I got back to the office that I realized somehow during the lunch I'd started thinking of Caroline's exposé as ''our story''—Nick's and mine.

EIGHT

I ended up calling Paul Marshall that evening to see if I could find the missing journal. The housekeeper, Mrs. Gates, told me, with a certain sour satisfaction, that Mr. Marshall and Jonathan were not home. All the books and papers from Mrs. Marshall's office, she said when I asked, were now at Mrs. Rogers's house.

Caroline's stepmother answered her phone on the fifth ring. She'd just love to have a chance to visit with me, Celia said, but the files from Caroline's office were over at Gertrude Stone's house. "Gertrude and I are dividing the work. She said she'd start with Caroline's work files to see what's worth keeping."

I thanked her for her help and called Caroline's Aunt Gertrude. The woman who answered the phone sounded out of breath and rather hoarse. I remembered Caroline mentioning her aunt had a heart problem.

When I explained what I wanted, Gertrude said she'd read about half the files but hadn't seen the journal in question. "Now let me understand you, Liz—did you say you were planning to finish Caroline's story?"

"Well, no, not exactly . . ." Gertrude Stone had spent her entire working life as a high-school English teacher, and her I-will-brook-no-nonsense tone brought back unpleasant memories from my adolescence. Nevertheless I managed to explain that I was helping Nick out with some mental-health background. "I work at a mental health center in public relations."

"Yes, I remember. You were Caroline's college roommate, weren't you?" She still sounded vaguely disapproving, as if she were also recalling a criminal record I was trying to hide.

"Yes," I said and waited. I sensed that Gertrude, unlike Celia Rogers, would not be moved by pleasantries or sentimental appeals.

"I'll look through her files and see if I can find anything about psychiatrists." Gertrude's tone made clear that her opinion of psychiatrists was not a high one. "If I find anything, I'll call you."

"I'd appreciate that." I hung up, thinking that that would be the last I heard from her.

Her phone call the next morning woke me from a dream in which I'd arrived in a big classroom only to find all my classmates working diligently on a final exam I knew nothing about. "Liz, this is Gertrude Stone," she announced unapologetically, as if everyone was up and about at 6:05 A.M.

"Yes?" I answered groggily.

"I think I might have found what you're looking for. When would you like to pick it up?"

At this hour of the morning I was doing well to remember my own address, much less the day's schedule. "How about tonight? I could come right after work, if that's convenient."

"That would be fine." She gave me her address. "Why don't you come for dinner? It won't be anything fancy, but it will give us a chance to talk."

Still half asleep, I thanked her for the invitation and said I'd be there by six. I spent the next half hour drinking coffee and wondering what Gertrude had found, before I roused myself enough to get ready for work.

By the time I pulled into the driveway of Gertrude Stone's small red-brick house I had grown less excited about the missing journal. Maybe it was just my inherent pessimism (The Power of Negative Thinking, I called it: If you keep your expectations low, you are seldom disappointed). Or my talent for imagining each of a dozen ways in which the visit could turn awkward. A less introspective type would call this phenomenon Getting Cold Feet.

I had a chance to inspect the street as I waited on the front porch for Gertrude to answer her doorbell. It was an unpretentious block of small, mainly brick houses, a middle-class neighborhood of the forties that looked like it was now going to seed. Two houses down from Gertrude's immaculate lawn, a rusting Ford of seventies vintage sat in a weedy front yard.

Gertrude was smiling but looked pale when she opened the door. Wondering how bad her heart problem was, I followed her through a tiny and very neat living room into a plant-filled sunroom at the back of the house.

"Another plant lover," I said, admiring a blooming geranium in a hanging basket. "Did Caroline pick up her passion for plants from you?"

Gertrude smiled, motioning me to a faded chintz couch. "My sister Mary Ann, Caroline's mother, was an ardent gardener too. She was the one who encouraged Caroline."

I hesitated, then decided to go ahead. "Jonathan told me that Caroline's mother was schizophrenic."

The level gray eyes suddenly looked less friendly.

"Yes," she said in a flat voice. "She was."

"And Jonathan said she killed herself."

Gertrude nodded. "A tragedy. She was only thirty-two."

The same age as Caroline. What had Dr. Houssman said—history repeating itself? "How old was Caroline then?"

"Ten. But her mother had been sick, hospitalized several times before that. Caroline must have been eight when Mary Ann first started having symptoms—hearing voices, having delusions of being persecuted. Overnight, it seemed, Mary Ann changed into another person."

"That must have been extremely upsetting for Caroline."

The gray eyes flashed, the lines around her mouth deepened. "It was extremely upsetting for all of us. Mary Ann was a beautiful, vivacious, intelligent woman. Very talented. She always wanted to be an actress but gave up that dream when she married."

With effort Gertrude managed to push herself out of her straight-back chair. "Let me show you," she said, walking to an oak chest in the corner of the room.

She returned with a brown leather-covered photo album. "I'd like you to see Mary Ann," she said, opening the album and handing it to me.

Gertrude remained at the side of the couch as I studied a page of old black-and-white photos of Mary Ann as a teenager, maybe seventeen or eighteen. "She was gorgeous," I said. The tall, leggy girl in one picture sat on a wooden dock in her bathing suit, grinning flirtatiously at the camera. Her glamour-girl pose. Another picture showed her standing, arms linked with a thin, dark-haired Gertrude. The two of them were laughing.

Like Caroline, Mary Ann was blond and slender, with a face defined by high cheekbones and large eyes. But Mary Ann's beauty was more unusual, more delicate than Caroline's. While Caroline was classically pretty, her mother was a knock-out. She looked like a young Grace Kelly.

Gertrude turned the page and pointed to a photo. "Here Mary Ann is playing Katharina in *The Taming of the Shrew.* It was her senior year of high school. She was wonderful in the role. Everyone said they expected her to go on to become a professional actress."

I studied the picture of Mary Ann, legs astride, hands on her hips, glaring at a Petruchio who looked more like a kid embarrassed to be standing in the middle of a stage wearing a pair of tights. Mary Ann, though, was utterly convincing: feisty, defiant, a grown woman brimming with rage.

Caroline's mother definitely had had stage presence. In all the photos Gertrude showed me—Mary Ann in other school plays, Mary Ann beaming as she accepted the audience's applause—the delicate, blond young woman dominated the stage.

But throughout the country there were hundreds—probably thousands—of talented high-school performers who dreamed of becoming movie stars or Broadway actresses and instead became teachers, housewives, or businesswomen. Mary Ann was hardly unique in deciding to become a full-time mother instead of an actress.

I turned the page to Mary Ann's wedding photo. She was a lovely bride, wearing a full-length satin wedding gown and a lacy veil. In the picture she was gazing adoringly at an earnest-looking young man, who seemed equally smitten by her. "Did she never act again after high school?" I asked. "She looks as if she got married very young."

"She'd just turned twenty. But actually Mary Ann did do some acting. After high school she went to New York for a year and a half. She even got several small parts in Broadway plays. But she met John when she came home to Houston for Christmas the second year. They got married a month and a half later, on Valentine's Day."

Gertrude gazed out the window for a moment, lost in her thoughts. "Mary Ann liked to say she was swept away by romance. And, of course, she was an impulsive, emotional girl, very dramatic, and John was handsome, and wealthy, and very much in love with her."

"But—?" I prompted when she didn't go on. I could tell from her voice that there was more to the story.

Gertrude sighed. "Personally I always felt that the marriage was an easy way out for Mary Ann, even if she didn't admit it to herself. She'd been struggling for over a year, going to audition after audition, working as a waitress to pay her rent. Though it's true she had done remarkably well for a beginner—even a small speaking part in a Broadway play is very hard to come by—I think Mary Ann had assumed she'd have a starring role by then. I think she was ready to give up, and when John appeared at that juncture, it provided her with a convenient excuse." This time Gertrude did not bother to hide her disapproval. "She had a new role now, Mrs. John Rogers."

Gertrude flipped ahead several pages. "Here's Caroline when she was a few weeks old." The two young parents, the smiling, beautiful blond mother and the serious-looking, dark-haired father, gazed down at their sleeping infant.

On the next pages I saw Mary Ann playing with her little daughter, Mary Ann catching a two- or three-year-old Caroline at the bottom of a slide, Caroline blowing out three birthday candles while her mother applauded. "She looks like a good mother," I said hesitantly, not sure what else to say.

"She was," Gertrude agreed. "For Caroline's first eight years—before Mary Ann's illness—she was a wonderful mother: loving and playful and sensitive to what Caroline needed. Caroline and Mary Ann were very, very close."

The kind of mother that Caroline had been to Jonathan. I glanced up and saw the pained expression in Gertrude's eyes.

"These are some of the later pictures," she said briskly. "There aren't very many of them. Mary Ann didn't like to have photos taken of her then."

I could tell it bothered Gertrude to show them to me, but her sense of duty was so ingrained that she couldn't envision skipping the painful part. I glanced at a picture of a stiff, bewildered-looking woman holding hands with a pretty blond girl who watched her mother with a concerned expression that seemed much too grown-up for a second-grader. I wondered why there had been no photos of Caroline's father from the time she was a toddler. Did Gertrude just not want any reminder of the man who divorced her sister? Or had earnest, successful John just disappeared from their lives?

Gertrude took the book from my lap. "I didn't mean to waste your time with these," she said, setting the book on a wicker end table and returning to her chair.

"You didn't waste my time. I enjoyed seeing them."

Gertrude continued to study me for a minute, then apparently decided she believed me. "You know, I think I've talked about Mary Ann more in the last six months than I did in the twenty years before that."

"Why is that?" I asked, intrigued.

"Well, for years Caroline didn't want to talk about her mother. As much as I tried to get her to open up, she just refused to discuss Mary Ann. Finally I decided that that was the way Caroline dealt with her grief, and I had to respect it.

"But then, out of the blue, Caroline started talking about her mother. About six or seven months ago, I think. She said it was part of her therapy. Suddenly Caroline wanted to know everything about Mary Ann: what she was like before she was ill, how she had felt about Caroline as a small child, even"—Gertrude's voice faltered—"how she'd been acting the last few days before she died."

I could imagine Caroline, with her passionate interest, her reporter's persistence, interrogating her aunt, totally oblivious to Gertrude's discomfort. I wondered what Caroline had learned and how she reacted to what Gertrude told her.

"But I didn't know that Caroline ever talked to Jonathan about Mary Ann," Gertrude continued. "You say he told you Mary Ann was a schizophrenic. What else did Jonathan tell you about her?"

I remembered that Gertrude had been the person who helped Jonathan out of the church when he became so upset at his mother's funeral. I hesitated. "He said his grandmother killed herself because she was mentally ill, but his mother wasn't sick, and she didn't kill herself."

Gertrude closed her eyes. Why hadn't I kept my questions to myself? I was deceiving myself if I thought that finding out more about Caroline would help Jonathan—or anyone else.

"I find it hard myself to accept that Caroline would do such a thing," Gertrude said finally. "So I guess I shouldn't be surprised that poor Jonathan feels the same way."

She seemed to rouse herself, remembering her duties as hostess. Quite possibly she was also telling herself that she was revealing too much to this nosy stranger. "But you must be hungry," she said. "I was going to serve appetizers out here, but it's getting late. Perhaps we should just eat now."

Wincing slightly, she pushed herself out of her chair and led me to a small formal dining room where a fine old rose-wood table had been set for two.

Her dinner was delicious: chicken salad with a light tarragon sauce, iced tea, rolls, cold marinated vegetables, followed by a tangy lemon mousse and coffee.

After our emotionally unsettling conversation in the sunroom, Gertrude steered the conversation to a safer topic: me. I answered questions about my job, my journalistic interests, and the kind of books I enjoyed reading. Gertrude was surprisingly knowledgeable about the intricacies of newspaper journalism, and obviously she read a great deal—newspapers, magazines, and books. But even as we discussed our favorite mystery writers, I still sensed an underlying tension.

"Have you finished sorting through Caroline's files?" I finally asked. It was, after all, the reason I was here.

"Oh my, no." Gertrude sighed. "I think that girl kept every story she ever wrote, starting in college."

"Well, I appreciate your finding the file for me—for Nick, actually. Did Caroline talk to you much about her therapist story?" From the anecdotes Gertrude had related it was clear that Caroline told her aunt a lot, at least about her professional life.

The watery gray eyes met mine. "She did ask me what my reaction was to psychiatrists having intercourse with their patients."

I couldn't resist it. "And what was your reaction?"

"I told her that I thought it was morally reprehensible. A woman who is seeking psychiatric treatment is obviously troubled; certainly she is vulnerable. Then this man whom she trusts to help her, to whom she's confided intimate information, propositions her? That is a heinous violation of her trust."

Gertrude regarded me over the rim of her china coffee cup. "And Caroline agreed with me. She said she hadn't felt that way originally. At first she thought that sex between consenting adults was their own business and not worth a story. But she changed her mind after she talked to some of the women involved, who were very disturbed by the experience."

"Did she mention anything about the woman who gave her the journal?"

Gertrude shook her head. "No, she didn't tell me about

anyone specific. Often she didn't, until the story was finished.'' She paused, staring with unfocused eyes into her coffee cup. ''She probably wouldn't have told me a lot about this story anyway. She knew how I felt about psychiatrists—even the ones who don't proposition their patients.''

She might have explained her animosity if the doorbell hadn't rung just then. Grimacing, she pushed herself out of her chair. ''If you'll excuse me for a minute . . .''

She returned with Celia Rogers. Watching the two of them enter the dining room, I couldn't imagine two more dissimilar women. Celia, heavily made-up and with the well-toned body produced by regular attendance at aerobics classes, wore black wool slacks, black high-heeled pumps, and a red sweater with a decorated Christmas tree embroidered in the middle. In contrast, Gertrude with her plain gray dress, short gray hair, and no makeup, looked like a drab sparrow.

''Liz, how nice to see you again!'' Celia said with a smile. ''I was just coming by to bring Gertrude my house plants. I have no green thumb at all, and I was hoping she'd be able to revive them. Then Gertrude was kind enough to offer me a cup of coffee.''

Celia sat down across the table from me while Gertrude went to pour coffee. ''Did you find what you were looking for?''

''I think so. Miss Stone found the file, but I haven't seen it yet.''

''Well, Gertrude would be the one to find it in all of that mess. I never would have, I can assure you.'' She smiled at Gertrude as she served the coffee. ''Have you read all of those files of Caroline's, Gert, and all of those old diaries?''

The older woman—or perhaps just the older-looking woman; it was hard to gauge Celia's age—shook her head. ''Only about half the files, and I haven't felt up to reading Caroline's diaries. I did notice, though, when I was sorting through them that her diary for the last year seemed to be missing.''

''Maybe she didn't keep a diary that year,'' Celia said.

"Caroline certainly wasn't acting like herself those last few months."

I glanced again at Gertrude's drawn face and felt a surge of sympathy for this well-intentioned woman who, Caroline once said, had raised her after her mother died. "I really need to go," I said. "I didn't realize how late it was." I thanked Gertrude for the dinner and for searching through the files for me.

Gertrude didn't quite manage to hide her relief when Celia announced she had to be leaving too. At the doorway, she handed me a manila folder on which someone had printed THERAPIST/PATIENT SEX in block letters. "I hope this is what you need."

I thanked her again and walked with Celia to our cars. Hers, parked behind mine on the street, was a late model white Cadillac.

Celia smiled and squeezed my arm. "It was so nice to see you again, Liz."

I hesitated, then decided to plunge in. "You mentioned that Caroline had been acting strangely for several months. Strangely in what way?"

"Oh, I can't explain it very well. I was afraid that Caroline might be becoming schizophrenic too—like her mother, you know. She and Mary Ann were alike in so many ways, and then when Caroline started becoming so moody and short-tempered and very suspicious . . . Well, Mary Ann acted like that too. Caroline and I were never very close—I think she blamed me for her parents' divorce, which, of course, is ridiculous—but even I could see the difference in her. She seemed like she was turning into another person."

Those were the same words Gertrude had used about Mary Ann. But surely Dr. Houssman would have realized if Caroline was experiencing symptoms of schizophrenia, wouldn't he?

Celia glanced at Gertrude's house, then laughed rather nervously. "But I shouldn't keep you like this. Maybe we can talk some other time."

As I got into my Toyota, I thought I saw the drapes move

in Gertrude's living-room window. I had the sharp, biting suspicion as I drove back to my apartment that there were many things I didn't know about Caroline Marshall, sides to her I never would have guessed.

NINE

I phoned Nick when I got home, but only his answering tape talked to me. When I hung up I idly started paging through Caroline's file. There were four typewritten pages with handwritten notes scribbled in the margin: ''Omit this?'' next to one long paragraph, ''unclear—explain'' a few paragraphs later.

I started to read. I felt a bit voyeuristic, but managed to rationalize my guilt. I located the file, didn't I? Certainly I had the right to read what I'd gone to so much trouble to find.

Even with some sections of the journal obviously omitted, the account was well-written and thoughtful. The writer (there was no name on the manuscript; she referred to herself only as ''I'') began sleeping with her therapist—''Dr. X''—without much thought. She'd had affairs before and was, she wrote, ''quite casual—too casual, I see in retrospect, about sex.'' She was attracted to Dr. X, and ever since she'd told him about an affair she'd had with a colleague, he'd become increasingly flirtatious. When finally, at the end of a therapy session, Dr. X told her how attracted he was to her, how much he wanted to sleep with her, she'd agreed to meet him the next day for lunch. She was aware that the restaurant he'd picked was next door to a motel.

Leaving Dr. X's office, the woman felt euphoric, immensely flattered that this man who knew her so well—''my resentments, rage, and endless pettiness''—was nevertheless attracted to her.

I read the next section, caught up in her story. She had, of course, met Dr. X for "lunch"; they'd bolted their Szechwan chicken and spent most of the lunch hour writhing on a motel bed. Dr. X was a disappointment as a lover: "Why had I assumed that his wry sense of humor and sensitivity to nuance would translate into great sex? It didn't. In bed he was an aging and not very imaginative lover, who seemed much more concerned about his own performance than about me." (It was here that Caroline had written "Omit this?")

Dr. X wanted to sleep with her again. They'd continue her therapy, he said; she still needed to work through her problems with her mother. Their sexual relationship would be entirely separate, and would not affect the course of her therapy.

But after a second lunchtime rendezvous, the writer was convinced that the affair was a mistake. "Why do I leap into sex so unthinkingly, so totally oblivious to possible—and likely—repercussions?" she wrote. "I wish I could discuss this self-destructive behavior—my need to be adored by every semi-attractive man I meet, followed quickly by my inevitable crushing disillusionment with the man. But the obvious person to discuss this problem with is Dr. X. And at this point he is hardly likely to be objective on the subject."

Even the therapy sessions that once were so helpful now seemed "like a farce." She saw Dr. X now as an actor, "nodding, chuckling, running his fingers through his hair whenever he secretly disapproved of something I'd said—all the things he used to do. But this time it seemed as if he were only going through the motions while he fantasized peeling off my clothes."

The phone rang before I finished reading the last page. It was Nick, wanting to get the file. "It's too late," I said, glancing at my watch. By the time he got to my apartment it would be after midnight. We agreed he'd come to my office the next morning.

"So have you read it yet?" Nick asked, sounding excited.

"Most of it." At least he'd assumed that of course I'd pry into someone else's papers.

"So how is it? What do you think?"

"It's well written, and she's more sophisticated than the woman you interviewed. Her therapist didn't tell her that the sex was part of her therapy. They continued their regular sessions and met in a motel another day."

"So what's she saying? 'I screwed the guy, and it was no big deal'?" Nick sounded disappointed. Detachment did not make for good copy.

"No." I skimmed the last page. "She's saying sleeping with him ruined her therapy. When she tried to break off their affair, he turned on her, using the stuff she'd told him in therapy against her. She started skipping her therapy sessions, but the psychiatrist kept calling her, trying to convince her how desperately she needed his help."

Nick whistled. "I look forward to reading this."

After we hung up I reread the whole story, trying to envision myself as a typical newspaper reader seeing it for the first time. Would most réaders find both Dr. X and the writer so unsavory that they wouldn't care what happened to either of them? I wasn't sure. *I* found the story intriguing and perplexing. By refusing to paint herself as an innocent victim, the writer had, I thought, made her case more convincing, a story of complex characters rather than an evil villain and hapless maiden. Even her account of Dr. X turning on her made us see his bewilderment at his lapse into unprofessional behavior. "I don't do things like this," he'd told her. "I've always behaved with impeccable professionalism toward my patients."

"Until now," the woman pointed out.

But then, rather than questioning his own behavior, Dr. X seemed to blame her for sexual "acting out," telling her he hadn't seen at first how "truly disturbed" she was. The typical shrink method of arguing, I'd observed in my years at the mental health center: Diagnose your adversary's psychopathology while ignoring your own.

I put the pages down, wondering what had happened to the author. Her account ended with a few sentences about the destructiveness of the affair, how she'd left therapy feeling even more uncertain, more depressed, than when she'd started. Had she gone on to therapy with someone else? Or, disillusioned with the process, had she managed to weather this crisis on her own? There were so many details missing from the account (when, for instance, had this happened?) that I felt as if I were glimpsing an intricate, fascinating puzzle in which a quarter of the pieces were missing.

Nick appeared at my office first thing the next morning. Perched on the edge of my desk, he scanned the journal. "Dr. X," he said scornfully at one point. "Sure." He finished reading and placed the pages back in the manila folder without comment.

"So what do you think?" I asked.

"I can't use this. No identification of the author or the therapist. This is journalism, for God's sake—who, what, when, where, why—all the little details the writer seems to have forgotten about. I don't know what possessed Caroline to think the paper would run this."

Nick sighed and stood up. "I need to get going. I'm starting on another story." He smiled. "Just a nice union corruption story, no psychological nuances. My kind of story."

We walked together out into the hall, where the custodian was setting up a tall, artificial Christmas tree. "Thanks for getting the journal for me," Nick said.

The insufficiently journalistic article he'd never use. Well, *I* liked it.

I spent the rest of the morning in a long-winded meeting on the center's next psychology symposium. While the clinical psychologists argued among themselves, I had a lot of time to wonder if Nick was about to abandon Caroline's story now that he'd started on a new one of his own. Wondered too why the thought of his giving it up bothered me so much.

But something else was bothering me as well. It wasn't until late that night when I was lying in bed, my mind wandering as I tried to fall asleep, that I realized what it was.

I sat up in bed, groping for the light. I searched for the

journal article that Nick hadn't bothered to take with him. Hands shaking, I read the piece once more.

Caroline had written that story! We'd been in too many journalism classes together, critiquing and editing each other's stories, for me not to (eventually) recognize her writing. That was why the tone of the piece, the voice of the anonymous author, had seemed so familiar. It wasn't Caroline's standard journalism style, but, now that I was sure of my hunch, I could see signs of Caroline in every sentence.

But why had she written it? Had the real Ms. Anonymous's journal been so incoherent or badly written that Caroline had decided to rewrite the whole thing? Or had she invented this "journal," taken what the woman had told her and put it into a more dramatic form? A flashy little side-bar instead of a few paragraphs of dull quotes? I didn't know, but I fell back into a fitful sleep wishing that I had more answers.

TEN

"Well, *you* certainly don't have much Christmas spirit this year," Margaret told me from behind the eight-foot pine tree occupying half a wall in her den.

"No, I don't," I admitted. As a matter of fact, this year I had a definite Christmas phobia, a desire to turn tail and run whenever I heard the jingle of sleigh bells or ho-ho-hoing Santa Clauses. It was a feeling, however, I wasn't about to explain to my sister, who had always been, as she put it, "into Christmas."

Margaret adjusted a strand of tinsel and then shifted her narrow-eyed appraisal to me. "It's the divorce," she said knowledgeably. "No one likes to face being alone for the first time during the holidays."

When I didn't respond, she added, in the voice of someone jollying a cranky preschooler, "But Liz, you don't have to be alone. You can stay with us for a couple days. That way you can go to Christmas Eve services with us and, after the kids go to bed, you can help Raoul and me put out the toys from Santa Claus. And we can all get up real early together on Christmas morning, open our presents, and then have a big breakfast. . . ."

Unfortunately, I was no longer a preschooler. "It's nice of you to offer," I said, not wanting to tell her that even hearing about her Christmas made me feel tired. "But Christmas is a long way away."

"Only three and a half weeks," Margaret said.

"I need to get going." I pointed to the top of her tree. "And, by the way, one of the lights in the first strand is burned out."

"Wait a minute. You can't go yet," my sister ordered. "We haven't discussed our Christmas plans yet."

I sent her a homicidal look, which Margaret, of course, ignored. "I don't want to discuss Christmas plans now—mine or anyone else's."

"It's only going to take a minute. I promise." Margaret paused long enough to yell at her twins to be careful with *those ornaments!* "I've already written Mother to invite her to spend Christmas with us. Do you think that she'll come this year?"

It was a touchy question, one that I had neither the time nor the inclination to answer. Last year Mom had turned down Margaret's Christmas invitation and instead went on a week-long cruise to the Bahamas with one of her friends, another widow. Margaret, who'd always had a rather volatile relationship with our mother, chose to take this decision as a personal rejection. Which was just one more thing I loved about The Holidays: Otherwise sensible people, who were perfectly happy having nothing to do with their relatives during the rest of the year, suddenly took on Family Togetherness as their new religion every December 24. And every December 26 they were furious that Pa was still as cantankerous as ever, and convinced that Ma should get an Academy Award for best supporting martyr role.

"I really don't know what Mom is planning to do this year," I said. Which was partially true. I strongly suspected, from her last letter to me, that she was going to take another Christmas trip with her friend Dot. But since they hadn't bought their tickets yet, I didn't feel morally obligated to share this information with Margaret.

"If she can't make it for Christmas, you could always invite her to come visit another holiday. Say for Valentine's Day, Saint Patrick's Day, or Easter." I knew I shouldn't start on this, but I couldn't help myself. "You know Mom never was a big Christmas person."

"You're telling me? Even in grade school I can remember all those other mothers who baked ten kinds of Christmas cookies and had Christmas wreaths on their front doors, and little mangers on the mantel, and Christmas cards taped to a door in the shape of a Christmas tree. *We* were lucky if we had a Christmas tree and Christmas presents that were wrapped."

I shrugged. "Yeah, that was Mom. Not exactly the Happy Homemaker." But for some reason my mother's eccentricities hadn't bothered me in the way they had Margaret. For all her decidedly slipshod housekeeping, Mom was an affectionate mother who read us books for hours when we were little and, when we were older, took us on long summer camping trips around the country the day after school let out. By the time I was twelve I'd set foot (and often a tent) in forty-seven states.

"So you want to give her the kind of Christmas you wished you'd had but never did," I, the trained Mental Health Communicator, explained to my sister. So what if I knew this conversation was futile?

Margaret's lower lip jutted out and her eyes flashed in an expression familiar to all sisters who have to put up with the antics of incorrigible siblings. "You think I'm just trying to rub her nose in it, don't you? That's what you think, isn't it? That I just want to show her up!"

Well, now that you mention it . . . Fortunately, I did not have to respond to this question before Margaret answered it herself.

"Well, I don't!" she said hotly. "I just want everything to be nice and festive. I want us all to be together as a family for the holidays."

"I know you do," I said, leaning over to pat her shoulder. And she did. Margaret had also believed in the tooth fairy and the Easter bunny until she was in the sixth grade. I figured it was a minor aberration in an otherwise well-functioning personality.

"I *do* need to get going," I repeated. I didn't want to give Margaret a chance to get started again on The First Christmas After a Divorce. "I told Jonathan Marshall that I'd take him out to lunch today."

"That's nice," Margaret said. Nice was an important concept to my motherly little sister. "Maybe you could bring him over here sometime. You think he'd like to come to our Christmas open house? There's always a lot of kids who come."

Somehow I couldn't see Jonathan getting a kick out of crawling under the buffet table's red and green embroidered tablecloth with the other kids this year. "I don't know. I'll have to check to see what his plans are."

I kissed the twins, their faces sticky with white cookie frosting, goodbye, and promised Margaret I'd give some thought to spending Christmas Eve at their house. Then I drove to the Marshall house to pick up Jonathan.

"Christmas sucks," Jonathan said when I asked him when his school vacation started. He didn't look at me when he said it, but instead stared straight out the car window.

I sighed. "Yeah, I've been feeling that way myself this year." But when I was eight years old, I had been filled with holiday anticipation, envisioning all the loot I'd receive on Christmas morning.

I studied the small pale face so determinedly inspecting the empty street. "So what are you going to do during your vacation?"

At first I thought he wasn't going to answer. But finally, as I turned off his street onto Buffalo Speedway, he said, "I'm going to Aunt Gertrude's for a week, and Celia told me that she'd take me Christmas shopping and let me pick out my own gift."

"That sounds like fun," I said cautiously.

"I guess."

I figured it might be best to drop the subject. But, hell, let's face it, never in my life had I been able to resist pursuing a better-left-unasked question. ''Don't you like to go to your Aunt Gertrude's house?''

''It's not that,'' Jonathan mumbled, now developing an intense interest in his pumper tennis shoes.

''So what is it?'' I persisted, doing my old journalism professors proud.

I waited a long time for the answer. ''It's Dad,'' he finally muttered. He didn't say anything else until I'd pulled into the parking lot of Ninfa's, the Mexican restaurant he'd picked for our lunch.

I found a parking place and turned off the ignition. ''You and your dad having problems?'' I asked in as casual a tone as I could manage.

He nodded, avoiding eye contact, looking on the verge of tears.

''Want to tell me about it?''

He obviously wasn't sure about that one. I let him think about it for a few minutes. Finally he said, ''He doesn't care that Mom is gone. All they ever did was fight. He's glad that she'd dead so now he can spend all his time with Jennifer.''

''Jennifer?''

''His *girlfriend.*'' Jonathan made it sound like a disease, a virulent and particularly repellent one.

For once I didn't know what to say. I waited to see if Jonathan wanted to add anything else. He didn't seem to. After a longish silence I suggested that we go into the restaurant, and the two of us walked together into the one-story white stucco building.

Jonathan ordered chili con queso and a Sprite, while I chose tacos al carbon and a margarita. I wished Jonathan were older so I could buy him a margarita too. He looked as if he could use one.

''So have you played any new video games?''

He shook his head. ''No, but Celia said she'd buy me a new one next week.''

''Which one are you going to buy?''

''Don't know yet.''

"Sometime you're going to have to teach me how to play."

He looked at me. "Okay."

Behind us I heard some little kids laughing. "Santa Claus!" one of them shouted.

I turned to see a somewhat underweight Santa Claus moving from table to table, stopping wherever there were children. Jonathan glanced at him too, his face expressionless.

The waiter had just arrived with our food when Santa got to our table.

"Merry Christmas, young man." Up close the guy's beard looked as if one too many little tykes had yanked on it. "What do *you* want for Christmas?"

Jonathan sipped Sprite from a straw. "Get lost," he told Santa.

There was a cactus decorated with tiny red Christmas balls sitting in the middle of Dr. Houssman's chrome-and-glass coffee table. It was the only holiday decoration in either his office or waiting room. Although the cactus was a little too cutesy for my taste, I had to at least give Dr. H. credit for downplaying the signs of holiday cheer.

"Bet this is a busy season for you," I said.

He nodded. "Every December it's the same, wall to wall clients. Speaking of which, how are *you* handling the holidays?"

"Badly. My sister thinks that I'm reacting to being alone for the first time at Christmas. She wants me to move in with them and have their Christmas."

"How do you feel about that?"

"I don't want to do it, but I don't know how I can get out of it without hurting Margaret's feelings. Christmas is very important to her. She works for months to pull everything off."

"What kind of Christmas would you have if you weren't worried about hurting Margaret's feelings?"

I thought about it. "I'd like to get away somewhere, just by myself. Not my apartment, but maybe some place out in the country where I could take walks and sit by the fireplace reading and listening to music if I felt like it."

"You don't think you'd feel lonely or depressed out there by yourself?"

I shrugged. "Maybe, but I feel lonely and depressed when I'm surrounded by people who are so determined to be happy. I don't want to be jolly and festive and tingly with anticipation. I just want to be left alone."

Dr. Houssman nodded, waiting. When I didn't continue, he said, "So you want to be depressed without the Christmas decorations."

I smiled. "Something like that. And you know it's not as if Max and I had such wonderful Christmases together. We usually shuttled back and forth between relatives' celebrations. Christmas Eve dinner with Margaret and Raoul and the kids, then Christmas Day with Max's mother. Max didn't like being around Margaret. Her bossiness irritated him—Max always thought he should be the only one allowed to issue ridiculous orders. And I hated spending a whole day with his mother. All she ever did was complain about how everyone was neglecting her."

"So why *don't* you have the kind of Christmas you want?"

"Because my sister would kill me."

"She'd survive. You need to start thinking about your own needs. Margaret has lots of other people to organize Christmas for."

This, of course, was somewhat like dismissing an upcoming hurricane with a little shrug, but I decided to keep that thought to myself. I did need to start thinking about what I wanted.

But now what I needed was to change topics. I was sick of even thinking about The Holiday Season. "You know, I've met a man," I said because I couldn't think of anything else to say. "Actually I met him a while ago—he was a friend of Caroline's—but I never spent any time with him until now."

"Oh?" Dr. Houssman leaned forward in his chair, looking interested.

I told him about Nick and how he'd got me involved in the

therapy articles. ''At first I thought I just wanted Nick to finish the story for Caroline's sake, and that was why I'd hunted up her journal for him, why I was so interested in everything. But then when Nick said he was going to drop the story to work on another one I got upset. *Finally* it occurred to me that perhaps it wasn't Caroline's article I was so interested in.''

I expected Dr. Houssman to smile. He didn't. ''Maybe the two of you can share some interest other than Caroline's exposé. The story sounds questionable anyway. I'm not surprised that this Nick decided to drop it.''

Leave it to a shrink to think that any ''exposé'' of therapists was questionable. ''I'm not sure what other interests we do share, other than a journalism background and both of us knowing Caroline.'' Put that way, it didn't sound like much of a basis for romance—or much of anything else, for that matter. ''I like Nick—he's funny, kind of quirky, independent and unpredictable. And he disapproves of workaholics; he was once married to one, too. In fact in a lot of ways—in outlook and even in appearance—Nick is almost the exact opposite of Max.''

This time Dr. H. did smile. ''I guess I can see the appeal of that. So now that the story you both were working on is dead, what are you going to do to continue this relationship?''

I shrugged. ''I don't know. I can't think of any professional reason to call Nick; I don't contact investigative reporters with feature ideas. And somehow I don't see myself saying, 'Hey Nick, how 'bout coming over to dinner Saturday night?' ''

Dr. Houssman ran both hands through his curly black hair. He peered at me with a Lord-give-me-patience look. ''Why not? He's already taken *you* out to dinner, hasn't he? I thought you were going to start taking some active steps to change your life.''

He was reminding me of Margaret and her Get-Out-There-And-Mingle speeches. ''I'm just not sure that this is one active step I want to take.''

''You'll never be sure. Do it anyway.'' He took a puff from the pipe he'd just lit. ''How's that for nondirective therapy?''

I grinned. "Nondirective you're not."

"You seem very involved with Caroline," he said, sending me a level look. "You're what? Reading her notes, getting involved in her story, visiting her relatives, taking her son on outings. What do you think is going on here?"

Obviously he thought the answer was of some significance. Is that why I promptly veered off into nitpicking? "It wasn't Caroline's notes," I said. "It was the journal of some woman who had an affair with her therapist."

Dr. Houssman blinked, and then grinned boyishly. "Would you be revealing a professional confidence if you told me which therapist?"

"Don't know. The woman, who was also anonymous, just called him Dr. X." Did I catch a look of disappointment cross Dr. Houssman's face? I decided to feed him my tidbit of gossip. The man couldn't ethically reveal what I told him, could he? "The only therapist's name that Nick found in Caroline's notes was Tom Fowler."

"Tom Fowler?" Dr. H. shook his curly head, looking incredulous. "He's always bragging about his impeccable professionalism. I certainly never would have suspected him of sleeping with one of his patients."

That's what Amanda had said about her supervisor who prescribed sex therapy for his depressed patient. I wondered what a therapist had to do to be considered sexually suspicious: walk around with a perpetual leer, pinch fannies on elevators?

"But getting back to your involvement in Caroline's affairs . . ." he said.

Something was nagging at the back of my mind, something I couldn't put a finger on. Probably Dr. H. would say I was going off on another tangent to avoid dealing with his question. "I guess I never thought about it like that, being involved with Caroline, I mean. I started seeing Jonathan, and then Nick asked for my help." Maybe I was just missing the point, but I didn't *feel* overly involved with Caroline.

Dr. Houssman was wearing his blank therapeutic mask. He ran his hands through his hair.

I stared at him.

"You don't feel that for someone who a few months ago was an estranged friend, someone who seldom even saw Caroline, that you've suddenly gotten extremely involved with her family and her work and her friend?"

"What? I'm sorry . . ."

He repeated it.

"I guess." I tried to concentrate. "You think I'm doing it out of guilt over Caroline's death—right?"

"What do *you* think?"

I didn't know what I thought anymore. Maybe it was just a coincidence. Maybe there were two therapists who ran their fingers through their hair when they disapproved of what their clients were saying. Maybe hundreds did. Perhaps they *all* were imitating some hair-obsessed therapy mentor. Or maybe Caroline had made up the journal. Perhaps there was no real patient, in the same way that *Washington Post* reporter had invented the poignant drug addict for *her* Pulitzer-winning investigative series. Maybe Caroline, inventing "Dr. X," had just used some of Dr. Houssman's mannerisms.

"Is something wrong, Liz?" The eyes turned toward me were kindly, filled with concern.

"No, no. I'm just not feeling very well." I made an effort to stomp down the sudden burst of burgeoning emotions. Like Scarlett, I'd think about this tomorrow. Or at least an hour from now. "I guess I must be coming down with something. I think I'd like to cut the session short today."

"Sure, fine." Dr. H. stood up and walked with me to the door.

I stopped at the doorway. "Oh, I just wanted to ask you one more thing. Do you think Caroline was showing any symptoms of schizophrenia? Her stepmother mentioned that she thought Caroline was starting to act like her mother had when she became ill."

Dr. H. shook his head. "None that I saw." He thought

about it for a minute. "No, I wouldn't have missed that, even in the end." He stopped, looking—or was I imagining it?—embarrassed. "Hope you feel better, Liz," he said, patting my shoulder.

Me too. "Thanks." I walked out the door, not looking back.

ELEVEN

"You know what I keep thinking?" I said to Amanda. "Dr. Houssman never even flirted with me!"

Amanda, to her credit, did not say, Don't be stupid. At least *you* got the therapy you paid for.

Instead she nodded sympathetically and let me talk. We were in her study, a pale green, book-lined room with a battered walnut desk and two faded corduroy chairs. On the table beside Amanda were a bottle of white wine and her wineglass. My own glass was in my hand, and I was doing my damnedest to empty it as quickly as possible.

"Isn't that terrible?" I went on. "The minute it hits me that Caroline was writing about her own affair with Dr. Houssman, I start getting jealous. Was I so unattractive, so asexual, so unalluring that he could only be professional with me?" I started to laugh, but suddenly, unexpectedly, found myself on the verge of tears.

Amanda leaned forward and grasped my hand with her warm, big-boned one. "I know it hurts," she said gently. "I'd feel betrayed too if someone I trusted acted dishonorably. And I'd probably feel jealous too. Transference generates some pretty strong emotions."

She released my hand and straightened up. "But Liz, honey, you don't even know that he *did* have an affair with Caroline. Maybe she made up a case to illustrate the points in her article. You know, trying to make her story more interesting. Or maybe Caroline was writing a composite of several people she interviewed."

"Maybe." I knew I had no actual proof that Caroline was writing about herself, but ever since my therapy session that morning, I'd known—intuitively, viscerally—that Caroline was writing about herself and Dr. Houssman. The woman's impulsiveness described in the journal, her compulsive seductiveness, the need to act on her whims no matter what the cost—that was Caroline to a T. I hadn't known that she was having affairs, but the fact that she did didn't surprise me.

"Don't you think if Caroline were writing for the newspaper about a real affair that she'd use Houssman's name?" Amanda asked. "You said she was using Fowler's name. She wanted to expose him."

I finished my wine, held out my glass for a refill. "But that situation was different. Houssman didn't tell Caroline that sleeping with him was therapy. He didn't bill her for the sex."

"But it ruined her therapy." Amanda scanned a section of Caroline's anonymous journal. "And any experienced therapist would know that was exactly what would happen. Houssman was only deluding himself if he thought real therapeutic work could continue after that. It would hardly be unreasonable if Caroline did blame him. After all, he initiated the affair, he was the professional. Hell, if it were me, I'd be angry at myself, but I'd be one hell of a lot angrier at my therapist."

And how would I have felt if Dr. H. had come on to me during therapy? Flattered, scared, appalled? Probably all of the above. But I don't think I would have slept with him. (I could hear Caroline's voice in my head, "You never had any guts, James.")

"Probably Caroline just wanted to protect herself," I said. "If she ran Houssman's name, she'd have to run her own too, and Caroline always was a very private person."

Amanda tucked her long blue-jeaned legs under her. "How does all this affect your therapy?"

"I don't think I want to see him anymore." I knew it was a childish impulse—I'm going to take my ball and go home, so there—but it was *my* childish impulse.

Amanda raised an eyebrow. "You know you *could* confront him about this and tell him how you feel. You might find out that he didn't have an affair with Caroline. Or maybe he did, but you can go on without it affecting you."

Why was it that every therapist's solution was to "discuss your feelings"? Ever since my divorce I'd been discussing my feelings until I was blue in the face, and what good had it done? I didn't want to discuss anything with Houssman. I felt like a kid who'd gone to tell Santa what she wanted for Christmas only to find, when it was my turn to jump onto Santa's lap, Santa turning with a big leer and exposing himself.

I'd expected Dr. Houssman to be totally empathetic, constantly understanding, someone who appreciated me and nurtured me and pushed me toward growth. The perfect parent who no one ever had. The fact that I knew those feelings were unrealistic, that every day I dealt with dozens of therapists who clearly were just as flawed, petty, and self-centered as everyone else, didn't make me feel any better. If anything, it just made me feel stupid as well as betrayed.

"Do you think it's possible that Houssman missed seeing that Caroline was having schizophrenic symptoms because he was too involved with her?"

Amanda thought about it. "I guess it's possible. Some symptoms can be fairly subtle, with a person functioning reasonably well except for, say, delusions of persecution."

I remembered Caroline in my apartment on the last afternoon of her life. Something awful was going to happen to her, she'd said. But was that a delusion? Something awful, in fact, *had* happened to Caroline that night.

"Because of her mother's illness," Amanda was saying, "Caroline was probably well aware of the symptoms."

"And would have been so frightened that she'd end up like her mother in a mental institution that she wouldn't have told anyone what she was experiencing," I interrupted. "I could see Caroline killing herself rather than face what she might have seen as a lifetime of mental illness."

A knock on the door was a welcome interruption to my thoughts. Amanda's husband, Daniel, stuck his balding head into the room. "The beef bourguignon is ready. I've set an extra plate for you, Liz."

"Oh, I wish I could stay," I said. Not only did I enjoy their company, Daniel was an excellent cook. "But unfortunately I have to go to a Christmas party." I checked my watch. "It started half an hour ago."

"Sure you don't want to forgo the party?" Amanda asked with a narrow-eyed appraising look.

I laughed. "I didn't drink that much. And while I'd love to skip the party, I am chairman of the Medical Center Public Relations Committee and need to at least make an appearance. I'll stay an hour, eat some hors d'oeuvres and go home to bed."

"Drive carefully," Amanda said.

I stood in the polished wood hallway of the Doctors' Club, watching my colleagues chatting up each other, thinking how much I'd prefer to be soaking in a hot bathtub.

Behind me another group of holiday revelers—or hungry doctors—got off the elevator. I turned when I heard someone say, "Hello, Dr. Fowler."

It was *the* Dr. Fowler. I recognized him from his photo in the medical society newsletter. In person he looked tired and older, a tall, pale, jug-eared man in his fifties wearing horn-rimmed glasses and a nondescript navy blue suit that looked too big for him. Maybe the stress of seducing his female patients was getting to him.

"Tom, you remember Eileen Gould from the neurology department, don't you?" a deep-voiced woman asked.

I set my face in that glassy-eyed expectant look of a woman waiting for someone to get off the elevator and turned to check out the speaker. It was definitely Mrs./Dr. Fowler, the pediatrician pictured in the newsletter. She was a tall, big-boned woman in a well-tailored red wool suit. She had gray hair cut in a short, no-nonsense cut, very large teeth, and she looked tired too. I bet living with Tom would do that to you.

They moved on after the introduction. It was not a memorable moment for anyone. But it set me wondering as I joined the party whether Mrs. Fowler knew about her husband's affairs. And did Mrs. Houssman, the woman her husband never mentioned to me except occasionally as "we," know about Caroline? (Never mind Amanda's doubts about the affair; I was sure.)

Reluctantly I joined my party. As I smiled at people on my way to the buffet table, I had a mental flash of Dr. H. sitting across from a slender woman with graying shoulder-length hair. *Sweetheart, I feel so guilty*, he was saying, leaning forward in his chair, sending Mrs. H. his sad, beagle-eyed appeal for understanding. *What can I say? It was a typical, middle-aged male thing, needing to prove that I hadn't lost it, I wasn't over the hill yet. God, I'm such a shit!*

"Liz!" It was Melanie Bent, head of public relations at Presbyterian Hospital, advancing on me with an aggressive smile. I often thought that Melanie took the public perception of what PR people are like much too seriously. "I haven't seen you in ages," she gushed. "How are you *doing*?"

I didn't tell her. Instead I said, "Isn't that Rob Jamesson over there in the corner? Now this is strictly in confidence, Melanie, but I heard that he's thinking about taking an offer from the Cleveland Clinic. I can't imagine who they'd promote into his job, can you? But of course it was just a rumor, and maybe I misunderstood. . . ."

I watched Melanie's heavily mascaraed eyes swivel over to Rob, then back to me. "We need to have lunch real soon, Liz," she said, squeezing my arm. "Great seeing you."

I figured I'd be long gone by the time Rob figured out that I was the one who sicced Melanie on him. In the meantime I filled a plate with lots of cheese puffs and sausage balls.

I forced myself to stay forty-five minutes. After another glass of wine it wasn't that bad.

I was getting out of the elevator into the club's underground parking lot when I heard the argument. First a woman's voice, hrill, upset; I couldn't understand the words. Then the unnistakable sound of a slap. A brief silence was followed by nuffled sobs.

An older couple was on the elevator with me. The two of nem looked at each other, then stayed on the elevator. I got ut. The elevator doors closed behind me.

I walked out into the parking lot. Mrs. Fowler stood next o a white BMW, her hand on her cheek. Her husband was lready sitting in the driver's seat.

She heard my footsteps and glanced at me, biting her lip. 'erhaps I was imagining it, but the expression I saw on her ear-stained face was relief—I wasn't someone she knew. Starng straight ahead, she got into the car.

A minute later I was almost to my car when the BMW sped round the corner of the garage. I had to jump back to avoid eing hit.

"Hey, watch it!" I shouted at the back of the car. But neiher of the occupants looked back.

I was just out of my hot bath and reading an Elizabeth 'eters mystery in bed when Nick called. It was 11:03—I glanced at the digital clock beside my bed when the phone ang.

"Sorry I'm calling so late," he said. "I phoned earlier but 'ou weren't home. I didn't wake you, did I?"

I said he hadn't, then told him about what I'd seen in the Doctors' Club parking lot.

He whistled softly. "Everything Mary Jo told me about 'owler made him sound like the classic bully: domineering, nanipulative, only interested in what he wants."

Exactly the kind of man you wanted for your therapist. 'Did he hit her too?"

"She never mentioned that. He seemed more verbally abuive, threatening to commit her to a psychiatric ward when she omplained she was still having anxiety attacks."

"You know, I can kind of understand why Mary Jo started leeping with him, but I can't imagine why his wife puts up with his abuse. She's a well-known pediatrician, certainly able to support herself. And if Fowler is willing to hit her in a public place where he's very likely to run into his colleagues, I hate to think what he's doing to her in private."

"She's probably terrified of him. I know Mary Jo is. I talked to her today, and she's getting cold feet, thinking about what Fowler might do to her when the story comes out."

"After seeing him in action tonight, I can see her point," I said. "The man *is* scary. He almost ran me over in the parking garage tonight. I had the sense he feels somehow entitled to eliminate anything standing in his way. So did you decide to finish the story after all?"

Nick groaned. "I don't know what I've decided. Mary Jo is so damn vague about specifics—when things happened, what exactly Fowler said to her. Caroline clearly intended to include other cases, but I don't know who they were. Maybe she hadn't interviewed them yet, or maybe she was trying to talk that journal-writing woman into revealing who Dr. X is."

I started to tell him about Dr. Houssman, but something stopped me. Maybe residual loyalty to Dr. H. Or maybe just my journalism background kicking in to tell me that newspaper stories should be based on fact, not just one person's suspicions.

"What are you doing for Christmas?" Nick asked.

I was relieved he'd changed the subject. "Don't know yet. Maybe go to my sister's or to a friend's. Maybe take a trip."

"Where?"

I sighed. "Anywhere. I'd just like to get away. I don't feel like celebrating the holidays this year. I guess I just want to bury my head in the sand somewhere."

"Come bury it with me."

I blinked.

"My family has a cabin in the Hill Country," Nick was saying. "I plan on going there on the twenty-third and coming back on the twenty-sixth. I'd sure like to have you come along."

When I didn't immediately respond, he added, "If you

want, I won't even tell you Merry Christmas."

I tried to laugh. "It's a tempting offer, but I'm just not sure if I can escape from my family." I was also not at all sure how I felt about going to a cabin with Nick.

"Well, think about it and let me know."

I could tell from his voice that he was hurt and trying to cover it up.

Maybe it was because I was still upset about Caroline and Dr. Houssman. Maybe because I'd drunk way too much wine that night or because I can't stand to see anybody hurt. Whatever the reason, I said, "I've thought about it, Nick. Yes, I'd love to go to the cabin with you."

That night I dreamed of being alone in a cabin. Suddenly Tom Fowler broke in the door and started chasing me around the bedroom. I woke up shaking, too terrified to go back to sleep.

TWELVE

For Christmas I'd bought Jonathan a book about improving your Nintendo game, and I wanted to drop it off before Nick and I left for his cabin the next day. When I phoned, Mrs. Gates said Jonathan was staying at Gertrude's. Gertrude, when I called, said that Jonathan was out shopping with Celia. "But by the time you get here, he'll probably be home."

He wasn't home by 6:15. I wanted to leave the gift with Gertrude, but she insisted that I stay for a cup of coffee. "Jonathan really should be back any minute. I expected them an hour ago, but with Celia's new-found wealth, she'll probably buy him everything in the store."

"New-found wealth?" I asked. "Where did she find it?"

"A new trustee for her trust fund," Gertrude said. "Someone who's more tolerant of her shopping sprees." Gertrude's expression made clear her view of Celia's shopping.

Lucky Celia. I finished my coffee and glanced at my watch. I still needed to pack. "I'm sorry, but I really have to go. Tell Jonathan I'll see him after Christmas."

"Oh, I know he'll be so disappointed that he missed you," Gertrude said. "He talks about you all the time." Painfully she pushed herself up from the straight-back mahogany chair. "At least let me phone Celia to see if they're back at her house yet."

She returned in a minute. "They just got home. I told Celia that you'd drop the gift off at her house. It's right on your way," she added, as if sensing a balky student.

Reluctantly I drove to Celia's house, thinking about the strange relationship between these two older women. I couldn't imagine two more dissimilar people, but they seemed to get along splendidly, if you overlooked a little behind-the-scenes grousing about each other's eccentricities.

Celia lived about five miles from Gertrude, in a subdivision that seemed light years away. While Gertrude's street had the unmistakable look of a middle-class neighborhood gone to seed, Celia's was filled with huge new multistory houses set in carefully tended lots.

Celia's house was one of the largest on the street, a three story red-brick Colonial that couldn't have been more than five years old. I vaguely remembered that Celia and Caroline's father had moved there a few months before he died. It seemed awfully big for two people, much less one.

Celia answered the door. "Oh, you have to come in for a minute," she said. "Jonathan is expecting you, and it will give me an excuse to make us both a drink."

I passed on the drink, but followed her down a long hardwood hallway, past a cluster of poinsettias arranged at the bottom of a lovely, curving staircase, and into a large, cheerful room at the back of the house. Two mauve couches faced each other on opposite sides of a fireplace, separated by a huge Oriental rug of mauve, green, and violet that looked as if it cost about one year of my salary.

"Hi, Liz," Jonathan said, smiling shyly at me from a corner of one of the couches. "Look at all the stuff Celia bought me today."

"Wow, you sure did rake it in," I said, sitting down next to him. I was pleased to see him so happy. Celia had bought him a Game Boy ("Now I can play video games wherever I go"), three games for it, and a plastic carrying case. Every kid needed a relative like this.

"I guess I did go a bit overboard," Celia said, sounding pleased with herself. She looked chic as usual, in a red knit suit with a chunky necklace of silver beads. She smiled fondly at Jonathan. "But it was such fun to go shopping with him."

"It was great," Jonathan agreed, then looked questioningly at the package in my hand.

"Maybe you should save it and open it another day," I said.

But delayed gratification is not an eight-year-old trait. Jonathan opened the present.

"Hey, great!" he said, paging through the book, stopping to read a section. "Thanks a lot."

I was happy that he seemed to like it. After Celia's gifts I was afraid that he'd be bored with my paltry offering.

"You were sweet to bring it all the way out here," Celia said in a tone of voice which made clear that she, at least, found it a pretty chintzy gift. But then all of us were not in her tax bracket.

"I'm going out of town for Christmas. I wanted to see Jonathan before I left."

"Where are you going?" Jonathan asked.

"Oh, to a cabin in the country with a friend." I stood up. "I need to get home. I still have to pack."

Celia stood up too. "Well at least I know *you'll* be having a Merry Christmas." She raised an eyebrow, smiling coyly. "With your 'friend.' "

I hoped.

Jonathan searched through his pile of packages. "Look what Celia found," he said, pulling out a Christmas stocking decorated with a needlepoint Santa. "This was Mom's Christmas stocking when she was little."

He stared at the stocking for a long time, his hand rubbing back and forth against the chubby, red-suited Santa.

"I told Jonathan he can have his old stocking at his house, and this one here," Celia said with a smile. "Maybe we can trick Santa into filling both of them."

Jonathan sent me a look that said he wasn't buying the Santa routine but was too polite to disillusion his innocent step-grandmother. Or maybe he figured he might not get the extra presents if he confessed that he was no longer a believer.

The two of them walked me to the door. When I turned

back to wave, Celia had her arm draped around him, and Jonathan was smiling.

Nick's cabin was located about forty miles outside of Austin, in a town so small I'd never heard of it, one of those places with a few stores clustered around a cute town square that made those of us who didn't have to live there buy into the romance of small towns.

The cabin itself was a small stone structure overlooking a lake. I was relieved to find that while the place was tiny—essentially two rooms: a long glassed-in porch with a pull-out sofa, and a big kitchen/bedroom—it did have functioning indoor plumbing, something my still-angry sister had reminded me that rural cabins often did not. ("And remember how you hated Girl Scout camp because you couldn't stand all the bugs?" were Margaret's parting words to me.)

My own anxieties centered less around insects and outhouses than around the question I'd been asking myself ever since I woke up this morning: Whatever had possessed me to agree to spend three days (and nights) alone with a virtual stranger?

Not that The Stranger hadn't been pleasant. Ever since he'd picked me up at 8:15 that morning he'd been chatty and funny and interested in what I had to say. He'd even brought a thermos of coffee. Still, as my ever-supportive sister had pointed out, "My God, Liz, even serial killers can be charming at first. How do you think they entice their victims?"

After we'd brought in our suitcases, ice chest, and bags of food (Nick, I was pleased to see, had packed enough for a visiting army; my own contributions were limited to a can of coffee, pumpkin pie, and a container of Cool Whip), Nick suggested we take a walk by the lake.

"This was my favorite place when I was a kid," he said as we walked down the hill to the lake. "We came here four or five times a year and stayed for a week every summer. The cabin was my uncle's, but he always let Mom use it. He'd usually come out on the weekend and take me fishing."

He pointed toward the lake. "We'd spend the whole day in his boat, fishing, eating junk food, talking about whatever was on our minds. It was great. Uncle Ned was the publisher and editor of a weekly newspaper. I think it was all his stories about putting out his newspaper that got me interested in journalism." He grinned at me. "I thought journalists spent all their time drinking coffee, smoking cigarettes, and telling funny stories."

"I've known some who do. Do you still go fishing with your Uncle Ned?"

"No, he died a couple of years ago. I miss him."

The two of us walked past a rickety wood pier. "Do you like to fish?" Nick asked. "We've still got the boat."

Sitting in a boat, talking, and eating junk food: just my kind of sport. "Sure. I haven't done it since I was a kid, but it sounds like fun."

We walked companionably alongside the lake. "You didn't mention your father when you were talking about coming here," I said as we passed another pier.

"My dad died when I was seven. My mother really struggled to support us, my sister and me. She worked two jobs, and my sister and I were alone a lot. Coming here was a welcome change for us. My mother was around and everybody was more relaxed. The best times of my childhood took place here."

We were across the lake from the cabin now. In the waning afternoon light it looked like a squat and hardy survivor, sitting alone at the top of its hill. "Is it your cabin now?"

"No, it's my Aunt Edna's. But she lets me use it whenever I like. She comes out a lot during the summer, but once it gets cold, she stays away. I think she's happy that I'm checking the place out."

"And miss Christmas? They're not having a big family dinner that they desperately want you to attend?"

Nick shrugged, his face expressionless. "My mother will be with my sister and her family in Abilene, and Aunt Edna's going to visit her son in Atlanta. If I wanted to go to Abilene—which I don't—I could spend Christmas with Mom and Ellen and her family, but no one expects it. We get along fine, but we don't have a lot of expectations of each other."

He should tell that to my sister, who probably wasn't going to speak to me again until Valentine's Day. As we trudged back to the cabin, the wind at our backs, I felt glad that I'd come here.

We spent the evening playing Scrabble and eating popcorn. Then, around ten o'clock, we took a chilly, moonlit walk around the lake.

"This is great," I said, teeth chattering, wishing I'd thought to add a sweater under my lightweight jacket.

Nick laughed. "You look like you need warming up." He moved closer.

For a moment I thought he was going to wrap an arm around me. Maybe both arms. Instead he took off the knit scarf he was wearing and wrapped it around my head. "Keeping your head warm will help," he said.

I smiled weakly. "Thanks." Why did I feel disappointed?

So just what was the sexual agenda here? More importantly, what did I want it to be? I mulled over the questions as we walked, but unfortunately, no answers came to mind. Admittedly I was attracted to Nick—and growing more attracted by the moment. But I wasn't ready yet to be involved with another man.

So what the hell was I doing here?

The will-we-or-won't-we issue was resolved an hour later. After a warming cup of decaf, Nick and I said good night a bit awkwardly and then headed for our separate beds.

The next morning all traces of that momentary awkwardness seemed forgotten. The two of us, dressed in jeans and sweat shirts, took our coffee outside and sipped it while we watched the sun rise over the lake. The hot coffee mug warmed my hands as we rocked back and forth on the old wood porch swing, listening to the bird calls.

We spent most of the morning out in the boat trying to fish. A nice idea, but finally, even with the thermos of coffee and multiple layers of clothes, we gave in to the cold. Fishless.

It wasn't until the afternoon, during dinner preparations, that I started remembering Christmases with Max. Not last year's strained and silent holiday, but earlier Christmases, when Max had tickled me awake so he could finally give me the gold necklace I'd once admired (and never expected to get) in a jewelry store window. Or one year when it had snowed on Christmas—a once-in-a-decade occasion in Houston—and we'd spent hours walking together, gaping like kids at the ground's wondrous white mantle. This year I didn't even know what Max was doing for Christmas—the person I'd promised to stick with through better or worse, and now did not even exchange Christmas cards with.

"Is something wrong?" Nick asked, glancing at me with concern.

I shook my head, and started to chop carrots again. "No, just memories of Christmas past."

"It's tough the first Christmas after your divorce."

I looked at him. "That means it's easier next year?"

He smiled. "A little. More like a dull, throbbing pain instead of a raging toothache."

"That makes me feel a lot better."

"Any time you need some words of reassurance, you just come to your old Uncle Nick." He opened his arms and pulled me close for a hammy hug.

We stayed that way, arms around each other, for considerably longer than was necessary. Then he kissed me, a gentle, questioning kiss. I pulled him closer and began my own explorations.

Nick kissed the side of my neck and slid his hand down to unbutton my flannel shirt. I froze, suddenly stripped of desire, envisioning the sight of my nude body, unfirm, overweight, the "before" photo for a weight-loss ad. Only two other men had seen me completely naked, and I'd been married to one of them.

Nick glanced at my face and stopped fumbling with the buttons. "Want me to stop?"

"It's been so long," I whispered, feeling on the verge of tears. I clutched at my open shirt. "Different. I was always trying to get pregnant." Sex was associated with my handy bedside thermometer, the pillow for under my hips.

I didn't think I was making sense, but Nick seemed to understand. He cupped my head in his palm and tilted it so I had to look at him. "It's okay," he said quietly. "We don't have to."

My lips started to tremble. "But I want to!" Or at least five minutes ago I had wanted to. Very much.

Nick smiled weakly, managing, with great restraint, not to roll his eyes. "What do you suggest?"

"Total darkness."

He nodded. "I think that can be arranged."

Unbelievably we ended up spending the rest of the afternoon in bed, generating our own warmth against the cold and darkness outside.

"We never ate the steaks," I said as I lay limp and sweaty and exhilarated in Nick's arms.

"Hungry?" He kissed behind my ear, the nape of my neck.

"Ravenous." I rolled over, and savored the look, the feel, the smell of him. Wondering how I'd ever had sense enough to do something so uncharacteristic—and right.

THIRTEEN

"Didn't we meet at one of Caroline's Christmas parties?" Nick asked the next morning as he slathered a bagel with cream cheese. He had fulfilled his promise and not wished me "Merry Christmas."

I washed down a mouthful of bagel with excellent French Market coffee. "I think so, but was it last year or the year before?"

Nick chuckled. "I must have made a big first impression on you."

I loved the way he laughed, eyes crinkling and a dimple appearing at the right side of his mouth. "I remember meeting you at a Chinese restaurant at lunch one day. You and Caroline were walking out when I was coming in."

"That was the second time. The first was at the Christmas party. You were wearing a green dress, and you and Caroline and I talked about mystery novels."

"Okay, now I've got it." I poured us both another cup of coffee. "I was pissed off at Caroline, and furious with Max, who at the last minute decided he needed to go to work that afternoon. Everything else sort of washed right by me. Did I seem testy?"

"Let's just say I thought you had very passionate views on mysteries. You practically leaped down Caroline's throat when she said Kate Fansler was pretentious."

"I wanted to leap down her throat all right, but not for that. I like Amanda Cross, but I'm not generally moved to attack people who don't. I was angry with Caroline because she'd just given me this lecture about how I needed to pull myself together and save my marriage. She had this wonderful therapist who would help me do it."

"Houssman?" Nick looked disapproving.

"The irony is that he did help me. I think I went to him mainly because he wasn't connected with the mental health center. I didn't want to be in therapy with someone I saw every day at work. But he turned out to be a good therapist for me."

"I couldn't see that he did much for Caroline."

"He might have helped her if she hadn't been sleeping with him." It came out sounding as if I blamed her for their affair. Did I? Caroline's "journal" said it was Houssman who made the first move, and there was no reason not to believe her. Of course she hadn't exactly *resisted* his invitation. . . .

It took me a minute to notice Nick's face, blanched of color. "Caroline was sleeping with Houssman?" he asked in a small, tight voice.

"I think so." I told him about all the clues I'd spotted after reading the Dr. X piece. "Didn't you recognize Caroline's voice when you read the journal?"

"No, I should have. I guess I didn't see it because I didn't want to know."

I nodded. "It was a big shock to me too. Dr. Houssman seems like the last person in the world to pull that sort of thing. He was never anything but professional with me."

Nick drank his coffee without speaking. Outside, the lake glistened in the sunlight, a fine, bright Christmas morning.

"She dumped me for Houssman!" Nick suddenly burst out in an incredulous voice. "All that bull about needing to work on her marriage, to really commit to it, were just lies. Instead she's fucking this fat, married old lech, who's supposed to be helping her patch up her marriage."

I stared at him. "You were having an affair with Caroline?"

He nodded, still looking ill. "For four or five months; we broke up last summer. It was stupid of me, I know. We'd worked together for years. I knew what she was like. But there was something about her—so sensual and fierce, but vulnerable too.''

He was still in love with her. I could see it in his face, in his shaking hands cupped around the red coffee mug.

I jumped up from the table and rushed to the bathroom, knowing I was going to be sick.

When I returned I said I really wasn't feeling very well. Nick, I thought, looked relieved.

''I feel as if I might be coming down with something too,'' he said, avoiding eye contact. ''Do you think we should leave?''

''Maybe that would be a good idea.''

We were out of there within half an hour, leaving a day earlier than we'd planned. In the car we tried to chat: weather talk. Finally we just gave up. Nick turned on the radio.

From the corner of my eye I could feel him glance at me, but he didn't say anything. He probably didn't know what to say any more than I did.

As we neared Columbus, Nick asked if I'd like to stop for lunch or coffee.

''Sure, that would be nice,'' I said, even though I wasn't the least bit hungry.

We had to settle for a McDonald's that was right off the highway. The two of us ate our Christmas cheeseburgers and fries in silence until Nick said, ''Listen, Liz, I'm really sorry that things turned out like this. This certainly isn't the way I anticipated our trip ending.'' He looked awful, pale and tense, as if he really were coming down with something.

''I know,'' I said, finishing my coffee. ''It's not your fault. I'm sorry too.'' Sorry that I'd mentioned Caroline, sorry that I'd thought this weekend could have worked out, sorry that right this minute I wasn't sitting in my own apartment.

''But sleeping with her psychiatrist!'' Nick said, more to himself than to me. ''How could she do that?''

I didn't try to answer.

Bing Crosby was singing ''White Christmas'' as we hit the outskirts of Houston. I suddenly remembered a Saturday night two years earlier when Caroline had invited Max and me to dinner. I was almost four months pregnant, starting to "show," finally wearing maternity clothes. Max and I arrived at the Marshalls' precisely on time, but when Caroline opened the door, she was wearing a wet and very brief bikini. "Sorry I'm not dressed yet," she said, grinning at us, not looking a bit contrite. "I put dinner in the oven and finally had a few minutes to swim my laps."

I could still recall, as if it were today, the look in Max's eyes as he inspected that taut, sleek body, the perfectly flat belly. I could remember too how much I hated Caroline at that moment. Caroline who had to be the center of attention always. Caroline who had to have every man in the vicinity panting for her, and would do almost anything to assure that they did.

The weather had turned hot and muggy again. Typical Texas winter weather: chilly in the morning and sweltering by mid-afternoon, a nice contrast to the other seasons, in which it's hot and humid all day long.

Nick parked his car in one of the visitors' parking spaces at my apartment complex. We had spoken barely a dozen words—none of them significant—since we'd left Columbus. I didn't feel much like breaking the silence now, but Nick was getting out of the car.

I watched him pull my canvas suitcase from the trunk. "Thanks, I can get it from here," I said, reaching for the bag. I didn't think I could take Nick walking me to my apartment.

He shrugged, looking embarrassed. "Well, okay." He glanced at me. "I *am* very sorry, Liz."

"Me too. Goodbye, Nick." I heard his car's engine as I started up the stairs to my apartment.

In front of my door I put down my suitcase and fumbled through my purse for my keys. I could feel the sweat trickle down my back under my wool sweater.

I hated hot weather, particularly the humid, subtropical variety found in Houston. Intense, muggy heat made me feel limp and headachy, ready to take a day-long siesta. I'd read once that in the days before air conditioning foreign diplomats received hardship pay when they were posted to Houston. They deserved it. Understandably, it wasn't until the introduction of affordable air conditioning that the city's first big growth spurt took place.

I could feel tears welling in my eyes. I found my key, jammed it in the lock. Once inside, the first thing I did was turn on the air conditioner. Then I poured myself a Diet Coke with lots of ice. I drank it quickly, telling myself sternly I was not going to cry.

There were two messages on the answering machine, one from my sister, one from Jonathan. The message from my sister—"Call me. We need to talk" sounded so petulant, I decided to wait until tomorrow to call her. Instead I phoned Jonathan.

"Liz!" At least Jonathan sounded happy to hear from me. "Can you come and get me? I need to tell you something."

"Well . . ." Surely Paul would not want me butting into his Christmas plans with Jonathan, and I really wasn't in the mood for company myself. "I have tomorrow off, Jonathan. Why don't we get together then? I'm sure your dad doesn't want you leaving him alone on Christmas."

"Right," Jonathan said bitterly. "Dad isn't even here. He took Jennifer out for lunch."

"Oh." Such a sensitive guy, that Dad. I glanced at the clock: 4:05. "If it's okay with Mrs. Gates, maybe I can take you out for a little while."

Jonathan came back to the phone, assuring me that it was fine. I said I'd pick him up in twenty minutes.

He was riding a bike up and down the driveway when I arrived. I was sure the bicycle—an expensive-looking mountain bike that sported a canvas duffle bag on the back and a plastic water bottle on the front—was new. But the minute Jonathan spotted me he jumped off the bike, dumped it in the front yard, and ran to my car.

"You got a new bike for Christmas," I guessed as he slid into the passenger seat.

"Yeah."

"It's cool."

Jonathan shrugged.

"Is something wrong?"

"Can we go to Hermann Park? Or to Baskin-Robbins?" He was looking around as if he expected someone to leap out at him any second and drag him from the car.

I put the car in reverse. "I'm not sure if any ice cream place will be open today. I guess we could take a walk in the park, though."

"Okay." He settled back in the seat, his arms wrapped around his T-shirted torso. I'd changed out of my sweater, into a short-sleeved plaid cotton blouse.

"How was your Christmas?" I asked. "Did you get the presents you wanted?"

"It was okay. I got some video games and the bike."

A few days earlier I probably would have pumped him for more information. Today I didn't feel much like talking either.

We drove in a not unpleasant silence to the park. To my surprise, several parents with small children were there, pushing their kids on the swings or catching them at the bottom of the slide. Probably burning off some of the Christmas goodies, or dealing with that anticlimactic Christmas afternoon thud when all the presents were opened and cabin fever set in.

"Let's walk over there." Jonathan pointed toward the duck pond, where a teenaged couple was pretending they were there to feed the ducks.

"Did you have a good Christmas?" Jonathan asked politely as we walked.

"Parts of it were nice," I said. "I liked being out in the Hill Country." And, I thought to myself, I would have had a lot better time if your mother—as vividly present as if she had shown up in person—hadn't intruded.

Jonathan didn't pursue the subject and we lapsed into silence. It occurred to me with some surprise that I no longer associated Jonathan with Caroline. It was as if the two of them now occupied separate airtight compartments in my head.

Jonathan I liked. I worried about him, and felt an increasing attachment every time we were together. And Caroline? Right now, I was so furious with her that I could hardly think straight. I'd never known anyone who was as selfish and sexually provocative as Caroline. Was there no man I knew who hadn't slept with her—or at least wanted to? *That's called envy, honey*, the Caroline voice in my head taunted. I suspected she was right.

"I have something I have to tell you," Jonathan said, glancing over his shoulder to be sure that no one was following us.

"Tell me." I tried to smile my encouragement.

"I was riding my bike, and this lady who lives next door, Mrs. Hunter, called to me. She's real old and she hardly ever goes outside, but she said that when she heard what had happened to Mom, she remembered that she'd seen a white car at our house that night and a man—a big man—walk up to the door. She wanted me to tell Dad that—about the man who came to the house."

I stared at him, noticing how nervous he seemed. "Did you tell your dad?"

"Yeah, I told him." Jonathan's nervousness was suddenly transformed into anger. "He said it wasn't important, and I should forget about it."

Good old Paul. Maybe he'd thought it was harmful for Jonathan to brood so much about Caroline's death. Maybe—and more likely—Paul just didn't want to be bothered.

"Did Mrs. Hunter tell you anything else? Like what time the man came to the house? Or how long he stayed? Or what he looked like?"

Jonathan shook his head. "She said it was dark and she didn't see him good. But she told me she went to bed that night at a quarter to nine, and the man came right before that."

So the man, whoever he was, could have stayed for ten minutes or three hours. Could have had a heated argument with Caroline that proved to be the last straw, or an innocuous conversation that was notable only because it didn't convince Caroline that there was any reason to go on living.

A bald man in a T-shirt and shorts jogged past, breathing in loud, tortured gasps. I waited until he was far ahead of us, debating what to say. ''What do you think about what Mrs. Hunter told you?'' I finally asked.

Jonathan stopped and fixed me with an intense, unblinking stare. ''I think he might have been the man who killed Mom.''

Oh, God. ''He might have just been a friend who came to visit,'' I said as gently as possible. ''He might have stayed a few minutes and left.''

Jonathan looked as if a light had gone out behind his eyes. He started walking again. ''You don't believe me either.''

I grabbed his arm and pulled him around to face me. ''I know how much it hurts to lose someone you love a lot.''

He seemed to consider what I said, then decided it wasn't what he wanted. ''But you don't believe that someone killed my mom.''

I shook my head. ''I can't accept it without some kind of proof. Just because a man came to see your mother on the night she died doesn't mean that he shot her.'' I paused, considering. ''Did Mrs. Hunter say if she heard''—I stopped, remembering my audience—''anything?''

''No. She doesn't hear very good.''

Jonathan turned around, and I followed him back to the car, wishing that I could think of something that would make him feel better. But I couldn't. The sight of a giggling toddler on the swing, squealing as his dad pushed him higher and higher, intensified my feeling of having failed him.

Jonathan was waiting at the car for me. ''What if I could prove to you that someone shot my mother?'' he said. ''Would you help me then?''

''Sure. But how can you prove it?'' The only person I was aware of who could ''prove'' what happened was lying in her grave.

He shrugged. ''I'll think of something.'' I thought of the mystery novels I'd seen him read—the Hardy boys, Encyclopedia Brown. The kid detective marches in and solves the mystery, one-two-three. If only real life was that easy.

"You're not thinking about doing something silly like chase after every man you see in a white car, are you?"

"No, that would be stupid. I was thinking about talking to our other neighbors to see if they saw or heard anything."

I wondered if that's what Encyclopedia Brown would do. "Don't talk to anyone you don't know," I said, sounding like my overprotective sister lecturing her kids.

Jonathan must have been used to it, though. He shrugged. "I won't," he said, sliding into the passenger seat.

At least he seemed in a better mood than when I picked him up, I thought as I pulled into his driveway. Maybe the thought of his investigation had cheered him up. Or maybe it was just getting out of that huge, silent house.

I walked him to the door and waited while he rang the doorbell. To my surprise and, I think, Jonathan's, Paul Marshall opened the door.

"Hello, Liz. Come inside, Jonathan." Paul stepped aside to let Jonathan pass, but did not invite me in. I noticed a muscle twitching at the right corner of his mouth. Was he angry that I'd taken Jonathan out this afternoon? Or maybe his lunch with Jennifer hadn't gone well.

I said goodbye to Jonathan and turned to walk back to my car. I was startled when Paul started walking with me. "I suppose Jonathan told you all about the man in the white car?" he said.

I nodded. "Do you know who he was?"

"Hell, no. It could have been one of a dozen people. Caroline knew lots of men. Intimately."

I looked at him but said nothing. I thought I smelled liquor on his breath. It had been a long and trying day, and I didn't want to make it any more unpleasant.

I opened my car door and slid into the driver's seat. "Goodnight, Paul. Merry Christmas."

He didn't leave. "I'm going to get married in February. To Jennifer Layton, an old friend."

Well, that didn't take long. "Congratulations," I said, putting my key in the ignition.

"I think Jonathan is going to be upset by the news. I haven't told him yet."

I looked at him. "Yes, he will be. Maybe if you give him a while to get used to the idea . . ." Maybe if you could wait more than one month to choose wife number two.

Paul shook his head. "I told Caroline I wanted a divorce. As soon as it was final, I was going to marry Jennifer."

Oh, that put it all in a better light. We're just talking about some long-term adultery, not an unseemly quick jump into remarriage. What did the man want from me?

"You and Jonathan are spending a lot of time together," he said, his eyes narrowing. "I hope you decide to help him adjust to the new situation."

So here was another task he couldn't be bothered with, like sorting through Caroline's clothes or her papers. If the job was tedious or vaguely unpleasant, you could always delegate. I took a deep breath. "I think what Jonathan would appreciate the most is your spending more time with him."

He stared at me, not bothering to hide his dislike. In the light from my car, his large features looked coarse and weathered. "I don't have more time to spend with him, Liz. Some of us have a life to get on with."

Without saying another word, he walked back to the house.

FOURTEEN

The pounding on my apartment door woke me from a deep, dreamless sleep. I peered at my alarm clock: 7:20 A.M. I'd stayed up until 1:30 last night, watching *Rebecca* on the late show, and had planned to sleep in. What kind of jerk showed up unannounced at seven in the morning anyway?

I pulled on my terry-cloth bathrobe and stumbled to the door. Peered through the peephole and moaned. On the other side of the door was Nick Finley, looking wide-awake and intense. A man with a mission.

I briefly considered going back to bed. But the loudness of the pounding made me realize the futility of that idea. Nick was not the kind of man who could be ignored.

"What do you think you're doing?" I snapped as I opened the door. "Do you realize what time it is? Have you ever heard of the telephone?"

"Did I wake you?" he asked, sounding surprised but not especially remorseful. When I didn't answer—did I look wide awake?—he added, sheepishly this time, "I was afraid if I called you, you'd hang up."

"So instead you figured if you came over at the crack of dawn I'd be too groggy to tell you to get lost?" My heart wasn't in it, though. I was bare-footed, shivering in the chill wind blowing from the north. When you also took into account the unmistakable smell of coffee wafting from the brown paper sack Nick was carrying, there were a lot of good arguments for inviting the man inside.

"I wanted to explain things to you," Nick said when we were seated across from each other at my kitchen table. "About Caroline and me, I mean."

"You don't have to explain anything," I said, sipping surprisingly good coffee from a plastic foam cup. Whatever he was going to tell me, I sensed, I wasn't going to want to hear.

"No, I want to. I owe it to you." Nick gulped the rest of his coffee before continuing. "I was hurt when Caroline suddenly decided we shouldn't see each other anymore. It seemed like everything was great—we'd even managed to spend a couple of weekends together out of town when we were working on a story—and then, out of the blue, she announced it was over. Just like that. And I was supposed to accept it: We were no longer lovers, just colleagues and friends. Time to revert to our former positions, and pretend that nothing had ever happened between us to change that."

The level of anger in Nick's eyes startled me. I wondered why he was telling me this now. "She didn't give you any explanation of why she wanted to break up?" I asked.

"She said that our personal relationship was interfering with our working together, that our stories were losing their edge." Nick spoke quietly, but his face was pale and grim.

"And she said she needed to focus on her marriage. She and Paul were having problems, and she needed to try to solve them, not just run away from them with me."

Glancing down, I noticed his right hand had clenched into a fist. I wondered if Caroline actually had intended to work on her marriage or if she'd just used it as an excuse to brush Nick off. Somehow I suspected that Caroline, despite all her evident infidelities, would not take the dissolution of her marriage lightly. My biggest argument with her, after all, was over her unrelenting nagging that I patch things up with Max, no matter what the cost.

Even I, as depressed as I was at the time, had still thought Caroline's behavior odd, uncharacteristic of such a seemingly independent woman. "What you're saying is that I'm better off miserable with Max than alone," I'd finally snapped at her. "That's ridiculous. Nobody believes that anymore."

Caroline had shrugged, stony-faced, unyielding. "I'm not saying be miserable. I'm saying work out the problems. Everyone I know who's gotten divorced starts out talking about how great it is to be free and independent, to do what you want to do whenever you want to do it. But what they end up being is lonely and unconnected, Liz—free to spend hour after hour staring at the walls of their apartment."

But I didn't think that Nick wanted to hear Caroline's idiosyncratic views on marriage at the moment. Particularly when her idea of marital problem-solving seemed to involve sleeping with her therapist.

I broke off a piece of one of the blueberry muffins Nick had brought. "Just why are you telling me this?"

He studied his empty coffee cup for a long time before he answered. "I didn't know about Houssman, though I probably should have guessed. It seemed, when I heard about it, a double betrayal from Caroline." He looked up from the table, searching my face. "You can understand that, can't you?"

I nodded, but didn't say anything.

His eyes still held mine in a steady gaze, as if from sheer force of will he could elicit the information he wanted from me. After another long pause, he said, "But what happened between Caroline and me has nothing to do with my feelings toward you. That's what I came here to tell you."

I raised my eyebrows, openly skeptical. "I find that kind of hard to believe, Nick. We met through Caroline. We've been spending so much time together because of Caroline's story. Our entire connection is based on our mutual acquaintance with Caroline. So don't tell me this has nothing to do with her."

"I know that. What I'm saying is that you're the first woman I've been attracted to since I broke up with Caroline. And that has nothing at all to do with her, and everything to do with you."

I sighed. "I'd like to believe that . . ." I was surprised at how much I would have liked to believe it.

He finished the sentence for me. "... but you don't." When I nodded, he said, "So what if we both knew Caroline? Certainly she was what brought us together, but that was the extent of it. I invited you to the cabin because I wanted to be with you, not because I wanted to share stories about Caroline. Hell, I've had enough of Caroline to last me a lifetime. Two lifetimes."

"I know what you mean." Driving home from the Marshalls' house I'd thought how much less complicated my life would be now if I'd walked into my freshman dorm room that first day and encountered a different roommate, some sunny, easygoing young woman who, years later, I'd chat with occasionally on the phone, telling her how much I'd enjoyed the annual Christmas photo of her kids.

Nick was looking at me expectantly. "So what do you think?" he said finally. "Can we start over? I had a great time with you at the cabin. And the end—that had nothing to do with you. I'm sorry I let that ruin our weekend."

"You didn't ruin it." It was like assuming blame for bad weather, a leaky roof, a freak electrical fire. "It just happened. And"—I smiled, feeling suddenly shy—"up until the end I had a good time too." A very good time, I mentally amended, recalling our walks around the lake, the feel of his arms clasping me tight.

He grinned at me, looking suddenly boyish, all the tension gone. I intended to say, Look, just because I had a good time doesn't mean that I think we should get involved. It's too soon for both of us. We need time to recover from our past relationships. But I didn't. Partly, I suppose, because he was looking so happy. But also because I wanted to believe he was right, that we could step away from all the emotional debris and forge our own relationship, unencumbered by our pasts.

I got up to make us a pot of coffee. Nick followed me into the kitchen, offering to scramble some eggs.

"You're not working today either?" I asked as he cracked eggs into a Pyrex bowl with flowers on the side.

"I might go in for a few hours this afternoon to go over

my notes, but everyone I need to interview has the day off." He added milk, salt and pepper, then beat the eggs with a fork. "And I was thinking I might see if Houssman is in today."

"What?" I set down the paper coffee filter. "I thought you were talking about giving up that story, and working on the union corruption piece."

"That was before I got this new information."

Right. I felt as if he'd just thrown a glass of ice water in my face. And who was it who gave him this new information? I fought to keep my voice level. "And just what do you think Dr. Houssman is going to say—'Sure, Nick, I'm glad you asked me about Caroline. I've been needing to get this off my chest'? You'll never get any proof of their affair. The only person who might tell you about it is dead."

The stubborn set to Nick's jaw, the glint in his eyes, told me what he was going to say even before he said it. "I still have to talk to Houssman. I've got to try."

"Why?"

He didn't meet my eyes. "I owe it to Caroline."

"Yeah, I can see how you've gotten over her."

"It's not like that, Liz. You don't understand."

Oh, but I did. "You really think that if it hadn't been for Dr. Houssman, you and Caroline wouldn't have broken up, don't you?"

His eyes met mine. "I don't know about that. I do think that if Houssman had been doing his job instead of fucking her, Caroline might still be alive today."

And if Nick had been doing *his* job instead of sleeping with Caroline, maybe he and I could now be starting something of our own.

Did I believe that? I wasn't sure. What I did know—what I was sure of—was that I couldn't endure this roller coaster ride of emotions: Passion. Hopefulness. Hurt. Anger. Jealousy.

Enough.

I'd been hurt, badly hurt, by the months and months of gut-wrenching emotions during my breakup with Max. I'd barely emerged intact. After my divorce, I had resolved that I would never ever subject myself to such pain again.

My hand, I noticed, was shaking. I pointed at the door anyway. "Please leave, Nick," I said. "I don't want to see you anymore."

FIFTEEN

I watched as Nick, white-faced and silent, stalked to the door and out of my life.

Angrily I brushed the tears from my face, filled with self-loathing. "Some of us have a life to get on with, Liz." Paul Marshall's barb, intended more to rationalize his neglect of Jonathan than to skewer me, suddenly seemed eminently true. I was too involved with Caroline's family—now even Caroline's ex-lover. Let's face it, Caroline's life had always been more exciting, more glamourous, more deeply hued than mine.

I poured myself another cup of coffee. It was time that I created a life—a satisfying life—of my own. Since my divorce from Max I'd never strayed far from the safety of my comfortable, sterile cocoon. My excursions outside—to my job, to my sister's, to old friends' houses—had been to familiar places and with people I'd known for years. And that had been okay for a while. I needed that security blanket, that private place to lick my wounds when my world seemed to be disintegrating around me. All those statistics about the prevalence of divorce had not equipped me for the sheer psychic pain of the process. In response I'd retreated, I hid, I grieved—and I ate. Until Caroline Marshall arrived unannounced on my doorstep to disturb my stifling peace.

Resolutely I pulled out a plastic garbage bag and opened my pantry doors. Pepperidge Farm cookies, cheese potato chips, a devil's-food cake mix all went into the bag. Minutes later the inside of my freezer yawned, empty except for two cans of orange juice, after I'd dumped a half gallon of Rocky Road and my stash of Sara Lee cheesecake and croissants.

Before I changed my mind I took the bulging plastic sack outside and heaved it into the dumpster behind my apartment. It was a start.

After that I took a walk, tromping through the chill drizzle, trying to discover the new direction for my life. I thought about a speaker I'd heard at the center, a Jungian analyst, who'd said that the tasks of the second half of your life should be those things you'd left undone in the first half. People needed to develop the facets of themselves that they'd previously ignored. That sounded good. By that criterion I should be preparing myself to become an athletic, confident, flirtatious bimbo. At this point that didn't sound half bad.

Working on one undeveloped facet of myself, I went that afternoon to my tae-kwon-do class. I could see the look of surprise on Master McCrae's beefy face; I hadn't attended class in over a month.

There weren't many students there, mainly a sprinkling of kids who hadn't gone out of town for Christmas. The low attendance must have made Master McCrae even more irritable than usual. As I huffed and puffed through our warm-up calisthenics, I envisioned him as the Great Santini in a karate suit. The thought also crossed my mind that perhaps my athletic facet was better left unexplored.

I was still gasping for breath when our *sabum nim* announced the sparring partners. "Shit!" I muttered under my breath. I had to spar again with Seth, the psychopathic seven-year-old.

The little dear was up to his old tricks again. Sending me the evil eye from beneath his mop of red hair, he executed a jumping side kick that landed a couple of inches above my waist. It hurt.

Without thinking, I took a step forward and aimed a front snap kick at the kid's thigh. He tried to dodge the blow but didn't move fast enough. It landed with a loud thud on his scrawny little butt.

Seth started to cry.

Master McCrae came over, scowling at us. "What's the problem here?"

"She kicked me!" Rubbing his posterior, Seth pointed an accusing finger at me.

I turned to the instructor. "I'm so sorry, sir. I was trying to kick to the side of him. I guess I'm out of practice."

McCrae, apparently unwilling to believe that the wimp had turned violent on him, nodded disapprovingly. "Tae-kwon-do is a discipline, Liz. You need to practice three or four times a week minimum. This isn't a tea party, you know."

Trying to look properly chastened (a *tea* party?), I made sure that the rest of my kicks were six inches away from Seth's wiry body. And the glowering little brat did the same for me. As I left the *do jang*, feeling sore and sweaty, I reflected that kicking a kid was probably not the kind of midlife change that the Jungian analyst had in mind. I knew I should feel ashamed instead of what I did feel: triumphant but trying to hide it.

I felt less triumphant the next morning when I awoke, every muscle aching, with stern thoughts about child abuse. A hot shower made me feel marginally better, but I was glad to be able to go to my PR job instead of continuing the work on my undeveloped facets.

I spent most of the morning finishing the copy for a brochure about the center that we planned to hand out to new patients. I was sufficiently engrossed that the knock on my open door startled me.

"Sorry." Dr. Houssman smiled apologetically at me from the doorway. "I was wondering if we could talk for a few minutes."

"Sure. Come on in."

He entered my office, stopping to close the door after him. I thought he seemed tense, or maybe, as the shrinks would say, I was projecting.

I watched him sit down on the molded plastic chair at the side of my desk. His large body looked incongruous in it—an adult trying to squeeze into a child's chair.

"Would you like some coffee?" It was not just knee-jerk politeness on my part. I had a sudden strong suspicion that whatever Dr. Houssman was going to tell me, I didn't want to hear.

He smiled. "Thanks, I could use some. I take it black."

I had to go down the hall to the coffee pot. When I returned, Dr. H. was standing in front of my bookshelves, checking out the titles.

"Your office looks like you," he said as he accepted the coffee.

"Cheap posters, piles of books, and unrelieved clutter remind you of me? Now, that's flattering," I said, remembering the pristine neatness, the carefully selected *objets*, in his office.

He shook his head. "The mixture of the books—a medical dictionary next to the Lillian Hellman autobiography—and the different styles of art—O'Keeffe's starkness and Monet's soft, flickering light—reflect your personality. It's a charming, inviting place."

For some reason I was reminded of my gorgeous Aunt Helen telling me as an adolescent that I had "a very interesting face." I sipped my coffee, and waited for Dr. Houssman to tell me what was on his mind.

"A reporter, Nick Finley, phoned me this morning," he said. "I remember you mentioned that you knew him."

I nodded.

Dr. Houssman stared into his coffee, as if searching there for a message on what to say next. "He apparently has decided to go ahead with that story you were telling me about on therapists who have sexual relations with their patients."

He stopped, studied my face for a reaction. When apparently he saw none—or at least not the one he expected—he continued, in a peculiarly flat voice. "He wants to interview me."

The coffee I gulped was lukewarm and too sweet. The intense irritation I felt with my old therapist seemed incongruous: This selfish, manipulative man was someone I'd adored less than a month ago. Hell, I'd thought he was Dr. Perfect-In-Every-Way. Who turned out to be not so perfect after all.

"Did you agree to the interview?" I asked, as if I didn't know what was coming next.

"No." Houssman watched me, his face expressionless. "But on second thought, I'm not sure that that was a wise decision. Perhaps it would be beneficial to talk to the man in order to express my views and find out what slant he's taking on the story."

Yeah, I could see how that would interest him. Are we taking the impersonal, global view here, Nick—my professional opinion on the ethics of patient-therapist intimacy? Or are you interested in something a little more, well, specific?

"I guess you'll have to make that decision," I said. "Whether or not it would be beneficial for you to talk to Nick."

He obviously hadn't expected this reaction. For a second Dr. H. looked startled. Probably he thought I'd be only too happy to help out the noted Dr. Ted Houssman, flattered to finally offer some tidbits of my own expertise in gratitude for all his support, encouragement, and sparkling insights.

"What I wanted to know," he said, recovering quickly, "is can Finley write anything I tell him? I know you deal with the media a lot. Is there any way to tell him something strictly in confidence, with the condition that he doesn't use it in his story?"

"You can say you want to talk off the record," I told him. "You need to say that before you start discussing the subject." We won't mention what that delicate subject might be. "If Nick agrees to that—and he might not—then he won't use anything confidential that you tell him."

He nodded, then glanced away, his eyes narrowing. "Say Finley agrees to let me talk off the record. What's to stop him from going ahead and printing the information anyway?"

"Nothing," I said coldly. "I guess you have to trust in his professional ethics. Kind of like when you go to a therapist. You have to trust that he'll not betray your confidence or take advantage of you when you're vulnerable."

Houssman blinked twice, rapidly. When he spoke again he

looked suddenly tired, an overweight, middle-aged man who wasn't aging well. "How long have you known?" he asked.

"I knew at our last session. I saw you making all the gestures that Dr. X made in that anonymous journal I'd found in Caroline's file. I thought all along that Caroline had written it, and then suddenly all the other pieces fell into place."

Dr. H. nodded his head sadly. "You said you weren't feeling well. I can see why."

He seemed for a moment to have reverted to the man I thought I'd known, a nice, empathetic sort, a good guy. The man I wished I still believed in.

"How could you have done such a thing?" I blurted out.

He winced. "I don't know. I keep asking myself that. For what it's worth, it's never happened before. A year ago if someone told me that I'd have an affair with a patient, I would have laughed in his face. There are all the glib answers, of course. My wife and I were having problems. I'm a fifty-two-year-old man, married early, faced with an attractive, seductive woman who made a point of letting me know that she was very casual about extramarital sex."

He said it before I could. "Yes, I know. That was all the more reason for me not to sleep with her. To help her deal with this problem, her compulsive seductiveness, instead of exploiting it the way I did. Believe me, I've told myself that a thousand times."

For a minute I thought he was going to cry. He didn't, but his voice broke as he continued. "I told myself that I could still be Caroline's therapist, could still help her. That I was experienced enough, professional enough, to keep the two relationships separate. Which was absurd, of course. From the moment we slept together, our therapeutic relationship deteriorated. I could see Caroline withdraw. I knew she had to be withholding information, no longer sharing her feelings with me. But nothing I could do or say seemed to make any difference."

To my surprise, I felt sorry for him. Dr. Houssman had never claimed to be anything other than human. In fact, he'd worked hard to show me his frailties. "Everyone has problems, Liz," he'd said. "Everyone is vulnerable about something." I just wished that his weakness hadn't been Caroline.

"Did you realize that Caroline was contemplating suicide?" I asked.

Dr. Houssman shook his head. With some effort, he pulled his bulky body from the too-small chair. "By the time she died," he said wearily, "Caroline wasn't telling me anything. Except, of course, by her every gesture, her every unspoken word, that I had betrayed her."

SIXTEEN

As usual, Gertrude Stone got right to the point. "Why don't you come to dinner tomorrow night?" she asked on the phone. "There are some important matters I'd like to discuss with you. I think it would be best to discuss them in person."

I didn't know how to refuse. A good girl (or unassertive wimp) until the end. The only point I managed to interject was that I was on a diet. Why didn't Gertrude let me bring the food this time?

No, Gertrude said. That wouldn't be necessary. She'd prepare a low-calorie meal. "I could stand to take off a few pounds myself," she added.

I told her I'd see her tomorrow. For someone who just yesterday had vowed to disengage herself from Caroline and her family, this wasn't a very auspicious beginning.

Another planning meeting for the psychology conference ate up most of the next afternoon, filled with the kind of endless bickering over trivia that made me want to scream. After that the sweaty exertion of my tae-kwon-do class, which I'd planned to attend that evening, seemed appealing. I wished I'd thought fast enough to make up an excuse to bypass Gertrude's dinner. I was not in the mood to spend an evening discussing Caroline Marshall.

Gertrude answered the door at my first knock, wearing the kind of navy wool outfit my mother used to call a "church dress." I had the sense that she'd been hovering by the window waiting for me.

"I'm so glad you could come, Liz," she said as she took my coat. "I know how busy you are."

God, what a selfish bitch I was! Here the poor woman had prepared a delicious-smelling meal, dressed in her good clothes, and was obviously happy to see me, and all *I* could think of was how I'd rather be somewhere else.

"It's nice of you to invite me," I said, accepting a glass of sherry. "Though you really didn't have to cook for me."

"Oh, I enjoy cooking. And what I wanted to discuss with you will take quite a while, I suspect."

She didn't offer a clue to the topic of our discussion until we finished our dinner. Until then, eating our green salad and delicious vegetarian lasagna ("It's a low-fat recipe my neighbor Helen gave me"), we talked about books we were reading and the Alley Theatre's version of *King Lear*, which she'd seen a couple weeks before.

"You know I always used to tell my students about how contemporary Shakespeare's plays are," Gertrude said as she poured our coffee. "How the conflicts and emotions depicted in his plays are as relevant today as they were in the 1600s."

She handed me my coffee in a delicate china cup covered with roses. "Every time I see one of his plays something different speaks to me. Always. Lear's brooding about his unfaithful daughter Regan: 'See what breeds about her heart. Is there any cause in nature that makes these hard hearts?' "

I wondered what it was about unfaithful daughters that so intrigued her. Had she been thinking about Caroline when she spoke? The passionate tone of Gertrude's voice when she recited the words and the way she glanced away from me in embarrassment, the minute she finished, made me suspect some personal connection to Lear's anguish.

"Excuse me for a minute, dear, while I get our dessert," she said before I could make any inquiries.

She came back with a platter of beautifully arranged fresh fruit—pineapple, strawberries, apple and pear slices, even some kiwi. She brushed aside my compliments. "I'm sure you're wondering why I was so insistent on seeing you, Liz."

She didn't wait for me to answer, but continued in what seemed like a prepared speech. "I'm concerned about Jonathan, and I know you've been seeing quite a bit of him lately. He's very fond of you."

I smiled. "And I'm very fond of him."

The watery gray eyes fixed on my face, and for a moment the sternness in Gertrude's face softened. "Yes, dear, I know you are. So I'm sure that you too can see the terrible strain the poor child is under with this obsession of his to find his mother's killer."

This time she waited for me to speak. I tried to choose my words carefully. "Certainly I can see how upset Jonathan is by Caroline's death, and I can understand how his insistence that someone killed his mother would be painful for you. But I guess I assumed that what he's doing is kind of acting out the stages of grief, doing the kid's version of denial right now. I figured that after he convinced himself, proved to himself that his mother wasn't killed, that he'd move on to the next stage: being furious with Caroline for leaving him."

Gertrude looked as if she was considering what I said. She sipped her coffee in silence, contemplating. "That's an interesting theory," she said finally. "I just wish I were convinced that Jonathan would move on to the next stage, as you call it, even if that meant facing his anger toward Caroline. And I know how painful that would be for the child. He loved Caroline very much."

I nodded. "Perhaps that's why he's so adamant about Caroline's having been killed. He doesn't want to face that anger, to acknowledge that Caroline willingly abandoned him."

Gertrude sighed, looking in that instance every one of her seventy-plus years. "That is one likely explanation. I must admit that at first even I had a very difficult time acknowledging that Caroline killed herself. Considering her own childhood, the terrible pain that her mother's death caused her, I would have thought that Caroline would be the last person in the world to commit suicide."

"But something made you change your mind?"

Gertrude nodded and glanced away again before bringing her eyes back to my face. "I found a file that Caroline was keeping about her mother. She had a notebook called 'Memories of Mary Ann.' There were also two cassette tapes, but I haven't listened to them yet. I read the essay Caroline wrote about Mary Ann's last day. That essay was what changed my mind. It was very disturbing."

I watched as, hands trembling, Gertrude brought her cup to her lips and sipped at the coffee. I waited but finally had to ask my question. "Did Caroline write that she was considering suicide too?"

"Not in those precise words, but she wrote a great deal about her mother's death, about how Mary Ann was the same age as Caroline when she died. I told you, didn't I, that Caroline refused to even talk about Mary Ann for years? And then suddenly she seemed obsessed with her. Caroline wrote pages and pages about her mother's death, noting every detail she could remember about that day—even the sound of the gunshot she heard from her bedroom."

"Caroline was the one who found her mother's body?" I asked, horrified.

"Yes. It was horrible for her. She was just a child, only ten years old and very protective of her mother, very attached to Mary Ann. I was there a few minutes later. I was walking over, bringing groceries, when I heard Caroline scream."

"My God." And I had assumed Caroline's life had always been privileged and easy, filled with admirers, designer clothes, and easily won successes. Even to imagine the horror of finding your mother slumped over, bleeding from a gunshot wound, made the nausea rise to my throat.

"Wait. I want to read something to you." Gertrude pushed herself out of her chair and walked into the living room. When she returned, she held a spiral notebook. A slip of paper marked the place.

"Here it is. Caroline is writing about Mary Ann: 'What did she think during those last minutes before she pulled the trigger? She had already written her note, kissed me and told me she loved me. Did she welcome death? Hold out her arms and embrace this final solution to her terrible problems? Did she see the cessation of pain, the closure to unanswerable dilemmas, the end to all the betrayals? I suspect that as she raised the gun to her head, she saw, after years of agony, a final peace.' "

"You think Caroline was writing about herself?" I asked. "Seeing suicide as the solution to her own problems?"

Gertrude sighed, looking old and exhausted. "I wouldn't have thought so before, but now—yes, I do. I know that she and Paul were having problems, though Caroline always sounded confident that they would work things out."

I shrugged. "Paul told me that he and Caroline were considering a divorce."

"*Paul* was considering it." Gertrude could not keep the bitterness from her voice. "Apparently he had a girlfriend, and he was pressuring Caroline."

"Caroline didn't want the divorce?"

"She was trying to convince Paul that they needed to try to solve their problems. Because of her own experience with the breakup of her parents' marriage, Caroline was very opposed to divorce, you know."

I knew.

Gertrude took a slice of pineapple from the platter. She cut it into tiny pieces with her knife. When she looked up, her face was determined. "So you see about Jonathan, don't you? All of this talk about finding Caroline's killer is just keeping him from accepting what really happened to Caroline. I don't think Jonathan needs to know all the details now, but if he could accept the fact that his mother was depressed and not herself when she committed suicide, I think it would be better for him in the long term. Right now the boy is running away from reality."

Sometimes reality was so bleak that running away from it seemed a healthy response. "What is it that you want me to do?" I asked.

"Discourage him from his fantasy about finding Caroline's

killer. Help him to understand that Caroline wasn't herself." Gertrude sighed. "That's what the doctor told us about Mary Ann, that her mental problems distorted her thinking. Everything seemed hopeless. She saw no way out of her misery, only more pain."

But Mary Ann's mental problems were a lot more serious than Caroline's. Certainly Gertrude was not saying that she thought Caroline also was suffering from schizophrenia, was she?

"I wouldn't normally involve you in this," Gertrude was saying, "but I'm afraid my health isn't what it used to be." The paleness of her face and her shaking hands gave credence to her words. "A couple of years ago I could have handled this entirely by myself, but this heart condition makes me feel so tired all the time. . . ."

"No, I'm happy to help," I interjected. So much for my plan to butt out of Caroline Marshall's life. At the moment, though, assisting this kind and decent woman seemed more important than my self-improvement agenda.

Gertrude smiled a small, tight smile. "I appreciate that. I considered talking to Paul, but he never was very good with Jonathan, and from what the boy tells me, he's too involved with his girlfriend now to be of much use." She shook her head, her lips pressed together in a straight line.

"And of course there's Celia, who, in her own way, is fond of Jonathan. But Celia is preoccupied right now, getting herself ready for her face-lift."

"A face-lift?" I asked incredulously, remembering Celia's taut face. "I assumed she'd already had one."

"She has. This will be her second." Gertrude smiled sardonically. "When I'm around Celia I'm glad I wasn't born beautiful. Plain women have to develop their other resources, and they're not so terrified of growing old."

I laughed. "I'll try to keep that in mind." As I was getting ready to leave, Gertrude said, "Oh, I meant to ask you before, how is the article about the unethical therapists coming?"

"I'm really not sure." I hadn't spoken to Nick since the

day he marched out of my apartment. It was actually only last week, but it seemed like months ago. "I . . . I'm not involved in the story anymore," I stammered.

"Good," Gertrude said. "I'm pleased to hear that." Apparently sensing my surprise, she added, "I was going to tell you to be careful. I meant to caution you before."

"Careful of what?"

"That man." Gertrude pulled on her ear lobe, looking annoyed. "I can't remember his name now. Caroline told me and . . ."

Was she talking about Dr. Houssman? "Was he—this man—a psychiatrist?"

"Yes. A vile man. He threatened Caroline."

I stared at her, my mouth open.

"Chicken?" Gertrude said softly, as if speaking to herself. "No, no. Fowl, that's it. His name was Dr. Fowl, or . . ."

"Dr. Fowler," I said. "Caroline told you that Dr. Fowler threatened her?"

Gertrude nodded. "He learned about the article she was writing. He told her that if she printed anything negative about him, he'd make sure she never wrote another word."

"Was Caroline frightened?" I remembered her standing in my apartment, telling me she couldn't take anymore.

"No, not Caroline." Gertrude shook her head, even managed a smile. "She said the man was a bully—all hot air. First he tried to intimidate her with some psychobabble analysis of her: how neurotic she was, that kind of thing. Then, when that didn't work, he called her managing editor to complain about her. And, of course, that didn't work either. Caroline couldn't believe this Fowler was naive enough to think the newspaper would kill her story just because he didn't like it."

"Doctors are like that," I said. Usually psychiatrists were less likely than, say, surgeons to believe that they were God brought back to earth in human form, but Fowler seemed to have received more than his share of arrogance along with his degree. "But I don't understand. If Caroline wasn't afraid of Fowler—"

''Why would I warn you about him?'' Gertrude finished my sentence. ''I'm not sure exactly. Intuition maybe, or perhaps just overprotectiveness. Dr. Fowler sounds sinister to me. I told Caroline to be careful too, but she just laughed at me.''

Gertrude suddenly looked very tired. I left a few minutes later, after assuring her that I'd talk to Jonathan soon.

SEVENTEEN

"You talked to Houssman!" Nick Finley blocked the door of my office, scowling at me.

"Yes, I did," I said and went back to the news release I was writing.

Uninvited, Nick stalked inside and plopped down into my molded plastic chair. He fit in it better than Houssman had, I noticed when I looked up.

"How could you do that?" His voice was quiet enough, but from the expression on his face it was costing him considerable effort not to shout the question at me.

"How could I do *what*? What exactly do you think I told him?" I didn't give him a chance to answer the question. "You make it sound like I revealed some deep secret, which I didn't. The only thing I told him was what 'off the record' meant."

Nick did not look mollified. "And of course now Houssman wants *everything* off the record. He won't even admit to being Caroline's therapist for the record. He says it's all confidential information."

I could see why he was pissed. "So you refused to keep anything off the record, and he refused to tell you diddly-squat," I guessed.

"You got it."

"But what did you expect? Certainly you didn't think that you'd just mention the name Caroline Marshall, and Dr.

Houssman would blurt out a confession? The man's not stupid."

Nick's eyes narrowed as he studied me. A muscle at the side of his mouth twitched. "Just whose side are you on, anyway?"

"No one's side." I glared back at him. "I don't want to be involved in this at all. I've had my fill of Caroline and her messes. I'm tired of raking up her past, sorting through all her garbage."

"And you think you can just walk away from it?" His eyes darkened as he stared at me, challenging me to disagree with him. When I said nothing, merely met his gaze, he added, "Don't delude yourself, Liz. You're as involved in Caroline's past as I am."

"Gee, I don't recall sleeping with her," I said.

"Is that what this is all about—me sleeping with Caroline? That's why you suddenly don't want to be involved?"

"No!" I must have practically shouted it, because a secretary passing by in the hallway stopped and glanced into my office, her eyes wide.

I got up to close the door, using the time to take several deep breaths. I managed to keep my voice down when I spoke again. "I don't want to get involved because I have my own life to get on with, something, I've only recently realized, that I've been avoiding at all costs. Getting so engrossed with Caroline's life—her family, her story, her past—is just another way of running away from mine."

"You're wrong." An unreadable expression crossed Nick's angular, finely lined face. "I think you need to deal with Caroline before you can get on with your own life. I think both of us, you and I, need to do that."

"And you think this story will somehow help me to deal with Caroline?"

He nodded. "Remember when I said I thought I was going to forget this story and instead spend my time on one of my own?"

"I remember."

"I tried that. Tried putting hers aside and starting on a new one. But I kept coming back to Caroline's. Not because I find it especially compelling—I don't; it's not my kind of story but because of this nagging feeling I have that Caroline needed it to be finished. I feel like I owe her this, to finish the job."

If it had been so important to Caroline to finish her story, she could have finished it herself. There was no deadline for shooting oneself. "Okay, that's why you need to finish it. But that doesn't have anything to do with me."

"Maybe not." Nick glanced around my office. At the stack of newsletters from other mental health institutions that I intended to read some day, the yellow phone messages on my desk that I needed to respond to.

Finally he looked at me. "But don't tell me that you're not hung up about Caroline too. Because I can see that you are."

Before I could ask what that had to do with Caroline's article, he anticipated my question. "I keep sensing I can get a lot of answers about Caroline if only I finish her story. Answers about what she was thinking, what she was afraid of before she died. Ultimately, I guess, why she shot herself. And you need to know that as much as I do."

I found myself studying some doodles I'd drawn in the margins of my notebook—labyrinths of varying-sized squares, strange formations of intersecting triangles. "I don't think you're going to find that out from a story about therapists who seduce their patients. At least not with the notes Caroline left."

Nick's voice when he spoke was deceptively gentle, a soft, wooing voice. "Did Houssman tell you about his affair with Caroline?"

I looked up finally, met those steely blue eyes. "You know I can't tell you that." I wasn't even sure that it made sense, but I knew that I couldn't tell Nick what Dr. Houssman had confided to me.

''Can't or won't?'' The voice was no longer gentle. Nick's face was white with anger.

When I didn't answer, he stood up. ''You're making a big mistake, Liz,'' he said before he walked out the door.

I spent the rest of the afternoon giving a group of high school juniors a tour of the center. We started, as always, with me giving my introductory spiel, a five-minute overview, in the auditorium. After that a staff member who I managed to coerce into speaking came to talk to the group. Today's speaker was Tim O'Brien, a slight, bearded psychiatric social worker in his thirties who enjoyed talking to groups and usually had something interesting to say.

Tim sat on the edge of the stage and told the kids about his job. He was a therapist in the adult clinic, which meant that in a typical week he led therapy groups, saw individual patients, supervised social work students, and dealt with massive amounts of paperwork.

''But I'm getting tired of just talking. I'd rather hear what's on your minds,'' Tim said, looking around the auditorium with a relaxed smiled. ''Anything you guys want to know? I'm open to questions.''

Last week when Tim had spoken to a group of teenagers from an exclusive private school one of the boys, dressed like all the other boys in white shirt, khaki pants, and navy school blazer, asked, ''Do you consider family therapy an effective mode of therapy, sir?'' Today's group, from a public high school in one of the city's poorest neighborhoods, favored the blue jeans and torn T-shirt look. The first question, from a gangly black kid, was, ''What's the most dangerous case you ever had?''

''You mean the most violent?'' Tim asked.

''Yeah.''

Tim pulled on his ear, thinking about it. ''I had this woman patient once, a big, muscular woman. She'd been sexually abused as a child by her father, but she'd repressed the memory of the abuse—she didn't remember what had happened. Well, she was in therapy with me, just sitting there talking, when the memory started coming back. And was she furious! She jumped up from her chair, her eyes wild, screaming. She hoisted this big, upholstered chair over her head and looked around for someone to throw it at. She wanted to heave it at her father, but he wasn't there—I was. And right then this woman had no use for men, any man at all.''

''What did you do, man?'' the skinny kid asked, his eyes bright with excitement.

''I got the hell out of there as fast as I could,'' Tim said. ''Let her smash the chair into my wall instead of into me.'' He waited for the murmurs to die down before he continued. ''And after that I referred her to another therapist, a female therapist. The two of them had good rapport and eventually the woman worked through her problems.''

I was aware that some of the kids, particularly the boys, were doing a poor job of hiding their disdain. What kind of man runs away from a feisty woman (even if she's bigger than he), the macho dudes were thinking. But Tim was unfazed by their reaction, and once he started answering the other questions (Should girls only see women therapists? Do you have to be crazy to see a shrink?), he recaptured his audience's attention.

I was left with an entirely different reaction to Tim's story. Faced with Caroline's seductiveness and his own attraction to her, Dr. Houssman too could have bailed out and referred Caroline to another therapist. Caroline's needs would have been met and Dr. H. wouldn't have compromised himself. Even after he'd slept with her and witnessed the disastrous effects on her therapy, Dr. H. still could have made sure that Caroline got the help she needed from another therapist. Instead he'd done nothing, while Caroline sank deeper and deeper into the quagmire of her misery.

I felt a distinct pang of relief as Tim answered his last question and I herded the students into the hallway for the rest of the tour. Obviously I didn't want to think too much about my reluctance to tell Nick what Houssman had disclosed to me. Originally I'd thought I was refusing to betray a confidence, and showing loyalty to a man who'd helped me through a crisis. Now I was beginning to suspect that it was vindictiveness toward Caroline that made me protect her betrayer.

EIGHTEEN

"You're *sure* you want to go to the zoo?" I asked as Jonathan walked out the front door of his house. It was a blustery 40 degrees today—subarctic weather by Houston's standards—and the idea of standing in front of the monkey cage, shivering, didn't do much for me.

"Yeah, it's great on days like this. Nobody else is there."

I forced myself not to say what I wanted to say: Sure, everybody else has some sense. It was the kind of comment I'd heard Margaret make to her kids dozens of times, the kind of thing my mother had said to both of us. It surprised me how difficult it was *not* to voice these words and assorted similar comments. (What? You think money grows on trees? I don't care what everybody else does! You're not everybody.) I couldn't stop myself, however, from asking Jonathan if he'd like to go back to get a hat or gloves. Maybe a jacket to wear on top of his sweat shirt?

"No," he said, taking in my down jacket, knitted hat, leather gloves, wool slacks, and leather boots. "I'm not cold."

No, *he* wasn't. I noticed his new bicycle lying on the driveway. Obviously he'd already been outside playing today. "Does Mrs. Gates know we're going to the zoo?" I'd told her on the phone that I'd take Jonathan to the Museum of Natural Science: an entertaining, educational—and warm—activity.

He sent me a look of barely contained impatience. "Yeah. Now let's go."

"So what have you been up to?" I asked when we were in

the car, heater blasting, en route to Hermann Park.

"I finally beat Ninja Turtles II."

"Terrific. Anything else going on?"

"Well, I've been riding around, talking to our neighbors about what they saw the night Mom died. Yesterday I talked to Andy Corman. He's in the sixth grade and lives in the house behind us."

I knew this was the point at which I was supposed to interject The Message—Gertrude's message, actually, but I'd agreed to repeat it. But I couldn't do it now, not when Jonathan seemed so happy. It would have to wait until later.

Jonathan was still talking. "I went back to talk to Mrs. Hunter, the lady who saw the guy in the white car. I thought maybe she'd remember something else."

"Did she?"

"Kind of. She said the white car looked like a box." Jonathan rolled his eyes at Mrs. Hunter's lack of sophistication. "She said she thought the man had on a black coat and that he was real big."

A big man in a black coat with a boxy white car. Nick, who was tall and owned a black leather jacket, drove a black Maxima. Dr. Houssman, who was heavy, had a black coat—but who didn't? I had no idea what kind of car he drove. Who did I know that drove a white car?

I spotted the outskirts of Hermann Park. "You're right. Nobody is here," I said as we drove by a playground that was usually swarming with kids. "Now what exactly do you like to do at the zoo, Jonathan?"

"First I feed the ducks in the pond." He pulled a smashed plastic bag containing a half dozen pieces of bread from his jeans pocket. "Then I ride the train. After that I visit the animals, if I'm in the mood."

I pulled into the zoo parking lot, which was half empty. Ahead of us a harried-looking mother was shepherding two bundled-up toddlers toward the steam engine which pulled a dozen or so open-air cars around the park.

"Mom always liked to come to the zoo when it was real

cold out,'' Jonathan offered as we trudged toward the duck pond. ''She said it was her favorite time to come.''

It would be. I grinned. ''Your mom always loved bad weather. She wanted to be right in the middle of it. I wanted to be safe inside with a warm cup of cocoa, but your mother had to be walking through the pouring rain, hiking through the snow drifts, or standing outside watching the cars slide all over the street when we had an ice storm.''

Jonathan smiled, transforming his too pale, too serious face for a moment into a little boy's face. ''Yeah, I like storms too. Once when it snowed here Mom and I walked for miles and miles, and I didn't even get cold. Mom said I was hot-blooded like her.''

''You certainly seem to be,'' I said, glancing again at his thin Nintendo sweat shirt, as the frigid wind bit at my nose and made my feet feel as if I were standing in a meat locker.

The ducks weren't especially interested in Jonathan's scraps of bread, but their indifference didn't faze him. ''Sometimes they're not hungry,'' he explained. ''Let's go to the train now.''

We were two of only a handful of passengers, but the train chugged valiantly around the leafless park. Jonathan's momentary enthusiasm seemed as fragile as the oblique sun which had slipped behind a cloud, making the day even colder. He sat in silence, inspecting the park with an unreadable expression.

''I saw your Aunt Gertrude last week,'' I said, trying to create conversation.

He looked at me, his expression wary.

''She's a nice person,'' I continued lamely. ''I like her.''

Jonathan turned away from me, ostensibly to look at the duck pond. He said nothing.

I sighed. ''How are you getting along with your dad? Things any better?'' As long as we seemed destined to have a touchy discussion, it might as well be on a topic I was interested in.

''No!'' At least I'd caught his attention. He turned back to me, his face flushed. ''Everything is worse. He's such an asshole.''

I'd always thought so. I was aware that Jonathan was sending me an appraising look: Was I going to call him down about using Bad Language? I decided to ignore it. ''How come it's worse?'' I asked.

''Well, yesterday when I was talking to Andy—you know, the sixth-grader—he told me that he was staying up late the Saturday night Mom died. Andy had a friend sleeping over, and they were watching *Friday the Thirteenth* on TV.''

Jonathan was warming to his subject. When the train stopped he climbed out of the car, not missing a beat. ''Andy said he and his friend Sam went outside just before the movie started to get some Cokes from the garage; they have this room over the garage that has an extra refrigerator. And when they were out there, Andy saw my dad coming home.''

I stared at him. ''But your dad was with you in Austin.''

''No, he wasn't. Not at night. He left before dinner; he said he had to go out to see an old friend of his. I stayed with Grandma and Grandpa. Dad wasn't back when I went to bed.''

I tried to think of some reason why Paul would make the three and a half hour trip to Houston and then turn around to drive back to Austin the same night. ''Was Andy sure he saw your dad? Maybe it was just somebody who looked like him. A lot of the time you can't see very well in the dark.''

''That's what my dad said. He said he wasn't here that night; he was in Austin with his friend. He said it would have been stupid to drive back to Houston, and he didn't get where he is today by being stupid.''

No, he'd gotten where he was by using his uncanny ability to suck up to powerful people. But if it hadn't been Paul who Andy saw, who was it that went into Caroline's house that night? ''Did Andy say what time his movie was on? Maybe he saw the same man as your other neighbor did.''

Jonathan shook his head. ''The man in the white car was here about eight thirty. This guy came around ten thirty, when the late show starts.''

"Maybe Andy saw the guy in the white car leaving." I remembered someone saying that the autopsy had shown that Caroline died between 10 P.M. and 2 A.M. If that was true, she could already have been dead by 10:30.

Jonathan's features settled into a look of dig in your-heels stubbornness that I'd seen on Caroline's face hundreds of times. "Andy said Dad was walking in the back door." He paused. "But when I said that to Dad he started yelling at me. He said I had to stop making things up and live"—his voice was heavy with disdain—"in the real world. And just because I didn't like something didn't mean I could pretend it didn't happen. That was the way crazy people thought, he said, and one crazy person in our family was enough."

God! I draped an arm around him, feeling his bony frame heave, his ragged gasps of breath. "You're not crazy," I said gently, smoothing the cowlicky blond hair down. "I don't think your mother was crazy either. She was probably very depressed, and when people are depressed sometimes they don't think straight. They think that they'll be miserable forever, and that anything they can do to stop the misery is worth it. The only thing they can see is how unhappy they are."

Jonathan pulled away from me. "But my mom didn't kill herself."

"Jonathan—" I hesitated, trying to find the right words. "You're never going to find proof that someone else killed her. Even if one man or two men visited her that night, that doesn't mean they shot her. Your mom came to visit me that afternoon and told me that she thought something awful was going to happen to her. I didn't understand what she was talking about, but I think she knew she was going to kill herself and felt powerless to stop."

I moved closer to Jonathan, but he backed away from me. "She wasn't thinking straight, sweetie. She wasn't acting like herself."

"You're wrong!" Standing in the middle of the zoo parking lot, Jonathan hurled the words at me.

I didn't see the car until it was ten feet away. Jonathan's back was to it.

"Watch out!" I grabbed Jonathan and pulled him out of the car's path. Barely in time.

The car sped past us and out of the parking lot.

"My God!" I held Jonathan tightly, not wanting to let go. The driver hadn't even seen the boy, hadn't even slowed down. What kind of person raced through a zoo parking lot, a place normally teeming with small children? If I hadn't seen the car, and grabbed Jonathan . . .

Jonathan pulled free from my arms. "Did you see it? Did you see what kind of car it was?" He sounded excited, not frightened at all.

"I'm not sure." Checking out the model of the car hadn't been high on my priority list.

"It was a white car, wasn't it?" Jonathan pulled on my arm, his voice high and urgent. "It was the same white car that was at our house the night Mom died. Did you see who was driving it?"

I stared at him. "The car was red," I said. "Bright red."

NINETEEN

I was worried about Jonathan. His fixation on Caroline's death seemed to have passed over some invisible line. We weren't talking about denial anymore—a normal stage in the grieving process. This seemed a bonafide obsession. Jonathan was consumed with finding his mother's murderer.

As I ate my dinner—a broiled chicken breast, steamed broccoli, and a huge salad—I kept thinking about the way Jonathan had acted at the zoo. When you start believing that a random reckless driver was the guy last seen talking to your mother, it was cause for concern.

I decided to phone Amanda. She was the expert on kids' crises, and at least would be able to tell me how serious this really was. She'd probably even give me some tips on how to deal with Jonathan. I picked up the receiver, then remembered that Amanda and Daniel had gone to the symphony. The Houston Symphony was playing a program called Back To Back Beethoven.

I phoned Jonathan instead. Maybe, I told myself as Mrs. Gates called him to the telephone, the kid had just been having a bad day last Saturday. Maybe—I hoped—I was the one who was overreacting.

''Jonathan, hi. It's Liz.''

''Hi.'' He did not sound thrilled to hear from me.

''Is something wrong?''

''Yeah.'' A pause. ''I can't ride my bike anymore.''

''Your new bike? Why not?''

"Somebody ran over it with their car."

"Oh, no, what a shame! I know how much you liked that bike."

"When I came home from school today, it was all crushed up in the middle of the driveway." Jonathan sounded as if he was crying. "Nobody even knows who did it."

I remembered seeing the bicycle lying in the driveway the day we went to the zoo. I wondered if Paul or Mrs. Gates had accidentally run over it and then refused to admit it. On second thought, though, I eliminated Paul from my suspicions. If *he* had mangled Jonathan's bike, he not only would have admitted it, he'd have immediately used the accident as an object lesson in What Happens If We Are Careless With Our Personal Property.

I waited until I was pretty sure Jonathan had stopped crying. "What does Mrs. Gates say?"

"She says the bike was fine when she came in the morning, but when she got back from the grocery store, around two o'clock, it was all mashed up."

I wasn't sure that I believed her, but I guessed it was possible that somebody had just pulled into the Marshalls' driveway to turn around and inadvertently run over the bike. "I'm sure sorry, Jonathan." The boy had more than enough problems without adding this to his list.

"You know what I think?" Jonathan said. He didn't wait for my answer. "I think it was that guy in the white car who did it. I bet he waited until he knew everybody was gone at my house, so no one would see him. He smashed my bike to stop me from riding around and asking questions about him. He doesn't want me to find out anything else about him. He thinks I know too much already."

Oh, God.

I'd just hung up the phone when someone knocked on the door of my apartment. Loudly.

I squinted out the peephole. Opened the door. "What the hell happened to you?" I asked Nick Finley.

He winced as he gingerly touched a deep purple bruise surrounding his right eye. "You referring to this?"

"Among others." I nodded at the angry red cut on his cheek and his swollen lip.

"If you invite me inside, maybe I'll tell you about it."

I figured he couldn't be hurt too badly if he could still be such a smart-ass, but I let him in anyway. "You want a drink?" He looked as if he could use one. "I've got Chablis or some light beer."

"I'll take the beer.

"It happened a couple of hours ago," Nick said after I'd returned with beers for both of us. "Two guys jumped me in the parking lot behind my apartment."

"You okay?" I asked, leaning forward to inspect him more closely. His face was a mess, and he was sitting as if other parts of his body hurt too. But other than that, he seemed all right. He didn't have that dazed, out-of-it expression I'd seen on people who'd recently been injured, the look that said they still couldn't comprehend what had happened to them.

"Let's put it this way," Nick said, "I'm sore, but there's no major damage. Nothing broken. I think someone just wanted to scare me."

I looked at him. "What do you mean *scare* you? Didn't whoever did this rob you?"

Nick shrugged, a gesture he instantly regretted. Wincing, he said, "Yeah, they took my wallet. There were two of them—real rednecks, white guys. One of them held a gun while the other guy—the big one—worked me over."

"What made you think they didn't just want your money?"

Nick sent me his Lord-give-me-patience look. "Right before the big guy punched me in the gut he said, 'I won't be so nice if I have to come back.' "

It could have meant a lot of things. My mind raced ahead, presenting possible explanations. Maybe these guys had intended to beat up someone else—a drug dealer, say, or someone who was welshing on his gambling debts. Or maybe they did mean to threaten Nick, but were referring to something other than his therapy story. Nick was working on other stories too. And union officials, for instance, seemed like a potentially more violent group than psychiatrists. Or hell—who knows?—maybe these two thugs went around the city telling everyone they robbed, "I won't be so nice if I have to come back."

"So you think someone sent these men to beat you up," I said, still trying to take it all in. "Who?"

Nick leaned back against the couch, gingerly crossing his legs. "My guess is Tom Fowler. But it could just as easily have been Houssman. Both of them have a lot to lose. They both have big, very profitable private practices. What do they charge now—one twenty-five, one fifty an hour? A lot of those affluent, yuppie clients might decide to go whine on somebody else's couch when they read about what a sleaze-bag they have for a therapist."

I sighed, but decided to let it go. Why waste my breath on a man who, even when he wasn't in pain, wouldn't listen to my rational, well-informed arguments? "Have you been to a doctor?" I asked instead.

Nick shook his head. "No, I'm okay. That's what I'm saying. They could have shot me, but they didn't. All they wanted to do was scare me off the story."

It was starting to seep in. Maybe Nick was right. "Gertrude Stone, Caroline's aunt, said Fowler threatened Caroline," I told him. It was clear from the look on Nick's face that he hadn't known about it. "He tried to intimidate her—verbally, I mean, nothing physical. He even called the managing editor to complain. Fowler told Caroline that if she ran the story about him, he'd see that it was the last one she ever wrote. Something like that."

Nick raised an eyebrow. "Did Miss Stone say how Caroline reacted?"

"She said Caroline just laughed it off. Said Fowler was full of hot air."

Nick took a long swig of his beer. "Yeah, that's what I would have thought too," he said. "Before tonight."

He left twenty minutes later. At the doorway he turned and

inspected my living room. "Hey, you changed something, didn't you?"

I couldn't believe he'd noticed, particularly with his right eye almost swollen shut. My decorative touches were fairly insignificant, just a big dieffenbachia I'd bought and set in front of the living room window and a bright quilt I'd hung on the wall that separated the living room and dining room.

"I like the quilt," Nick said.

"Thanks." He can't be in too much pain, I thought, feeling relieved and strangely pleased that he liked the quilt. "My grandmother and I made it the summer after my sophomore year of high school. Grandma said it was called a crazy quilt because we just kind of made it up as we went along." I studied the quilt, a hodgepodge of bright blues and greens mixed in with a lot of turquoise and lavender pieces—all my favorite colors. My apartment still looked empty, but with the addition of the quilt and plant, at least it had some color.

Nick tried to smile at me. It looked more like a wince. Yes, he assured me, he would be careful. No, he wouldn't drop the story. He'd call me as soon as he learned anything new.

It was only after I'd closed the door behind him, making very sure that the deadbolt was securely in place, that I realized Nick was talking as if it was *our* story again. A wrong-headed assumption if ever there was one. Surely the man was not deluded enough to think that tonight's incident would make me reconsider my decision to stay out of this mess? Me, the original coward, the woman who ran to get popcorn during the violent part of a movie?

I spent the rest of the night trying, unsuccessfully, to sleep. I kept hearing strange noises that I was convinced were the sounds of someone prying open a window or jimmying my flimsy front door.

Finally, at 3:15 in the morning, I got up and made myself a pot of coffee. I needed caffeine to keep me wide-awake and jumpy instead of jumpy and half asleep.

Sitting at my kitchen table, I sternly informed myself that what I was dealing with was a simple case of overactive imagination. An evening filled with too many ominous warnings—mangled bikes and swelling black eyes—had made me hear danger in every car driving through the parking lot, in every footstep that passed my door.

I wanted—desperately wanted—to believe that Nick was just imagining that Dr. Fowler or Dr. Houssman had sent those thugs, and that Jonathan's crushed bike was just a senseless accident. But this morning I knew in my gut that Nick, at least, was probably right. Someone wanted to shut him up, and there was a better than even chance that I was at least casually acquainted with that person. Someone possibly wanted to shut up Jonathan too, though I wasn't so sure about that one. Then, because it was 3:30 A.M., I tried to see how the two incidents could possibly be connected. I was very relieved when I couldn't come up with any connection.

Searching for calm, and for rational, reassuring answers, I gulped my coffee. It didn't do any good. My thoughts kept returning to one indisputable fact: Neither Nick nor Jonathan had any intention of backing down. I was terrified for both of them.

TWENTY

It was just another little Sunday afternoon shopping trip, I told myself. Except that ever since I'd left my car in the Galleria parking garage I had the sense that someone was following me. Which was ridiculous, of course. I'd checked twice, and no one was there, at least no one suspicious-looking. When you're walking in a gigantic shopping mall like the Galleria, there's *always* someone behind you. My sleepless night was just making me jumpy.

To squelch my fears I darted into a kids' shoe store. No one followed me in, and no one was waiting when I came out.

To be on the safe (read "paranoid") side, I checked again a few minutes later. This time the only people behind me were two teenaged girls. They were arguing about where to shop next.

"Liz!"

I jumped. But I knew the voice before I turned around. Certainly I had heard it frequently enough, a mellifluous baritone that too often held an undertone of petulance. Or at least it had seemed that way during the last couple years of our marriage.

"Hello, Max." He was wearing a Burberry raincoat, khaki slacks, and Topsiders—Max's idea of weekend casual—and carrying a Neiman-Marcus shopping bag. I thought he looked pale and tired, his round face a little fleshier than the last time I saw him.

His bloodshot brown eyes were taking me in, running a

quick tally of my appearance: grooming, dress, and—always important to Max—weight. "You're looking terrific," he said, sounding surprised. "You've lost weight, haven't you?"

I thought for sure he'd tell me how much. Max's mind ran to such analyses. I nodded. "I've been exercising a lot and cutting down on what I eat."

He tilted his head, his eyes narrowing. "Fifteen pounds?" he guessed.

"Fourteen so far."

"Well, you really look great. I like your hair that way too." He smiled at me, bestowing his approval.

I felt a familiar mixture of contradictory emotions—foremost irritation. Did I assess his appearance like a condescending beauty pageant judge? But yet, I blush to admit, I felt a distinct stab of pleasure too. Pleased that hypercritical, judgmental Max thought I looked good. Smug that on my own I was losing the weight that he'd begged me to chuck when we were married.

"Thanks. I guess I'd better get back to my shopping. It's nice seeing you, Max."

"Wait." He grabbed my arm as if he was afraid I was about to make a break for Lord & Taylor. "Do you have time to have coffee with me? Or lunch, if you haven't eaten yet."

I'd had my lunch already, half a cup of cottage cheese, some apple slices, and a handful of pretzels. Plus I really wanted to buy a pair of black slacks (my old ones were too big) before I went out to dinner with Amanda and Daniel. I hesitated long enough to catch a glint of desperation in Max's deep-set eyes. "Well, maybe a quick cup of coffee . . ." I told him.

Max picked a sandwich shop overlooking the Galleria skating rink. Once, he and I had gone ice skating there. Our ankles had given out after we'd circled the rink once, grimly clutching the railing for balance. "Next year the winter Olympics!" Max had announced as we came off the ice, laughing at our mutual lack of athletic ability.

"So what have you been up to?" I asked, after Max ordered a corned beef sandwich and two coffees.

"Oh, the usual. Work mainly."

"I thought partners put in fewer hours than the associates."

"Some partners do. I don't." Max stopped watching the skaters. "Still as compulsive as ever, I guess." He smiled at me.

"Why doesn't that surprise me?" I smiled back.

Max watched a pretty teenaged waitress set our food in front of us. "It was easier to leave the office when we were together," he said after she'd left. "I know it sounds corny, but I guess I had something to come home to."

So why hadn't he come home? I stared at him, wondering if he had somehow managed to forget all those weekends when we barely laid eyes on each other, when Max was so obsessed with his passion to make partner that even on those rare occasions when he was physically present, I ached with loneliness.

"You can't mean that you're working longer hours now than when we were married?" I said.

Max finished chewing a mouthful of corned beef. "Lately I have been. The last couple of months."

I was going to ask him what he'd done for Christmas, but then decided against it. I didn't really feel like hearing about the exotic, fun-filled trip he and that sexy associate, Lisa, had probably gone on. Nor, for that matter, did I feel much like telling him about my Christmas with Nick, a Christmas I was doing my damnedest to forget.

Max wiped a smudge of mustard from the corner of his mouth. "Paul Marshall tells me that you're seeing a lot of Jonathan."

I could feel myself bristling. "Yes, he seems to have a problem with that, though I'm sure he's already shared those concerns with you."

Max looked surprised. "He told me that he appreciated your spending the time with Jonathan. Said you had better rapport with the boy than he did."

"Anyone has better rapport with Jonathan than Paul does. He's not exactly an attentive father. And the last time Paul talked to me, he certainly didn't seem appreciative."

''But why? I'd think Paul would be glad that someone was taking an interest in the kid.''

I took a large gulp of coffee, then managed a condensed explanation of Jonathan's suspicions and Paul's reaction to them.

Max whistled. ''I can see how Paul would find that upsetting. He's a pretty controlling kind of guy, and he figures the issue is resolved. Then if Jonathan refuses to see it that way . . .''

''Only an ignoramus could assume that any child would view his mother's death as a resolved issue,'' I said angrily. ''What does Paul expect? Jonathan is just supposed to shrug his shoulders and say, Well, Mom has been dead almost two months, now I'll get on with my life?''

''That's what Paul is doing.''

''Paul is an insensitive bastard.''

Max blinked rapidly several times, a silent Morse code signaling his nervousness. This was our old impasse: my emotions versus Max's logic. When I started talking feelings—not cold, hard facts—Max wanted to bolt for the door.

Well, let him. I no longer had to try to translate my world into language that Max would understand, nor did I have to deal with the pain of realizing that Max didn't want to understand. But then why should he? Things were so much safer, so definite and concrete, in his black-and-white world. No one got hurt when you didn't acknowledge that you had any feelings.

''I understand that Paul is getting remarried soon,'' Max said.

''So I've heard. He told me that he'd asked Caroline for a divorce.''

Max's coffee cup stopped midway to his lips. ''Paul asked Caroline for a divorce? Are you sure?''

''I'm sure that's what he told me. Why? You thought it was the perfect marriage?''

''No.'' Max set down his cup. ''I thought he needed Caroline's money. And he wasn't going to get it if he divorced her.''

''Caroline's money?'' This was news to me. ''Surely she wasn't earning much as a reporter. And I thought Paul was making a bundle at the law firm."

"He was spending a bundle too. Every three or four years a new and bigger house. The Jaguar. His annual gambling trip to Las Vegas. He was living way beyond his means. And Caroline had a hefty trust fund that her father left her."

"So Caroline bailed them out financially?"

Max shook his head. "He wanted her to, but she refused to touch the principal. From what I heard, Caroline was pretty stingy with her own money. She'd help out enough to placate the bill collectors, but she always made it clear that the money in the trust was hers alone."

"And now it's Paul's?"

"It will be as soon as the will is probated. She divided her assets evenly between Paul and Jonathan."

"Another reason Paul has adapted so well to being a widower. Newly rich and about to be married to a twenty-three-year-old."

"She's twenty-seven," said Max, ever literal. "I met her a few weeks ago. She seems very sweet, not at all like Caroline. She's a high-school French teacher."

"Maybe they can honeymoon in Paris on Caroline's money."

Max ignored it. But at least he didn't explain that the will wouldn't be probated by that time. "You know, Paul isn't the only one who profited financially from Caroline's death," he said after swallowing a mouthful of corned beef. "From what I hear, Caroline's stepmother suddenly has a lot more money these days too."

I set down my coffee cup. "I can't believe that Caroline would have left Celia any money. Caroline couldn't stand her."

"Caroline didn't leave her money. But she was the administrator of a trust that her dad set up for Celia, who, from what I hear, is quite the little spender."

Before I could ask the predictable question, he added, "It's called a spendthrift trust. John Rogers wanted to make sure that Celia didn't spend all the money she inherited in one year. Apparently he made Caroline the trustee because he knew she wouldn't be swayed by Celia's charms."

To put it mildly. I could just imagine Caroline being only too happy to dole out Celia's money a dime at a time. Could Caroline's father really have viewed this as a loving solution to his wife's extravagance, giving his daughter financial rein over a stepmother she clearly disliked? "And now Celia has a more generous trustee?" I asked.

"Apparently. Paul said she's found some banker who she's wrapped around her little finger."

Which explained Celia's lavish Christmas gifts to Jonathan. I glanced at my watch. "I really need to get moving. I didn't realize how late it was." I leaned down to pick up my purse.

"Wait!" Max seemed to detect the note of desperation in his voice, and found it inappropriate. When he spoke again he was smiling uncertainly. "I was thinking how much I enjoy talking to you."

"Thanks." I could see the wariness in his eyes. Max had never been a good actor. Oh, well, I guess I could forget about my shopping, wear my baggy old slacks for a while. "Is something wrong, Max? Something you want to talk about?"

He looked relieved, then tried—not very effectively—to hide that too. "Not wrong, exactly," he finally said. "It's just that you're so easy to talk to. You're not so critical, so constantly judgmental like some women I know."

You didn't have to be a psychic to figure that one out. "You've broken up with your girlfriend?" I guessed.

He nodded sheepishly. "She was so aggressive, always wanting to call the shots. And God, was she self-absorbed—everything had to center around her."

I let him carry on about the unfeeling Lisa. Selfish. Bossy. Career-obsessed. Startlingly similar, in fact, to old Max himself.

But there seemed no point in sharing that insight with my ex-husband. He wouldn't see the similarities anyway. What was more interesting to me was my own reaction. I wasn't feeling any of the things I expected to feel, probably *would* have felt even a couple of months ago. I didn't feel gleeful, vindicated, triumphant over Max's failed romance, all tawdry reactions I was quite capable of experiencing. Instead I felt a muted (well, let's be frank, *very* muted) sympathy and not much else. After all the months of anger, hurt, the painful probing of good memories and the longing for the marriage we might have had, this reaction was a wonderment to me.

"What about you?" Max was asking. "Are you seeing any body right now?"

I shook my head. I had no desire to tell him about Nick, didn't know what I'd say even if I wanted to. "I'm sorry, Max, but I really do have to leave now. I'm meeting Amanda and Daniel for dinner in an hour."

"Well, give them my best," he said, looking doleful.

For a second I was tempted to invite him to join us, giving in to my knee-jerk sympathy for wounded animals, sobbing children, and unhappy adults. But then I remembered Amanda telling me how lucky I was to be rid of Max and Max's comments about what a sanctimonious bitch Amanda was. Reality intervened.

"Nice seeing you, Max." I patted his shoulder.

"Nice seeing *you.*" His eyes swept over me as I stood up to leave. "Get rid of another fifteen pounds, Liz, and you'll be a real knockout."

TWENTY-ONE

I answered the phone on the sixth ring.

"Liz? This is Gertrude Stone. Sorry to bother you so late."

She seemed breathless, or maybe upset. I assured her that it wasn't too late. I'd just returned from my dinner with Amanda and Daniel ten minutes earlier.

"I'm very worried about Jonathan," Gertrude said. "He spent last night with me. He's still talking about finding Caroline's murderer, you know. And when I told him that he has to stop dwelling on this, it's not healthy, he became very agitated and refused to speak to me."

It didn't surprise me. I'd tried to reason with Jonathan too, but nothing I said could convince him that Caroline had not been murdered. "I know that must have been upsetting for you," I said. It was upsetting for me.

"Yes, it was, but that's not why I'm calling." Her tone made it clear that she was not one of those silly women who needed their hands held every time a minor crisis occurred.

I could hear her take a deep breath. "I've been thinking things over, and I've reached the conclusion that Jonathan may be right. I'm not entirely certain, you understand, but some of the things I've learned recently point in that direction."

I wasn't sure that I'd understood her correctly. "Are you saying that you think someone *did* kill Caroline?"

There was a long pause. "I'm saying that someone *may* have killed Caroline," Gertrude said in a small, scared voice that didn't sound like her. "And if someone did kill her, Jonathan may be putting himself in terrible danger when he keeps talking all the time about finding her killer. He doesn't realize what trouble he could be getting into."

I took a deep breath. "Why do you think someone may have killed Caroline? Last week you were convinced that she committed suicide."

"I know, but since then I've acquired some new information. And there are things I've started to remember that put Caroline's death in a new light. I may be wrong, though. I need to check my facts before I make any accusations."

She was talking too quickly, rambling. I tried to imagine what could possibly have happened, what piece of information had turned up to upset her so. "It might help if you tell me about it," I said.

"Yes, yes. But not now. Not tonight."

So why had she phoned me—so she could not tell me what was on her mind? For the very first time I could see Gertrude's resemblance to Caroline: Something terrible is going to happen, Liz—but I won't tell you what it is.

The memory of that conversation made me try again with Gertrude. "You called to tell me what's upsetting you, Gertrude. I think you should let me know what it is."

"I will tell you. But not tonight," she repeated. "I'm afraid I've already told you more than I intended to. I want you to hear all the information for yourself, and then draw your own conclusions. I don't want to influence your opinion by telling you my interpretation right now."

Apparently making even that decision made her feel better. She sounded authoritative again, in control. "If you come to my house tomorrow, we can discuss the issue thoroughly."

Another of Gertrude's command performances? I was strongly tempted to decline the invitation. I was tired of being bossed around by this demanding old woman who'd apparently forgotten that I was not one of her high school students. And furthermore, I didn't believe for a minute that anyone had killed Caroline. But something—perhaps the memory of how I'd dismissed Caroline's complaints—made me agree to stop by Gertrude's house the next day after work.

"Fine. I'll see you around six-thirty then," Gertrude said. "Good night, Liz."

I'd just finished interviewing Jeanne Williamson when Amanda poked her head into my office. Jeanne, a young social worker who led a therapy group for pregnant teenagers, stretched her long, blue-jeaned legs and stood up. From beneath her halo of frizzy blond hair, she smiled at Amanda, then turned back to me. "If you have any more questions, Liz, just give me a call," she said as she headed out the door. "Enjoyed talking to you."

Amanda perched on a corner of my desk. 'So how's it going?"

"It was a good interview. But God, that sounds like depressing work. Jeanne says that lots of the girls—we're talking about fourteen- and fifteen-year-olds—decide they want to keep their babies. They're convinced that their babies are going to give them the unconditional love they never got from anyone else."

Amanda sighed. "And then when the baby *doesn't* give the girl that love—when he turns out to be the demanding, needy little creature he's supposed to be—the girl is frustrated and angry. Also frequently abusive. Children are not equipped to be parents. Hell, an awful lot of adults aren't equipped to be parents either."

"Jeanne's trying to give the girls a more realistic idea of what parenthood is like—not the pastel Mother's Day card version," I said. "But when I was talking to her I kept remembering how awful it was to be fourteen years old. Everything was terrible; I hated everybody, especially myself. And nothing particularly bad was happening in my life to make me feel that way."

Amanda nodded. "You were just fourteen."

"And then to think of adding a pregnancy on top of all that turmoil . . ."

We contemplated this grim thought for a moment before

Amanda broke the silence. "I came down here to see if you wanted to come hear the guest lecturer with me."

Every Monday afternoon some mental health expert—sometimes someone from the center staff, sometimes somebody from another institution—spoke in the auditorium. In theory, the speeches were designed for the students—psychology interns, social work graduate students, psychiatry residents—who were receiving some of their training at the center. But in practice any employee who was interested could sit in on the lectures.

"I don't know," I said. "I'm awfully busy."

Amanda raised her eyebrows. "You wouldn't want to miss hearing our friend Tom Fowler, would you?"

Dr. Fowler had already started speaking by the time we got to the auditorium. Amanda and I took seats at the end of a center row and settled back to hear what Fowler had to say about antipsychotic drugs.

It was boring. Or at least it was to me—someone who doesn't know the difference between chlorpromazine and thioridazine. The psychiatry residents who were there, though, looked interested enough.

I tuned out shortly after Dr. Fowler explained that no one knew exactly how the drugs used to treat schizophrenia work, although it's suspected that it's through their ability to block dopamine receptors in the brain. Instead I focused on the speaker himself.

He was wearing a white shirt, brown bow tie, and a brown tweed sports coat that looked as if it had been around for a while—sort of like his fifties-era crew cut. But despite his appearance—the bow tie, jug ears, and antediluvian haircut—the man did not seem ungainly. He was a good speaker (if, that is, you were interested in his topic), confident, and articulate. I remembered Amanda's telling me Fowler had the reputation of being bright and gregarious, a real networker. Today he looked as if he was enjoying himself on the stage, being the center of attention.

Amanda leaned over and whispered, "Too bad he isn't discussing the therapist-client relationship.''

Too bad he wasn't speaking on anything other than today's topic. I watched as Fowler fielded a resident's question about the effectiveness of the long-acting, injectable form of antipsychotics. Could this unfashionable, pedantic man have actually sent thugs to beat up Nick? Where would he have met such men? Watching him today, I couldn't imagine Fowler even being able to communicate with them: *You must calculate carefully the intensity of your blows, boys. I only want to intimidate this man, you understand.* I was starting to favor my original theory, that one of the union embezzlers Nick was checking out had sent that particular warning. Fowler seemed more likely to have someone slip a massive dose of Thorazine into Nick's coffee.

I didn't notice at first that Amanda was waving her hand in the air. ''What are you doing?'' I whispered, just as Dr. Fowler called on her.

''Wait and see.'' Amanda bestowed a beatific smile on me before turning her attention to Fowler. ''I'm wondering if we could extend the discussion to other areas,'' she said, ''now that we're all so well informed about antipsychotics.''

''Certainly.'' Fowler smiled down at the little lady in the center row. ''What did you want to ask?''

I braced myself.

''I read an interview you gave the *Chronicle* sometime last year about dealing with anxiety.'' She waited until Fowler nodded, yeah, he knew what she was talking about. ''You mentioned that when patients came in with high levels of anxiety, you were more likely to treat the female patients with drugs. With the men you tended to favor psychotherapy, relaxation techniques, or biofeedback.'' Amanda fixed Fowler with a look. ''I'm just very curious why you made this distinction.''

Behind me Bernard Baker groaned. Bernie, a balding administrator in his early sixties, had once spent twenty minutes telling me how an ''irrational feminist component'' at the center was disrupting meetings and causing dissension among the staff ("staff" meaning over-fifty, white male employees in white collar jobs). Amanda, needless to say, was not one of Bernie's favorite people.

Fowler took a deep breath but kept his cool. "I was misquoted in that article," he said. "What I actually was saying was that some of my patients come in with a quick-fix mentality. They don't want to work on the source of their anxiety; they just want a tranquilizer to make everything better. The patient I gave as an example of this mind-set was a woman. The reporter apparently assumed I was referring to all my women patients, which, of course, is absurd."

"So you're saying you treat your men and women clients in the same way?" Amanda asked.

"I treat all my clients conscientiously and professionally," Fowler responded.

I bet Mary Jo would be surprised to hear that.

On the stage Fowler hesitated, then decided to play it for a laugh. "But if you're asking me do I treat men and women differently, certainly." He smirked. "I'm a big believer in *Vive la différence.*"

Only Bernie Baker chuckled. A couple of rows in front of me a female psychiatry resident sent Fowler a glare that could have melted a glacier.

The whole thing was over in five minutes. Five minutes in which Wanda Smith, a middle-aged black social worker with a voice like Barbara Jordan's, demanded that Fowler clarify his male and female treatment plans. Five minutes in which Wanda refused to accept Fowler's snotty dismissal of her and her question, I whipped out my notebook and took fast and furious notes, and Nathaniel Reubens, the coordinator of the Monday lecture series, got up and thanked Dr. Fowler for his thought-provoking remarks at the same time that Fowler was stalking, tight-lipped, out of the auditorium. Someone a couple of rows behind me laughed. I knew, without turning around, it wasn't Bernie.

Amanda leaned over and patted my hand. "I told you he'd be an interesting speaker."

I left Amanda at the stairs that led to her office and headed down the corridor to my own.

"Miss." It took a moment for me to realize that the by-now familiar voice was speaking to me.

I turned to face Dr. Fowler.

He smiled at me, his lips curving upward but his eyes still angry. "I couldn't help noticing you taking notes in there," he said. "Are you with the media?"

"I'm the editor of *The Center News*," I said, noticing that his eyes had moved south of my face.

I could see him relax, visibly relieved. "Oh, I read that sometimes. A nice little newsletter." He turned, dismissing me, this person who was no longer a threat to him, and walked away without another word.

I stood in the middle of the hall, trying to figure out a way to use Fowler's gender quotes in the next issue of my nice little newsletter. I could not remember when I'd met such a vile man.

In my office I dialed Gertrude Stone's number, envisioning how Caroline must have savored the prospect of publicly humiliating this jerk. No one answered the phone.

"Damn." Gertrude was probably at the grocery store right now, buying something to fix for dinner. I'd meant to call her earlier to insist that this time I'd take her out to eat at some nearby restaurant, but, with one thing or another, I'd forgotten until this moment to extend the invitation.

I intended to call her again later, but by the time I finished my teenage-mother story it was after 5:30. I'd just have to convince Gertrude in person to put her meal in the freezer for tomorrow and let someone else do the cooking tonight.

My mind jumped from Fowler to unwed mothers as I drove to Gertrude's house. Since I'd had my last (and final) session with Dr. Houssman—an event which forced me to accept that I was now solely in charge of my own mental health—I'd refused to let myself fall into the interminable obsessing that used to be my specialty. It seemed a form of self-indulgence that I could ill afford at this point.

Tonight this meant that I could consider, but not dwell on, what had been in the back of my head ever since my interview with Jeanne. Namely, why did a teenage girl, who needed a pregnancy like a case of the plague, get pregnant so easily, while I, who'd spent years charting every ovulation and was even astute enough to realize that a baby wouldn't shower me with unending affection, remained childless? So I knew it was an unanswerable question. So what?

I made a big effort to think of something else. Like what I was going to have to do to convince Gertrude Stone that she was letting Jonathan's detective fantasies get to her. Tonight Gertrude could divert me from the topic of motherhood and babies and I could help her realize that her earlier instinct about Caroline's death had been the right one.

I pulled into the driveway of the little brick house, wondering why all the lights were off. Nobody answered the doorbell, so I pounded on the door.

My peripheral vision showed a movement in the next yard. "Excuse me!" It was another gray-haired woman, dressed in a faded pink jogging suit. She was waving her arm at me as she crossed the lawn.

"You've come to see Gertrude?" she asked, although I figured we both knew the answer to that one.

I nodded anyway. "Do you know where she is?"

"I'm afraid I do, dear." The old lady suddenly looked as if she were about to cry. "She died last night. I found her body this morning."

I stared at her, feeling as if I must have misunderstood what she was saying. "Did you say *died?*"

The woman pulled a tissue from the pocket of her sweat pants and wiped her eyes. "Her heart was very bad, you know. They say she had a heart attack."

"But I talked to her just last night," I said, talking more to myself than to her.

The woman, whoever she was, nodded sympathetically. "She died in her sleep, the paramedics told me. It was a real shame. Gertrude was a wonderful woman."

"Yes, she was." All at once I was freezing. I began to shake.

It wasn't until I was halfway home, my car heater going full blast, that I wondered what it was that Gertrude had wanted to show me.

TWENTY-TWO

Gertrude Stone's funeral was everything that Caroline's was not: small, heartfelt, with a lovely eulogy delivered by a gray-haired minister who'd obviously known and liked the lady. He spoke of Gertrude's impact on her high school classes, of the vast correspondence she'd maintained with former students who'd gone on to become English professors, lawyers, writers, high school teachers.

"Just yesterday I spoke to one of her former students, who called to tell me how much Miss Stone had meant to her," he said. "She said that Gertrude had made the characters they read about seem real to the students. 'Now what do you think Lady Macbeth is feeling here? Did you ever know anybody like her?' Gertrude would ask the class. But even more than teaching her students to love literature, Gertrude's gift to her students was to convince them they could go out of that classroom and accomplish anything they set their minds to. That young woman who called said it better than I can: 'Miss Stone believed in us and that made us believe in ourselves.' "

I sat toward the back of the church, feeling teary, wishing that this bright, determined woman were still around to phone at all hours and insist that I come to dinner.

The sanctuary, though small, was filled with mourners. I recognized some of them. In the front row were Paul Marshall and Jonathan, wearing the same navy blazer he wore to his mother's funeral, and Celia, again in black. A few rows ahead of me Gertrude's neighbor, the woman who'd found her body, sat with another older woman.

I was startled when someone in the row behind me tapped my shoulder. I turned around. "What are *you* doing here?" I hissed at Nick Finley.

Primly, Nick put his finger to his lips. It was an incongruous gesture from a man who still looked as if he'd recently been involved in a prizefight. "We need to talk," he whispered.

I turned my back on him and tried to concentrate on the rest of the service. It was only when the pallbearers pushed Gertrude's coffin down the aisle of the church that the outside world came back into focus. Watching solemnly, I was shocked to see the look of pure malevolence that Paul Marshall, a pallbearer, sent me as he walked past.

"Gee, you're almost as popular with Paul as I am," Nick said, leaning forward to talk as people started filing out of the church. "What did you do to get on his shit list?"

"I don't know," I admitted. "Sympathized with his kid's complaints about him, I guess."

I expected Nick to say something derisive. He didn't. "This must be a tough time for Jonathan. First his mother dying, now his aunt. I know how close he was to Gertrude."

"I didn't think you knew her," I said. Although I'd talked with Nick a couple of times on the phone since the night he was mugged, I'd tried to make clear that I didn't want to know every detail of his story. "Fine," Nick had said. But he still kept phoning me to talk about what was going on.

"I just met her a week ago. I phoned to ask her some questions for my story, and she invited me to come to her house for lunch."

The last mourners, a stooped, white-haired man and his stocky wife, looked at us curiously as they left the sanctuary. "Gertrude didn't by any chance mention to you anything about suspecting that Caroline might not have committed suicide, did she?"

Nick stared at me. "You don't mean she thought Caroline was murdered?"

I told myself that I needed to share my concerns with someone, and that Nick, because of his investigative training, was an ideal choice of confidant. This was an extension of our professional relationship, nothing personal. After this was all over—Nick's therapy story printed, me convinced that Jonathan was perfectly safe—we would revert to our old positions: having nothing whatsoever to do with each other.

"A few days ago," I said, "the night before she died, Gertrude phoned me and said that she'd learned something new that made her think Caroline might have been killed. She was very worried that Jonathan might be in danger. He's been going around telling everybody who will listen that someone murdered his mother."

Nick glanced around to see if anyone was in earshot. "Did Gertrude tell you what she'd learned that made her think that?"

I shook my head. "She said something about needing to think things through before she made any accusations. And she wanted me to hear the information and make my own conclusions. But when I arrived the next day to hear it, she was dead."

Nick seemed to be gazing at something over my shoulder. When finally his eyes returned to my face he said, "She said *hear* the evidence, not see it?"

"I think so. Why? It seems reasonable that she intended to tell me what she'd learned."

By this time the church was completely empty. "Do you have time to grab a cup of coffee with me?" Nick asked. "This place isn't exactly conducive to conversation."

"Okay." I felt reluctant and eager at the same time, a mixture of emotions I chose not to analyze. "But I need to be back at the office by noon."

I drove my own car to a delicatessen a few blocks away. When we were seated in a vinyl-covered booth, I declined Nick's offer of a bagel, ordered black coffee, and said as soon as the waitress left, "So what did Gertrude tell you about

Caroline? Anything to indicate what she was worrying about?''

''She said Caroline seemed obsessed by her mother's death.''

''She told me that too,'' I said, feeling disappointed. ''But that was what made Gertrude think that Caroline had committed suicide—she seemed to be romanticizing death, even saying it was a viable solution to her mother's problems.''

We watched the skinny, exhausted-looking waitress set down our coffee and Nick's cinnamon raisin bagel. ''Gertrude really didn't go into that much with me. I was more interested in the Houssman angle. Unfortunately, Caroline hadn't really discussed her therapy with her aunt, probably because Gertrude didn't have much use for therapists.''

Nick spread cream cheese on his bagel. ''Sure you don't want half?''

I shook my head, thrilled to realize that I didn't, not really. ''Did you tell her that Caroline had an affair with Houssman?''

Nick, chewing on his bagel, shook his head. ''There didn't seem much point in telling her. She was already angry with Houssman. Very angry, in fact. I really got the idea that she blamed him for Caroline's death. Said, What good were therapists if they couldn't stop their patients from killing themselves? Caroline's mother's therapist hadn't helped her either, Gertrude said. All he did was take her money.''

I sighed. ''I wish I knew what Gertrude wanted to tell me. I keep worrying about Jonathan. What if there *is* someone out there who wants to shut him up?''

Nick set down his white coffee mug. ''Come on then, let's go to Gertrude's house. Maybe we can find something—a note to herself, some papers of Caroline's, *something* that indicates what she was going to tell you.''

I looked at him. My common sense was telling me this was a useless endeavor destined to get the two of us arrested for breaking and entering. ''Give me a minute,'' I said. ''I need to call my office to tell them I'm taking the afternoon off.''

When we pulled in front of Gertrude's small brick house I

was happy to see her neighbor's navy Honda parked in her driveway. I had Nick wait in the car while I walked up to the little white frame house with the navy shutters.

The woman opened the door at my first knock, still dressed in the dark brown dress she'd worn to Gertrude's funeral. "I don't know if you remember me," I began, wishing I knew the woman's name. Was this the neighbor—Helen?—who'd given Gertrude the vegetarian lasagna recipe?

"Of course. You're Gertrude's friend, Liz," the woman interrupted. "Oh, by the way, I'm Helen Slater. You were a college roommate of Caroline's, weren't you?"

I nodded, surprised and grateful that she knew so much about me. I explained, as matter-of-factly as I could manage, that Gertrude had wanted to give me some of Caroline's papers, and I was hoping to get into her house to look for them. Did she have a key to Gertrude's house?

I waited, half-expecting Helen to refuse. Instead she nodded her tightly permed gray curls. "Just a minute. I'll get them for you."

She came back in a minute, carrying two keys tied together with a piece of red yarn. "Here you are. This key is for the deadbolt."

I was tempted to ask her if she had any idea at all what Gertrude had wanted to tell me, but decided it sounded too suspicious: *No, I don't know what I'm looking for, but I thought I'd just go inside and snoop around.* Instead I thanked her and said that I'd return the key as soon as my friend and I were finished.

Helen glanced toward the car where Nick was waiting. "Oh, yes," she said knowingly. "That's that reporter fellow who came to visit Gertrude. So you know him too?"

I nodded and left before she decided to come with us and help me and the reporter fellow look around.

The house was a bit musty-smelling, but immaculate as usual. Someone, I noticed, had taken away all the house plants. Everything else, though, looked the same as the last time I'd been there.

While Nick looked through the file folders that were stacked on the coffee table, I walked over to Gertrude's old roll-top desk in a corner of the living room. "I feel like a criminal," I said as I picked up a pile of letters. "This seems so sleazy."

Nick looked up and laughed. "You'd never make it as an investigative reporter, sweetie. Tell yourself you're ferreting out the truth, not poking your nose in other people's business."

Sweetie? "I'll try to keep that distinction in mind," I said. I forced myself to read a chatty letter from a former student who was thanking Gertrude for a baby gift.

Two hours later I thought I'd read every letter, notebook, and penciled list in the house (Gertrude was an inveterate list-maker). While I now knew a great deal more about Gertrude, I hadn't seen anything that raised any suspicions about Caroline's death.

Seated at the desk, I turned to Nick, who was slouched on the sofa, reading through a stack of Caroline's files. "How 'bout you? Found anything?"

He glanced up. "Not really. At least I don't see anything related to her death. Unless I'm missing something obvious."

"Did you find the folder about her mother? I think Gertrude said there was an essay about Mary Ann, and some tapes. Or what about a diary? Maybe Gertrude read Caroline's diary, and it said someone had been threatening her." The more I thought about it, a diary seemed like the most likely source of new information on Caroline's life. I vaguely remembered Gertrude saying Caroline's last diary was missing, but maybe she'd found it.

"I didn't see anything like that," Nick said. "Mainly what I've read is files with notes from Caroline's old stories." He pointed to the desk drawers to my right. "You didn't find anything in the desk? Maybe under some other papers?"

To make sure, I checked again. "Nope. Nothing."

We didn't discover a diary or the essay and tapes on Mary Ann in any of the other rooms we checked either. At the doorway to Gertrude's bedroom, I hesitated. This was the room where Gertrude had died. Even more than before, I felt as if I was violating her privacy, committing an act that would have appalled her.

Nick apparently didn't share my scruples. He walked right

past me and, kneeling, started sorting through the drawer of Gertrude's night stand.

I watched from the doorway as he opened books on the top of the night stand and then replaced them. From the drawer he pulled out a typed paper, which he skimmed, and then two cassette tapes.

"Hey, this might be something," he said, holding up the tapes. "It's Caroline's handwriting on the tapes, apparently interviews she did. She wrote the date on the tapes. Both are from late October, a few weeks before she died."

"Is there a tape recorder in the drawer?" I asked hopefully.

Nick looked. "No, unfortunately." He stood up. "But I think these are the most promising things we've found so far. Didn't you say that Gertrude said she wanted you to hear the evidence for yourself?"

I nodded, starting to pick up some of his excitement. Fifteen minutes later we left, the two tapes in the pocket of Nick's jacket.

As I returned the keys to Helen Slater, I told myself that Gertrude wouldn't have minded us snooping through the house if the end result would help Jonathan. I just hoped that we had found the right evidence to accomplish that.

TWENTY-THREE

Nick and I listened to the cassettes on the tape player in his car as we drove back to the deli parking lot to pick up my Toyota. The first tape was Caroline's interview with Mary Jo, Dr. Fowler's patient. Nick listened to it with gleaming eyes, while I tried to conceal my disappointment. "It's a good interview," Nick said when the tape ended. "Caroline got some information I didn't. I can use it in my story."

"But it's obviously not the new information that Gertrude wanted me to hear," I pointed out. "It doesn't have anything to do with Caroline personally. We already knew Fowler was manipulative and abusive. And Gertrude was the one who told me that Fowler threatened Caroline." It was possible, though, that the tapes had confirmed Gertrude's fears about the psychiatrist, shown her that he was indeed as sinister as she'd suspected.

Nick put on the second tape. It was an interview Caroline had conducted with Dr. Houssman, a bizarre kind of interview. It sounded more like a casual conversation in which Caroline suddenly started to interrogate Dr. H. about therapists' ethical responsibilities to their patients.

I could hear the increasing wariness in Dr. Houssman's voice as Caroline's questions grew more pointed. By the time she got around to asking him if there were ever any situations in which he could ethically condone a therapist sleeping with a patient, Dr. Houssman had shifted from wariness to anger. "Why are you asking me this, Caroline? What are you getting at?'' he demanded. ''The way I see the situation is that you are a rational, consenting adult who entered willingly into a sexual relationship with a man who, in another capacity, also happened to be your therapist. There were two separate relationships.''

''Bullshit.'' Nick looked at the tape with disgust.

On the tape Caroline's voice, calm and in control (and, I couldn't help imagining, enjoying herself immensely) replied, ''I doubt that most of your colleagues would agree that the therapeutic relationship can be kept separate from the personal relationship. Isn't that why most therapists go out of their way not to have any kind of outside contact with their patients?''

''What is this, an interview?'' Houssman inquired angrily.

''Yes,'' Caroline said. ''I'm doing a series of articles about psychotherapists who sleep with their patients.''

''What?'' Dr. Houssman roared, then added, obviously trying to regain control, ''You're not serious, Caroline.''

The tape stopped there.

I looked at Nick, feeling suddenly queasy. ''He must not have known she was taping him.''

Nick shrugged. ''It's easy to hide one of the small recorders in your pocket. I've done it myself. I guess this could have been what Gertrude wanted you to hear. Maybe she figured it gave Houssman a motive to murder Caroline. And when I talked to her, Gertrude *was* very hostile to Houssman.''

''But Fowler knew about Caroline's exposé too,'' I argued, unwilling to believe that Dr. Houssman would murder anyone. ''The articles would damage his career just as much as Dr. Houssman's—probably more, since Fowler coerced his patient into sex. And from what I saw of Dr. Fowler that one night at the Doctors' Club, he seems to have a pretty short fuse.''

Nick said something, but I didn't hear it. I was suddenly recalling where I had seen that boxy white car. ''Fowler drives a white BMW!'' I exclaimed.

''So?''

I told him what the Marshalls' neighbor had said to Jonathan, that she'd seen a big man in a white car enter Caroline's house the night she died.

Nick raised his eyebrows. "She say what time the man left?"

"Didn't notice. She wasn't feeling well and went to bed around eight forty-five, shortly after he got there."

"That's very interesting." Nick idly tapped his right cheek, thinking through what I'd told him. "There's one other thing, though."

"What's that?"

"Houssman drives a white Volvo."

I swore under my breath. After what seemed like an interminable discussion, Nick and I finally decided it was necessary to find out where Drs. Houssman and Fowler had been the evening Caroline died.

Nick said he'd speak to Fowler's secretary. "She hates the guy's guts and was perfectly willing to talk to me, as long as the big boss never learned that she was my source."

"I guess I could go see Houssman," I said, not exactly thrilled by the idea. "After all, he did come to my office to talk to me about your article."

"If that makes you uncomfortable, I can probably find out something on my own," Nick said solicitously. "I mean I know you like the guy. . . ."

"I'll do it," I said grimly. "He's more likely to talk to me than to you. And if Jonathan really is in danger, we need to work fast."

I started to get out of his car. "There's something different about you, isn't there?" Nick said, looking puzzled. His eyes scanned my face, took in my seventeen-pounds thinner physique. "You look nice. Did you get a new hair style?"

I laughed. "No, but thanks anyway. I'll talk to you as soon as I learn anything."

I couldn't stop worrying about Jonathan as I drove to Dr. Houssman's office. Now that I really thought about it, I was convinced that Gertrude would not have overreacted to Jonathan's suspicions. She was too bright, too level-headed for that. I also didn't think she would have concluded from the Houssman tape that he was angry enough to kill Caroline. At least not from that tape alone. There needed to be some additional link, some missing piece of the puzzle, to make Gertrude contact me. And I intended to find out what it was.

Dr. Houssman's receptionist, a friendly black woman with oversized gold hoop earrings, looked puzzled when I walked in the door. "You have an appointment, honey?" she asked after opening the frosted glass window separating her from the waiting room. "I don't have you down in the book."

"No, no appointment." I tried to look needy. "I was just hoping I could see Dr. Houssman for a few minutes between appointments. It's important and won't take long."

The woman nodded sympathetically. "Let me see what I can do."

I pretended to read *Newsweek* while I waited. At 2:50, just when I'd calculated his two o'clock appointment should be leaving, Dr. Houssman himself appeared in the doorway that connected the waiting room to his office.

"Liz, come on in." He was smiling, but I sensed something else too. Puzzlement, maybe, or wariness. "I only have a few minutes, but we can talk until my next client arrives."

"I only need a few minutes," I assured him as I followed him down the familiar gray-carpeted hallway to his office.

We sat down in our old seats, me on the gray tweed couch, he across from me in the black leather chair.

"So what can I do for you?" Dr. Houssman was still smiling, but up close I could see how tired he looked. His face, once ruddy, now looked pale. His brown eyes were bloodshot. I wondered if he'd been ill.

I don't know why I thought he'd tell me the truth if I just asked. Maybe I just wasn't clever enough to think of some sophisticated maneuver to trick him into telling me where he'd been the night of Caroline's death. Or maybe he'd just always struck me as a basically honest man.

"One of Caroline's neighbors saw a big man in a white car

go into Caroline's house the night she died,'' I began. ''Was that you?''

He hesitated for only a second, blinking rapidly. ''Yes,'' he said in a flat voice. ''I was there for about twenty minutes, half an hour at most.''

I waited for him to go on. When he didn't, I asked, ''So what happened? How did she seem to you psychologically?''

''She didn't seem suicidal, if that's what you mean. She was acting peculiar, though, almost manic.'' He sighed, ran his big hands through his curling black hair in the gesture Caroline had captured in her article.

''I went there to plead with her not to run the article about our affair. It would ruin my career, I told her. I'd never slept with a patient before, and, God knows, I'll never do it again. My affair with Caroline was a mistake—I admitted that—but I meant her no harm. And the damage had been as great to me as to her, though I'm not sure she believed that.''

''How did Caroline respond?''

''She laughed at me. Said how could I be telling her to think of the consequences of her actions when I didn't practice what I preached. When I pointed out that the article would hurt her too, certainly harm her already shaky marriage, she said she was tired of lying, tired of pretending to be the perfect, successful woman while always feeling like a fraud. For the first time, she said, she was just going to be herself. She was going to risk exposing herself, warts and all. Caroline said she'd decided to leave Paul, to take Jonathan and start a new life.''

I stared at him. This was the woman who just a few hours earlier on the same day, had been telling me that she was afraid something terrible was going to happen to her? ''That certainly doesn't sound like the speech of someone who's contemplating suicide.''

''For a long time that's what I told myself too.'' Dr. Houssman sighed, staring out the window. ''But now I'm not so sure. There was a definite manic undercurrent to all this that didn't sound like her. Caroline could be feisty, but she was also very emotionally controlled, too controlled, in fact. Then suddenly she decides she's going to be open and honest and revealing, to hell with her carefully constructed façade.''

Dr. Houssman turned to look at me. ''It sounds great, but change seldom happens that way,'' he said. ''Once all Caroline's bravado wore off, once she realized that she was destroying all her deeply entrenched defenses, she could well have realized how difficult this new life of hers would be. And for someone like Caroline, who was so used to being successful at everything she attempted, that knowledge might well have been devastating.''

''Devastating enough to kill herself?'' I directed the question at myself as much as at him.

''I didn't think so then.'' The bloodshot eyes met mine. ''Obviously I was wrong.''

I saw him glance at his little round crystal clock. The twin, I realized now, to the clock I'd seen in Caroline's office. Had she given it to him (the clock seemed more Caroline's taste than Dr. Houssman's) during an earlier phase in their relationship, before everything had turned sour? And was it at all significant that both of them had continued to use the clocks?

''So you left Caroline's at—when did you say?'' I injected quickly before he could say our time was up.

''I didn't say, as you well know. But I must have left before nine o'clock because I was back at my wife's cocktail party by nine fifteen. And any number of the guests can verify that time for you.''

He stood up, looking less friendly than he had ten minutes earlier. ''I'm afraid I have a patient waiting.''

There was something about the way he said it that indicated I was no longer one of those patients, no longer one of that group entitled to his empathetic attention, his little jokes, his nurturing. I was on my own now. He was only reaffirming what I already knew, but nevertheless for a moment I ached again with the loss.

''Goodbye,'' I said as I walked for the last time out of his office.

"Take care," he said, not meeting my eyes as I walked past him into the hallway.

In the dark parking garage, I sat in my car, trying to determine the significance of what I'd learned. I didn't believe that Dr. Houssman had killed Caroline, not at least in the legal, you-pulled-the-trigger-and-shot-her sense. But wasn't it possible that whatever he'd said to Caroline (who, he had admitted, was in a turbulent, volatile mood) had pushed her over the edge into self-destruction? Perhaps he had sneered at her plans. Or maybe he'd painted such a grim picture of the new life Caroline was fantasizing about—divorced, a single mother, no longer the young golden girl who'd never known a defeat—that she decided she couldn't face the future.

But that just didn't sound like Caroline. I could see her lashing out at Houssman and even—though this was harder to imagine—walking out on Paul. I couldn't see her reacting to Houssman's disdain by killing herself. She might shoot herself for her own reasons, but not because someone had jeered at her.

Which left me with the same nagging question: What had happened to Caroline Marshall from 9 P.M., when Dr. Houssman left her house, until the moment, one to five hours later, when the bullet entered her brain?

I had no idea how to find out, but on the theory that checking out Jonathan might decrease my anxiety, I decided to drive over to the Marshall house. It was around the time that Jonathan usually got home from school.

Mrs. Gates answered my knock. She told me that Jonathan wasn't home.

"When do you expect him?" I asked.

"Not until dinnertime," she said, and closed the door.

I'm not sure what made me doubt her. Mrs. Gates had never been exactly a beacon of warmth before, so it wasn't as if I sensed any big change in her attitude toward me. All I sensed was that she was lying.

I walked back to my car, loudly slammed the door, and

drove away. After circling the block, I parked four houses away and walked back to the Marshall house.

If Jonathan was at home, he was likely to be in the family room playing a video game. I crept to the back of the house, feeling like a bad actor in a spy movie.

Crouched in the bushes, I peeked through a long window. There was Jonathan, his back to me, playing Nintendo. I tapped on the window to get his attention.

He didn't hear me.

I tapped again, louder this time. Probably loud enough to send Mrs. Gates running to telephone the police.

Finally, after an extended interval in which I pictured a siren-blaring police car pulling into the driveway, Jonathan looked around and spotted me. I motioned for him to come out the French door leading to the patio.

"What are you doing here?" he asked when he got outside.

"I just wanted to make sure you were okay." I realized I was whispering. "*Are* you okay?"

"I guess. My dad doesn't want me to see you anymore."

Which explained Mrs. Gates's behavior. "How come? Did he say?"

"He says you're a bad influence on me. That when I'm with you I don't live in the real world."

"And he does?"

Jonathan ignored the question. "I *really* hate him, and he hates me too."

"He doesn't hate you," I said, not sure that I believed it. "He just thinks that he's the only one who knows what's best for you."

"He does hate me!" Jonathan's voice had grown so loud that I was sure Mrs. Gates would come running any minute. When I put my finger to my lips, he lowered his voice, but his face was flushed, his large, long-lashed eyes filling with tears.

"When I told Dad that he wanted to get rid of me the same way that he wanted to get rid of Mom, he slapped me across the face."

Before I could answer, we both heard Mrs. Gates calling Jonathan's name. I managed to duck into the bushes before I heard her halting steps walking through the family room.

The French door opened. "What are you doing out there, Jonathan? Come inside right now. It's too cold to be outside without a coat."

I motioned for him to go inside. "See you later," I mouthed, hoping he could read lips.

I heard the door slam shut. I stayed there, crouched in the bushes, for another five minutes. When I finally dared to peer through the window, the room was empty.

TWENTY-FOUR

I felt like an idiot knocking on strangers' doors, looking for a boy named Andy, but I was too panicky not to. I had to find an answer to some very disturbing questions.

At the first house I approached, a red-brick Tudor monstrosity directly behind the Marshalls', a skinny teenaged boy with frizzy red hair answered the door. "Hi, is there a boy named Andy here?" I asked with a smile, hoping I looked like a guileless adult rather than a sinister stranger. "He's a friend of Jonathan Marshall's."

"He lives next door," the kid said before slamming the door in my face. I chose to take it as a helpful gesture.

A boy of about twelve answered the door at the next house, an older, two-story wooden house that was smaller than most of the others in the neighborhood. The boy had a round face with a sprinkling of pimples on otherwise baby-smooth pale skin.

"Are you Andy?" I smiled at him.

He regarded me warily. "What if I am? Who are you?"

"I'm Liz James, a friend of Jonathan Marshall's." He still looked suspicious, but not enough to slam the door on me. Yet.

"What do you want?"

"Jonathan mentioned to me that you said you saw a man going into their house the night Jonathan's mom died."

"So?"

I couldn't decide if the kid looked scared or defensive.

"This is real important, Andy. I'm trying to piece together everything that happened that night. Did you get a good look at the man?"

Andy nodded. "Yeah, I saw him. It was Mr. Marshall. He was walking in the back door."

"You're sure it was him?"

The kid sent me a look of disgust. "I'm sure it was him. I was walking out to the garage, and I saw him going into the house. They had their back light on."

"This was around ten thirty?"

"Yeah, it was a little before ten thirty. My friend and I were going to watch *Friday the Thirteenth* on the late show."

I could hear a woman from inside the house calling his name. Andy turned back and yelled, in a voice that would have played to the balcony, "I'll be there in a minute."

"Just one more thing," I said before he had a chance to tell me he needed to go. "Are you absolutely sure this was the night of November fifteenth?" I remembered that it had been several weeks after Caroline's death when Andy told Jonathan about seeing Paul that night. "You don't think you might have seen Mr. Marshall on another Saturday night?" A Saturday night on which Mr. Marshall was not supposed to be spending the night in Austin.

"No, it was November fifteenth all right. It was my little sister's birthday that day. She was two, and the next day, when my mother told me that Mrs. Marshall had died, I remember thinking how weird it was that she'd died on the same day Sara was born."

This time I could hear footsteps walking across a wood floor. "Andy, what are you doing out there?" a woman's voice called.

"Guess I better let you go," I said. "Thanks for your help." I hurried down the porch steps. I'd gotten almost to the sidewalk when I heard the woman ask, "Who was that?"

I glanced back and saw a young Hispanic woman, another housekeeper, talking to the boy. She regarded me impassively, then closed the door.

By the time I got back to my apartment I was more convinced than ever that Jonathan was in danger. From whom was still the million-dollar question. Nick had left two messages on my answering machine. The first said he'd talked to Fowler's secretary, and he'd tell me all about it over dinner tonight. The second message was shorter: "Where *are* you? Call me."

I called him. "I was starting to worry that something had happened to you," he said, sounding a bit sheepish. "What took you so long? I thought you were going to phone Houssman."

I explained where I'd been and said no thanks to the dinner invitation. I felt too edgy to go out to a restaurant.

"In that case I'll bring the food to your place. How does Chinese sound to you?"

"Okay. I'm really not very hungry, though."

"I promise not to make you clean your plate. I'll be there in an hour."

He arrived in forty-five minutes, carrying a large paper sack filled with cardboard containers of Szechwan chicken, rice, and sweet-and-sour soup. "You look worried," he said, as he unloaded the food. "What did Houssman say?"

"That he went to Caroline's house on the evening she died to try to talk her out of writing the article. She laughed at him. She also told him she was planning to start a new life, taking Jonathan and leaving Paul for good."

Nick whistled. He took a minute to digest the news, then asked, "Did Houssman mention what time this conversation was?"

"About eight thirty. Said he stayed twenty or thirty minutes and was home to his wife's cocktail party by nine fifteen."

"And of course he's confident that you won't call his wife to verify what time he got home." Nick stopped pouring the soup into bowls and looked at me. "You believe his story?"

I thought about it. "As much as he told me, yeah. I believe that Caroline was alive when he left her. Incidentally, he said he thought she was acting manic. At the time, he never suspected she was suicidal.''

''But after the fact he saw all the telltale signs, right?'' Nick dug a spoon into the container of chicken. ''And you wonder why I think all mental health professionals are full of shit? Only in hindsight can they predict who's going to open fire in a crowded post office, or who's going to slit her wrists, or drown her kids. Hell, my thirteen-year-old nephew can do that too! 'Uncle Nick, that guy was sure acting weird!' ''

It was an argument I wasn't going to get into, at least not at the moment. ''What did you find out about Fowler?'' I asked as we carried the food to the kitchen table.

''That he was in London giving a paper at some psychiatric conference that day.'' Nick took a bite of his chicken, looking glum. ''Theoretically he might have hopped on the Concorde, driven from the airport to Caroline's house, shot her, and driven back to the airport and then flown back to London. But much as I would like to believe the worst of him, I don't think he shot Caroline. At least not personally.''

''You think he hired somebody?''

''It's possible. I wouldn't put it past him. He seems more the type than Houssman. Everyone I talked to either despises Fowler or is terrified of him. But I don't have any evidence that he did anything.''

I tasted the soup but felt too agitated to eat any more. ''I think that if anyone killed Caroline it was most likely Paul. He knew where their gun was kept, he had a key to the house, he could easily have typed her suicide note. He told everyone he was in Austin that weekend, but a neighbor kid saw him entering the house at ten thirty that night. Why did he drive all the way from Austin? He was coming home the next day anyway.''

Nick stared, unseeing, at my face. ''But why kill her if she was going to agree to the divorce?''

''If Caroline was dead, Paul had access to her trust fund. It wasn't community property, so he wouldn't have gotten any of it in a divorce settlement. But Max told me that in her will

Caroline split all her assets between Jonathan and Paul. Eventually I'm sure she would have changed her will, but she just hadn't got around to it yet.''

Nick looked as if he too had lost his appetite. ''You know it's also possible that Paul didn't actually shoot her. Maybe he just told Caroline something that upset her so much that she shot herself.''

''That's possible, I guess.'' But somehow I couldn't believe that Paul was not guilty—of something.

''Did that kid you talked to see Paul leave the house?''

I shook my head. ''He might have been in there three minutes or three hours. All Paul had to do was get back to his parents' house before Jonathan woke up Sunday morning. Of course Paul doesn't even admit that he was at his own house at all. When Jonathan told him that Andy saw him at the house that night, Paul blew up at him.''

Nick's intense blue eyes studied my face. ''You're afraid Paul is going to hurt Jonathan?''

I wasn't sure where the tears came from, but suddenly they were spilling down my cheeks. ''Paul has forbidden Jonathan to see me. He says I'm a bad influence.''

''You?'' At another time I would have found the incredulous expression on Nick's face amusing.

''Me. He even has the housekeeper primed to keep me away from Jonathan. When Jonathan needs me the most, he's not even allowed to talk to me. And I need to talk to him, Nick. I have to make sure he's okay, and I have to warn him to be more careful around Paul, to stop provoking him.''

I took a deep breath, but it didn't help. ''He's just a little boy, Nick.''

I heard Nick's chair scrape against the floor, and through the blur of tears saw him move toward me. He pulled me to him, let me bury my face in the white dress shirt he'd worn to Gertrude's funeral.

''Let me phone Jonathan,'' he said when my sobs had subsided to sniffles. ''The housekeeper doesn't know my voice. After she gets off you can set up a meeting with him. Maybe right after school or someplace near his house.''

''Okay.'' I wasn't sure it was going to work, but since I didn't have any better idea, it seemed worth a try.

I watched him dial the Marshall number. ''Hello. Could I please speak to Jonathan Marshall?'' he asked in a hearty, un-Nick-like voice.

He paused. ''This is John Lewis, a representative of Nintendo.'' Nick rolled his eyes at me.

''Jonathan, hi! This is John Lewis from Nintendo.'' I thought Nick was going to hand over the phone to me, but he shook his head, holding up one finger.

''How are you today, Jonathan? Are you still one of our loyal players?''

I couldn't figure out where Nick was going with this. Obviously he suspected that someone was listening on the extension. But did that mean from now on all of Jonathan's calls would be screened? That I'd have to skulk around in the bushes outside his house in order to get a few words with him?

''You're probably wondering why I'm calling you today, Jonathan,'' Nick continued. ''Well, I was hoping that you could answer some questions for us about the games you like best, things like that. In exchange for your cooperation we'll send you a coupon good for a ten-dollar discount off your next Nintendo game.'' He paused a beat. ''How does that sound to you, Jonathan?''

I'd hoped that by this time whoever was eavesdropping would have hung up. Apparently not.

''Now there's just one thing, Jonathan. This is a rather lengthy survey, which I can schedule at your convenience when you have the time. What would be a good time for me to call you back? Would tomorrow after school be good?''

I watched Nick listen. ''Okay. Not Saturday either? How about around three thirty on Monday? Good, I'll talk to you then. Thanks for your help, Jonathan.''

Shaking his head, Nick hung up the phone. ''God, I can't believe that any housekeeper would stay on the extension for all of that spiel. I did learn one thing, though. For what it's worth, Jonathan is going to be spending the weekend with Celia. She's going to pick him up after school tomorrow and take him to her house. Maybe she'll let you talk to the kid.''

''I hope so,'' I said, ''because I don't know what I'm going to do if she says no.''

TWENTY-FIVE

Celia, bless her, made it sound as if I was making the most reasonable request in the world. ''Why, of course, Jonathan and I would love to have you drop in on Saturday,'' she said in that honeyed voice that reminded me of the ladies in my mother's old bridge club. ''I know how fond of you Jonathan is, and I'd enjoy seeing you again, too.''

I wasn't sure if she was unaware of Paul's new attitude toward me or was choosing to ignore it. In either case I figured it was in my best interest to not bring up the subject. I assured her that I remembered how to get to her house, told her I was looking forward to seeing her too, and got off the phone before Celia had time to wonder why I didn't just drive over to the Marshall house and visit Jonathan there.

On Saturday morning Celia opened the door of her opulent house. ''Liz, come on in. How nice to see you!'' she exclaimed, dispelling my fears that since we talked, Paul would have left instructions to keep me away from Jonathan.

I smiled, telling her what an attractive outfit she was wearing—an expensive-looking beige knit dress, chunky gold chain around her neck, and the kind of excruciating, high-heeled pumps I'd given up years ago. Glancing down at my own jeans and turtleneck sweater, I wondered if the woman could possibly have gotten this dressed up just for me.

Over Celia's dainty little shoulder I could see Jonathan hovering in the hallway, wearing a shy, expectant expression on his pale face. I smiled, moving toward him, and was astonished when he ran over and threw his arms around me.

I hugged him back. "I've missed you," I said into his cowlicky blond hair.

"Me too," he said, his face still buried in my sweater.

When Jonathan finally pulled away, Celia suggested that we might like to visit in the family room.

"Or we could take a walk," I said, remembering Celia's high heels and hoping she wouldn't suggest coming with us. Much as I appreciated her hospitality, I still needed to talk to Jonathan alone.

Fortunately Jonathan said we could walk to a nearby park, and Celia didn't object. "We'll be back in an hour or so," I said, feeling as if I were trying to con some nice little old lady. Except, of course, that this "old lady" looked more like Joan Collins than Grandma Moses.

"So how are you doing?" I asked Jonathan as we set off for the park.

"Okay," he said, not looking at me. "I like being here with Celia."

"She seems a fun person to be around," I agreed. "But how are things with you and your dad? Getting any better?"

Jonathan shrugged. "He stays at work, so I don't see him very much."

"Max was like that too. A lot of the time I hardly ever saw him."

"Yeah, but you got rid of him. I'm stuck with my dad."

"For a while anyway, until you're older."

We walked the rest of the block in silence, while I tried to think of the best way to tell Jonathan what I'd decided I needed to tell him. "You know, your dad might be nicer to you if you stopped talking about how someone killed your mom. I think your dad gets upset when you talk about your mom like that, and then he gets angry with you."

Jonathan said nothing.

I tried again. "I'm not saying you need to stop talking about that altogether. You can talk to me about your mom any time.

I'd love to hear whatever you have to say.''

Jonathan fixed his large violet eyes on me. ''But Dad doesn't want me to talk to you.''

I'd already thought of that one. ''You can call me whenever you visit Celia. You could even call me from one of your friend's houses. You still have my home and office numbers, don't you?''

He nodded while I pictured slapping a tiny bandage on a large, gaping wound. Would Paul believe that his obsessed young son had given up his stubborn conviction that Caroline was murdered? And if Paul did believe it, would Jonathan be in any less danger from the man who might very well have killed Caroline?

Even as we spoke, Nick was talking to a police contact of his, seeing if the police would investigate the circumstances of Caroline's death. But both of us knew it wasn't likely. There was too little evidence to back our suspicions. Even if we could prove that Paul had come back to their house that night, that was still a far cry from proving he'd shot Caroline once he got inside.

''There's the park.'' Jonathan pointed at what looked like half a block of new playground equipment, surrounded by a few scrawny-looking new trees. ''Aunt Gertrude used to take me here sometimes. We brought a picnic once.''

''That sounds like fun.'' I was surprised Jonathan didn't seem more upset about Gertrude's death, considering how close I thought the two of them had been. His mentioning Gertrude, though, reminded me of something else I wanted to ask him. ''Jonathan, do you remember the last time you saw Aunt Gertrude?''

''Yeah.''

I felt as if I were inching my way through a mine field. ''Did you tell her about how you were asking your neighbors all those questions about the day your mother died?''

He nodded, but didn't volunteer any specifics.

''What did you tell her? Do you remember?''

''Just the same stuff I told you.''

"About Andy seeing your dad go into the house?"

"Yeah."

"Did Aunt Gertrude ask you any questions about that?" I was sure Gertrude wouldn't have revealed her suspicions to Jonathan. But, knowing her, I figured she would still want to make sure that what Jonathan was telling her was accurate.

"She asked me the name of my friend who saw Dad. And she wanted to know if Andy was positive he saw Dad and not someone else."

That was what I was afraid of. I tried to sound casual. "You didn't happen to see any tapes Aunt Gertrude was listening to, did you? Or see a diary or maybe a notebook that belonged to your mother? I was looking for them at your aunt's house, but I couldn't seem to find them."

Jonathan shrugged. "Aunt Gertrude had some stuff on her desk, but I didn't look at it."

"Just one more thing," I said, noticing that he was starting to look bored. "Did you learn anything else? Something you haven't told me yet?"

Jonathan glanced longingly at a wooden fort reached by climbing a ladder. "No, nothing else. Can I go play now?"

"Sure." I watched him scramble up the ladder, wishing I didn't feel so upset about confirming exactly what I'd expected to hear.

We stayed at the park a little over half an hour. During that time Jonathan didn't mention anything else about Gertrude, Paul, or Caroline, and I didn't press him. On the walk home we talked about a field trip his class had taken to the Museum of Fine Arts in which a kid in his class had thrown up on a piece of sculpture. "Was that gross!"

When we got back to Celia's, she was waiting for us in the living room, paging through a fashion magazine. "How was the park?" she asked with a big smile. When Jonathan said, "Fine," Celia turned to me. "Did I tell you I just got through remodeling my bedroom? Would you like to come see what I've done with it?"

Sure, I said, figuring it was the least I could do for her. The two of us headed for the stairs, leaving Jonathan in the den watching cartoons on TV. "I put some paper on the desk, honey, in case you want to do some more drawing," Celia called to him.

"Jonathan really is a very talented artist," Celia told me as we walked down a white-carpeted hallway. "In fact he appears to be talented in many areas."

I smiled. "I think so too. He's bright and very creative."

Celia turned her long-lashed eyes on my face. Her eyes were so intense a shade of blue that I wondered if she was wearing tinted contact lenses. "You really care about Jonathan, don't you?"

"Yes, I do."

Celia shook her head, rolling her eyes. "I don't understand Paul suddenly wanting to keep Jonathan away from you. It doesn't make sense at all. Do *you* have any idea what got into him?"

So she did know after all! "Not really," I admitted. I hesitated, wondering how much I should tell her, then decided that an abbreviated version of the truth would probably be the best tack. "Jonathan told me that Paul said I encouraged him not to face reality. I can only assume that means I listen to all of Jonathan's schemes and ideas, and Paul thinks some of them are pretty outlandish."

"Especially the ones about someone killing Caroline," Celia said sweetly, meeting my eyes.

It struck me that because of the way she looked and the syrupy role she chose to play, this woman had probably spent her whole life having her intelligence ignored. Even I, who should have known better, had assumed that someone so focused on her appearance must be on the low end of the IQ scale.

"Yes, Paul does seem to find that upsetting," I said mildly.

Celia stopped in front of a closed door. "Paul overreacts to things. I sometimes think he forgets that he can't dictate to his son in the same way he barks orders to underlings at the law firm. In any case, I want you to know that you can see

Jonathan any time he's at my house."

"Thank you," I said, genuinely touched.

Celia pushed open the door. "This is where I exercise each morning." I stepped inside to look at a carpeted room equipped with an exercise bike, treadmill, stair stepper, and an exercise bench with various-sized dumbbells nearby. There was also some Nautilus equipment—the only piece I could identify was a leg machine—and even a very hefty looking barbell. One entire wall was covered with mirrors.

"I try to work out for at least an hour every morning," Celia explained. "And then, of course, I go to my aerobics class four times a week too."

Of course. I (who felt like I deserved a President's Fitness Medal for now attending tae-kwon-do three times a week and taking a couple of long walks on the weekend) noticed for the first time the muscle on Celia's well-toned upper arms. I quickly calculated that Celia, a woman at least twenty-five years older than me, was spending roughly twice as long each week exercising as I was. And she had the body to prove it.

"That's very impressive," I said. Also a bit obsessive, but I suspected my assessment held a not-so-subtle strain of sour grapes.

Celia smiled. She closed the door and led me down the hall. "Now, dear, let me show you my new closet."

I wasn't prepared for it. Celia's closet was my idea of a small bedroom. It was attached to a frilly bedroom large enough to accommodate a peach-colored chaise longue and a flowered love seat as well as a queen-sized brass bed, night stand, and two large chests of drawers.

Celia led me through the bedroom into her mammoth closet. One entire wall was covered with built-in shelves. One section contained dozens of pairs of shoes, each pair in its own zippered plastic case. Another section contained drawer after drawer of sweaters. Through the transparent drawer fronts I could see dozens of sweaters and knit separates: black, beige, navy, red, white, and emerald-green. I couldn't imagine one person owning all these clothes—and I hadn't gotten any farther than the knit separates!

"Why this is . . . incredible," I said, searching for the right word. "Just incredible."

Celia, fortunately, looked pleased. "I've wanted a closet like this for years, someplace where I could spread out and get everything organized. Before, I always had to store my clothes in several different bedrooms. That was *so* inconvenient."

"I can imagine." I was still staring at the racks of dresses, each, of course, in its own garment bag. There seemed to be a section of evening dresses: hanger after hanger of floor-length gowns, some sequined, others beaded, strapless, gauzy, or elegantly tailored. Then the cocktail dresses, mostly black or black and white. Where in the world did Celia *wear* all these clothes? Next was a huge section of suits: tweedy, neutrals, a red wool, a black knit, a pinstriped gray wool.

"Why don't you sit down, dear?" Celia said graciously, nodding toward one end of the room-sized closet where two pretty flowered chintz chairs and a coffee table were arranged several feet in front of a three-way mirror. "I've brought up some tea and cookies for us."

I sat while Celia poured tea into two delicate flowered china cups from a matching china pot. I noticed the photos of her just after I bit into a delicious shortbread cookie.

The pictures were clustered on several otherwise empty shelves at the back of the room, on either side of the three-way mirror. They were all beautifully framed, many in silver art deco frames. All of them showed Celia at various stages of her life.

I swallowed the tea and cookie. "Do you mind if I look at your pictures?" I asked my hostess.

"Of course not, dear." Would anyone who had a closet like Celia's and was getting ready for her second face-lift mind if I looked at her picture?

One photo showed a slender, remarkably pretty teenager in high heels and a one-piece bathing suit being crowned with a sparkly tiara. "You won a beauty contest. Which one was it?"

Ceila smiled, and for a moment I saw the same look of raw

triumph that the teenaged Celia hadn't bothered to hide. "Yes, I was Miss Dallas and first runner-up for Miss Texas. The girl who won Miss Texas was sleeping with at least one of the judges."

I had the distinct impression it would be unwise to ask her what year that was. "You were gorgeous," I said instead, because I knew it was what she wanted to hear. And she had been beautiful—a knockout figure, lovely, luminescent skin, a face with classic, even features. Yet there was something about that young Celia, a palpable hardness or perhaps just an ambition so consuming that it burned in her eyes, that made me think I wouldn't have liked her then.

I looked at the other pictures. Celia as a young bride in a plain white suit and a smile that didn't reach her eyes. ("That was my first husband, Stanley," she said. "What a cheapskate he turned out to be.") A shot of her in a black-and-white polka-dot dress smiling up from behind her typewriter, a confident, tanned woman in her late twenties or early thirties. Someone who'd learned by this time how to hide her ambition behind a flirtatious grin.

"You were a secretary?" I asked. "Or a journalist?"

"I was John's personal secretary," she said. "That's how we met." She pointed to another wedding picture. Caroline's father—still earnest-looking, but heavier and with a lot less hair than in his first wedding photo—gazed down adoringly at his much younger bride. This time Celia wore a considerably more expensive cream-colored suit and a smile that made it to her eyes. "We were married six months later."

I wondered what had happened to Stanley, the cheapskate (Celia was wearing a wedding ring in the sexy secretary photo), but felt it was tactless to ask. I took in the photo of John Rogers and Celia and a ten- or eleven-year-old Caroline, all in their Easter outfits. Caroline was clutching her father's hand possessively, while Celia held his other hand.

The next family photo, maybe four or five years later, showed Celia looking elegant and well-cared-for while Caroline, in that gawky stage of early adolescence, glared sullenly into the camera. Probably she was pissed off about the babyish-looking white sailor dress she was wearing.

Celia saw where I was looking. "Poor child." She shook her perfectly coiffed head. "I tried to do what I could to help Caroline look more attractive, but there was only so much I could do. . . ."

I was going to say, Well, it was only a temporary stage. Caroline was lucky enough to outgrow it. But before I could open my mouth, Celia added, "Caroline was such a cute little girl. I never understood why her looks didn't jell. Her father had always hoped she'd be a beauty, though of course he never let Caroline know that he was disappointed."

I stared at her, not knowing what to say. Caroline *unattractive?* Glancing away from Celia's self-satisfied smile, I noticed that there were no other shots of Caroline in the group of photos, only pictures of Celia, and sometimes Celia and John, all dressed up and smiling at the camera. What looked like the most recent picture was a professionally posed shot of Celia. She was sitting in her living room, her posture perfect, dressed in a red wool suit and tastefully expensive chunky gold jewelry. Celia's elegant legs were crossed, her hair coifed, her face unlined, if a bit taut-looking. She looked only a few years older than she did in the family picture with the fourteen-year-old Caroline.

I set my teacup on the chrome-and-brass coffee table. "Maybe we should go down and check on Jonathan, don't you think?"

Celia cocked her head to one side and kept smiling. "Did Gertrude tell you much about Caroline and I?"

Caroline and *me*, I thought irrelevantly. "No, not really," I lied. I stood up, knowing that I didn't want to hear Celia's version of the story.

"Liz!" I heard Jonathan calling my name, heard his footsteps running down the carpeted hallway.

"In here," I called from the doorway. I smiled as he came running toward me.

"Look, look what I found!" Jonathan was calling, waving

something in my face. ''I found them in Celia's desk.''

He finally held his hand still long enough for me to see what he was holding. It was Caroline's leather diary and a notebook labeled ''Memories of Mary Ann.''

TWENTY-SIX

"Oh, yes, that's Caroline's diary and some of her notes." Celia was smiling at us, holding out her hand for Jonathan to give them back to her.

Instead Jonathan handed them to me. "Liz was looking for them," he explained.

"Well then, she should simply have asked me for them." Celia turned to me. "Remember the day we met at Jonathan's house when I was clearing out all of Caroline's papers? I still have them. I'm afraid I've been *very* slow about sorting through all of them."

"So you've had the diary all along?" I asked.

"Of course. But if you don't mind my asking, why were you looking for it?"

It was a reasonable enough question, but not one I especially wanted to answer in front of Jonathan. "Oh, Gertrude had mentioned wanting to show me something new she'd learned about Caroline, and I guess I just assumed she'd learned it by reading Caroline's diary."

Celia looked thoughtful. "It might have been in one of Caroline's earlier diaries. I know Gertrude took those home to read."

She held out her hand for the book. "Gertrude never read this one, though. She said she thought she'd find it too upsetting."

But if Gertrude had the earlier diaries, why hadn't we found them at her house? Reluctantly I handed Celia the diary and the spiral notebook. "You know when you first offered, I wasn't interested in reading Caroline's papers. But now I would like to read them." Although, if memory served, what Celia had *actually* offered was for me to look through Caroline's books to see if I wanted to keep any. I hoped she wouldn't remember that.

"Of course, any time." Celia smiled at me, but didn't hand back the diary or notebook. "I have boxes of papers for you to look at."

"What did Aunt Gertrude find out about Mom?" Jonathan asked me, looking bright eyed and interested.

"I don't know. Unfortunately she died before she had a chance to tell me." I could see the look of disappointment spread across his face, dousing the light in his eyes. "But it probably wasn't anything real important, Jonathan. Maybe she just wanted to tell me something she'd found in an old diary, like"—I sought for inspiration—"maybe what you were like when you were a baby."

I'd promised myself, at the beginning of my first pregnancy, that when I had a child I would never talk baby talk or patronize the kid, or lie to him for his own good. So how come my knee-jerk response was to fabricate this ludicrous story for a child who was too smart to believe it anyway?

"I'm sure Liz is right, Jonathan," Celia said. "If Gertrude had anything important to tell Liz, she would have told her over the phone. Isn't that what you would have done?"

Jonathan took a minute to think about that one. Celia's question made me wonder again what information Gertrude would have found so potentially explosive that she needed to think things through before confiding in me. Obviously it must have been something that could be interpreted in several ways. "I want you to hear all the information for yourself, and then draw your own conclusions," Gertrude had said.

Jonathan was apparently finished thinking. His bottom lip jutted out as he turned to me. "But you said Aunt Gertrude had new information."

"Maybe it was new to her, something she hadn't realized

before,'' I said, feeling as if I were digging myself further into a hole. From the corner of my eye I could see that Celia was not amused by Jonathan's persistence. ''I don't know what it was she wanted to tell me, Jonathan.'' Though I could make a few educated guesses, none of them fit for eight-year-old ears.

Jonathan dug in his jeans pocket and pulled out two cassette tapes. ''Oh, yeah, I found these too.'' He pointed to the label on the front of one cassette. ''See—that's Mom's handwriting.'' He squinted, reading the label. ''It says 'Death of Mary Ann Rogers.' ''

''Give them to me, Jonathan.'' Celia's voice was icy, almost as glacial as her eyes. ''This instant.''

I watched her march up to Jonathan in her ludicrously high heels and grab the tapes from the boy's hand.

It was one of those moments when you first realize that the sweet little puppy your toddler is playing with is actually a pit bull. That the harmless snake you've just stepped on with your bare foot is making strange, rattling noises. I recalled my last phone conversation with Gertrude. She'd said she had started remembering things that she thought she'd forgotten, things that put Caroline's death in a new light.

''Jonathan, why don't you go on downstairs and finish that drawing you promised to make for me?'' I suggested.

Jonathan, staring at the ground to hide the tears welling in his eyes, shook his head.

''Oh, Jonathan, don't cry,'' Celia said. Now that she had the tapes back, her voice had returned to its usual pleasant tone. ''I'm so sorry that I snapped at you. But it's very rude to be going through other people's desks.''

Jonathan, continuing to stare at the floor, didn't say anything.

With herculean self-control, I managed not to scream at him to Get the Hell Out of Here. When Celia moved back to her flowered chair, I walked over to Jonathan.

Kneeling in front of him, I forced the boy to meet my eyes. ''Come on, Jonathan,'' I said in what I hoped was a warm, supportive voice, but which to my ears held a definite undertone of hysteria, "I know you were trying to be helpful, honey, and that you didn't think you were doing anything wrong. Nobody is angry with you, so why don't you go downstairs and play now?"

I pulled him to me in a big hug. "Get out of here now," I whispered in his ear. "Don't ask me questions. Just run to the neighbor's house."

A sound behind me made me realize that Celia had moved from her chair. "Oh, I think it would be better if you stayed right here, Jonathan," she said.

Something in her voice made me jerk around. Or maybe it was the expression I saw on Jonathan's face when he looked up at her.

Celia held a gun. A revolver that was now pointed at Jonathan and me. "It's a shame, Jonathan," she said quite pleasantly, "that no one ever told you that curiosity killed the cat. Though of course with that mother of yours, I suppose we couldn't expect much else."

Jonathan's face was frozen in terror. I wanted to reach out to pull him to me, but was afraid to risk it. It was the sight of him—white-faced, eyes like saucers—that pushed me past my own immobilizing fears.

I stood up slowly, so I could deal with Celia at eye level. My voice, when I finally managed to speak, sounded unnaturally calm. "Celia, put the gun down. We can still work something out. We're all reasonable people here."

Celia's laugh did not bode well for the spirit of compromise. "I don't think so."

"You know you'll never get away with this," I said.

Celia smiled. "Oh, you'd be surprised how much I've already gotten away with."

That was what I was afraid of. With a soft, whimpering sound, Jonathan moved toward me and grabbed hold around my rib cage. I patted his back as he buried his face in my sweater.

I knew I had to buy us time. I pointed at the tapes Celia

was holding in her left hand. ''Is that what the tapes were about? Did Caroline discover that you killed Mary Ann?''

Celia did not look offended by the question. ''No, Mary Ann was quite capable of killing herself. All I did was send over one of John's pistols in a box of clothes and old family photos. I believe I slipped it under one of her negligees that I found in a trunk in the attic. It could well have been the one she wore on her honeymoon. Her wedding gown was also in the trunk. I sent that over too.''

I stared at her, remembering something I'd read once about how the Nazis on trial at Nuremburg—the sadistic concentration camp guards, Gestapo torturers, doctors who performed horrifying medical experiments on prisoners—did not look evil, merely ordinary. In Celia, though, you could see the evil if you looked very closely behind her beautifully groomed façade. You could see it in those chilling, amoral eyes. This was not a woman who was going to be talked out of a rash, violent act. She'd already committed too many other rash, violent acts to worry about two more.

I nudged Jonathan, who was still clinging to me. He needed to snap out of it, to dash to the stairs while I tried to distract Celia and (I hoped) wrestle the gun from her grip. But Jonathan was frozen in fear, unable to even look up at me.

Celia glanced from me to Jonathan, with a look that told me she was completely aware of what I was trying to do, and equally determined to make sure my plan didn't work. ''Mary Ann was once a very beautiful woman,'' she said conversationally, as if we'd just been discussing her predecessor's looks. ''By the time I met her, of course, you never would have guessed that she'd ever been even mildly attractive. She'd let herself go, and mental illness had ruined her face. But when I found those old photos of her, I saw how beautiful she'd been when she was first married.''

Celia nodded in Jonathan's direction. ''Jonathan, in fact, looks quite a bit like Mary Ann.''

I hadn't noticed it before, but she was right; Jonathan did look a lot like the early photos I'd seen of Mary Ann. ''Is that why you wanted to get rid of her—because she was so beautiful?'' I asked. At the moment, given what I'd learned about Celia, it didn't seem like an unreasonable question.

Celia considered. ''No, it was because she was costing too much. All those medical bills, maintaining two households. You can't imagine how expensive it was.''

''I bet it was.'' Particularly for a woman who lived to shop.

''Caroline wanted to keep my money too—the money that was rightfully mine. I don't know what John was thinking of with that ridiculous spendthrift trust he left me. He'd never denied me anything when he was alive, and then to do that to me when he died! Particularly when he knew how stingy Caroline was.''

I could feel Jonathan lift his head. When I turned to look at him, his lower lip was trembling. ''Did you kill my mother?'' he asked in a shrill voice.

Amusement briefly lit up Celia's hard eyes. ''Well, I guess there's no reason for me not to tell you now. After you've gone to so much effort to find out.''

The matter-of-fact way that she said it scared me more than anything else she'd said. ''Yes, I did kill your mother,'' she admitted in the tone of voice one might mention what time it was. ''And yes, I ran over your bicycle. I hoped you'd take it as a warning to stop this little detective act of yours.'' She raised a perfectly plucked eyebrow and sighed. ''But, unfortunately, you didn't.''

''Did you try to run him over in the zoo parking lot?'' I asked.

Celia looked puzzled. ''No, of course not. I never go to the zoo.''

She turned to me. ''Caroline's death was surprisingly easy, actually. Of course I had to wait until her visitor left—a heavyset man who looked quite angry with Caroline. But after that, everything went smoothly. I'd taken their handgun the last time I visited. I knew they'd never miss it; they just liked the idea of having a gun in the house for protection. Caroline let me in the house without question.''

Celia smiled at me. "All I had to do was wait until she sat down to go over my bills, and then I just walked up to the desk and shot her. After that I typed the suicide note on her typewriter and left."

She looked as if she wanted me to compliment her on her cleverness. Next she was going to share with us how she'd managed Gertrude's "natural" death and how she intended to get away with murdering Jonathan and me. I was so desperate to figure out a way to divert her long enough for Jonathan to make his escape that I didn't notice what he was doing.

I was too late to stop him. Jonathan had already started running at her, his fist raised. "I hate you!" he screamed.

Celia raised her revolver.

I leaped toward her with the blood-curdling guttural yell I'd learned in tae-kwon-do. A shot rang out, but I couldn't see if Jonathan had been hit.

"Run, Jonathan. Get out!" I screamed as I wrestled with Celia for the gun.

All those exercise classes had made Celia surprisingly strong. But I'd been exercising too, and adrenaline or sheer desperation had turned me into a fierce opponent.

Celia clawed at my face with her left hand as I tried to wrench the gun out of her right. She yelped as I twisted her arm, and the gun clattered to the floor.

I lunged for it, felt the hard metal in my hand. My fingers were grasping the trigger when Celia brought the weight of her stiletto heel down on my hand. Hard.

I shrieked in agony, letting go of the gun. Celia was on the floor in a second, grabbing for it.

Through the tears in my eyes I saw her, crouched on the floor, pick up the gun. This was it, I told myself. The end. Celia's fourth murder.

I hunched up on the balls of my feet and hurled my body at her in a feeble tackle.

She shot me.

It took a minute for the pain to sear through my right shoulder. But in those few seconds the gun blast echoed in my ears.

The look of triumph on Celia's face registered in my brain. I knew she was about to shoot me again.

I staggered to my feet, fighting the pain, taking loud, gasping breaths. Celia aimed the gun. I pictured the heavy punching bags in the *do jang* as I leaped up, smashing my heel into Celia's chest.

I heard the shot. Saw the look of pained astonishment on Celia's face as she crumbled to the ground. Then I passed out.

TWENTY-SEVEN

I came to in the ambulance. I looked past the young long-haired guy in white who was doing something painful to my shoulder. "Where's Jonathan?" I asked through gritted teeth.

"You mean the kid?" When I nodded, the EMT said, "He's back at the house."

I felt waves of pain washing over me. "Is he okay?"

"Yeah, he was pretty shaken up, but other than that, he's fine. He wanted to come with you to the hospital, but the police needed to talk to him."

I was going to ask him about Celia, but this time the wave pulled me under.

Two days later Jonathan ran into my room with an un-hospital-like whoop.

"Jonathan, you need to be quiet!" Paul, trailing behind his son, looked less overjoyed to see me, but I still gave him points for bringing Jonathan.

I managed to give Jonathan a one-armed hug, assure him that I was okay, and (at his request) let him see the bandage that covered my bullet wound.

"Is there always going to be a hole there?" he asked with great interest.

"I sincerely hope not." I told him that I was probably going home the next day, and then asked what he'd been up to.

While Paul sat silently, Jonathan told me about his science

fair project, his new best friend Byron, and the video game he'd rented last weekend. At the end of this recital, he added, "Did you know that Celia is in jail?"

"I heard that."

"I called 911 from Mrs. Thompson's house," Jonathan said. "When the police came, Celia said you attacked her first. But I told them she was lying, and I showed them Mom's diary and notebook and the tapes I found in Celia's desk. The police believed me, not Celia." Jonathan beamed at me, looking proud of himself.

"That's wonderful. You saved my life," I said, reaching out to give him another hug.

I turned to Paul. "Do you have any idea what was in the tapes or Caroline's diary?"

Paul nodded. "The police said the tapes were interviews Caroline had done with the nurse who took care of her mother and with a man who used to live in their neighborhood. Celia gave the guy—he was a kid then—a buck to take a box of Mary Ann's things over to her house. On the way there he tripped and dropped the box. Everything spilled out, and he saw the gun. He didn't think anything of it at the time; he was just worried that someone was going to blame him for dumping the stuff on the ground. I think Caroline planned to write an article about her mother's last days."

An article which, at the very least, would have ensured that Celia had very few places to wear all those fancy dresses. "I can see why Celia didn't want anyone else to hear the tapes." Poor Gertrude would probably still be alive if she hadn't heard them.

"I never knew Celia was so bad," Jonathan said in a sad, small voice. "I always thought she was nice."

"None of us knew that, Jonathan," Paul said from his chair. "Celia had a lot of problems that none of us knew about." He stopped, swallowed several times before continuing. "I wish to God we had."

None of us had much to say after that, and a few minutes later Paul said he thought it was time for them to leave. He told Jonathan to wait outside while "I talk to Liz for a minute about some grown-up things."

Jonathan didn't look happy about it, but after a goodbye hug, he left.

Paul closed the door and got to the point. "I want to thank you for saving Jonathan's life and to apologize for how badly I've treated you." He didn't give me a chance to respond, but continued in a resolute voice. Very much, I thought, like a schoolboy ready to accept his punishment, wanting to get it over with.

"I realize you think I'm an uncaring bastard, but I want you to know that I was convinced that Caroline did kill herself. I guess you know I came back from Austin the night she died. I wanted to have it out with her, to convince her once and for all that our problems couldn't be solved, that we needed to move ahead with the divorce. But when I walked into the study, she was dead, slumped across the desk with this typed note next to her."

Paul took a deep breath, glancing at the closed door. "I panicked. There's no excuse for my behavior. All I could think of was how bad it looked for me to be there when I was supposed to be in Austin visiting my parents. There was nothing I could do for Caroline; my staying wouldn't have helped her. So"—his voice hardened—"I got the hell out of there. Drove back to Austin."

"And officially found her body the next day," I finished in a neutral voice.

Paul nodded. "Except I made sure that Jonathan didn't come in the house with me."

His face begged for my sympathy, or at least my understanding. I didn't know if I could manage that yet, but I made an effort.

"So," he went on, "you see why I got so upset when Jonathan started saying Andy saw me going into the house that Saturday night."

I nodded. "But I don't understand what that had to do with me. Why did you tell Jonathan that he couldn't see me?"

Paul looked uncomfortable, but when he answered he made a point of maintaining eye contact. "I had the impression that you were encouraging him to believe that Caroline hadn't killed herself."

"I wasn't encouraging him. I was just listening to him, Paul Hearing what was on his mind."

"I realize that now. It was a mistake. I've been making a lot of mistakes with Jonathan. I hope I can make it up to him. I made an appointment for him to see that child psychologist you recommended." He stopped, suddenly overcome by emotion. "I I didn't realize how much Jonathan meant to me until I came so close to losing him."

Paul swallowed and, blinking, turned away. He raised his palm in farewell, staring straight ahead, as he walked out the door.

The first installment of Caroline and Nick's sex and therapy story ran Friday, the day I went back to work. It included some good quotes from Amanda and a few very cryptic ones from Dr. Houssman, but the main story was Mary Jo's experience with Dr. Fowler. Nick had managed somehow to nail down Mary Jo on the specifics, and the result was a sharp, well-documented account of sexual exploitation.

"Therapists are standing in the hallway talking about your story," I told Nick when he came to pick me up for lunch. "It's a terrific piece."

"Fowler has already phoned the publisher, saying he's going to sue." Nick sounded amused. "He doesn't seem to realize that truth is a defense against libel. And I think he'll be needing his money for the suit Mary Jo is bringing against him."

"What about Dr. Houssman?" I asked as we walked to Nick's car. "Are you writing about him and Caroline?"

Nick sighed. "Even with Caroline's tape, I didn't have enough for a story. No dates, no specifics. The Dr. X journal didn't say when, where, who. The best I could do is use some of Houssman's quotes in this story."

I was glad for Jonathan's sake that Nick hadn't run the part about Caroline; an eight-year-old didn't need this information about his mother. I wondered if Caroline might not have preferred it this way too. Would she really have wanted the world to know about her affair with Houssman—Caroline, who was so private a person?

"If it makes you feel any better," I said, "there's a lot of speculation in the hallways about Houssman's quotes, especially the part about his refusing to comment when you asked if he'd had an affair with any of his patients."

Nick grinned. "You don't know how glad I am to hear that."

"I think Caroline would have liked the story too." I'd thought a lot about Caroline when I was in the hospital.

Nick looked at me. His expression said this was dangerous territory; he wasn't sure it was safe to venture into it with me. "I hope so," he said finally. "I feel relieved that it's finished, as if I've fulfilled my obligation to her now."

I guess I could understand that. This last week I'd spent hours trying to decipher Caroline's words to me that last afternoon. From what I'd recently learned, I could see now why she had been feeling awful. Her marriage was collapsing, she was having to deal with an onslaught of long-repressed memories of her mother, and the therapist who was supposed to be helping her seemed more interested in her body than in her psyche. I doubted that I could have taken much more either.

But the part that still haunted me was when Caroline said, "You're convinced that something awful is going to happen, and there's nothing you can do to stop it." Had she known—perhaps just at some subliminal level—that Celia would never allow the story of her involvement in Mary Ann's death to be published? Had Caroline sensed that Celia, in fact, welcomed the opportunity to find a less stingy trustee?

I'd never know for sure what was on Caroline's mind that day. I hoped I could eventually manage to forgive myself for being too self-involved to listen to a friend who'd needed my help.

"I've been thinking about what Caroline said that last night to Dr. Houssman, how she wanted to start a new life," I told Nick. "I understand now how Caroline was always trying so hard to be everything her mother wasn't: married, successful in a career, never self-doubting or depressed. That's why she was so upset with me when I was depressed and getting a divorce."

I'd thought a lot about this too. "I think she was changing, though. I really believe Caroline finally was ready to just be herself."

But Caroline, the woman who had changed so many lives, never had the chance to change her own. I knew it was what both Nick and I were thinking as we drove in somber silence to Ninfa's.

We were each halfway through a margarita when Nick said he was planning to go up to his aunt's cabin for the weekend. Was I interested in coming along?

Was I? The question hung in the air, asking more than was said.

"I think I'd like that," I said with a smile. "In fact I'd like that very much."